NUADA

Gillian Bridé Madell

NUADA

by
Gillian Bridé Madell

1st Edition Trade Paperback 2018
All Rights Reserved

Dark Recesses Press

657 Craigen Road, Newburgh
Ontario Canada K0K 2S0

Edited by Kelly Dunn
Cover Art by Calvin Bailey
Layout and Inset design by Bailey Hunter

Library & Archives Canada
ISBN 978-1-988837-18-5

Dedication

For U, Nyree and Dylan for giving me space to write this book and to the rest of my family - Barry, Kyle, Sabrina, Iisis, Gabriel, Azriel and Mischa - for all giving me strength, light and inspiration.

Acknowledgements

I would like to especially thank my daughter Nyree and her partner, Dylan for taking the time during their busy work week to look after my young ones so that I had the ability to concentrate on writing "Nuada".

I would also like to thank my siblings and parents, for believing in me, even when I lost track of myself and helping to restore my faith in everything.

I thank the universe for bringing all things together, giving me this book and all others I write.

To you I give all the credit

NUADA

Gillian Bridé Madell

Table of Contents

✌ FOREWORD ✌

The story of the great Nuada is a phenomenal legend, but sadly it is a legend that has not been given the life, nor the respect, that it deserves. As stories go, some are fact, some are fantasy, but Nuada— he was real—as were the Tuatha Dé Danann: the Children of Danu. Ask any Irish man or woman. There are those who, to this day, claim lineage that can be traced back to Sreng, the noble Firbolg warrior. Who of us knows our full lineage?

The fact is, Nuada lived. As for his life before he and the clan of the Children of Danu arrived in Ireland, no one knows, except the gods. Nuada, through all his happiness and pains, along with his people the Tuatha Dé Danann, and the Firbolg and the Fomorian clans, helped make Ireland the great and beautiful nation it remains to this day.

Nuada was an intelligent and proud man, built as sturdily as the oxen the Tuatha people raised. His body bulged with muscles that flexed against the fight. His mind and words could direct his people in peaceful ways or lead them to succeed in a battle that would otherwise look to be a slaughter. Today was the day of battle.

Nuada's red hair glistened with three distinct different hues, the lightest of which appeared near gold in composition. He was every bit the man who would be expected to rule as king of one of the four islands of the Tuatha Dé Danann. His muscular torso was exposed except where it had been marred by fresh stains of blood, flesh and guts; his manhood was covered in torn cloth that had once been striped trousers of the finest blues and reds. The shredded remnant of his shirt hung down over his leather belt.

He held a short sword in one hand, an axe in the other. A shield was secured to his left arm and his feet were clad in dark leather. His hair, which had been pulled aside and secured behind the back of his neck, glistened with the traces of lost lives in the afternoon's sun.

Loose hair had fallen onto his unscarred face and stuck in the sweat and red ooze that clung to him as death clung to the air. His moustache lay flat, flaked with bits of his opponents' flesh, as though he had dined upon their corpses. Only to his mother, the queen Danu, did he ever really have to answer. On the fields of battle, he and his three brothers showed their absolute deserving of the titles they carried. Nuada stood to his full height.

His large hands were well-bloodied and his mind lusted for no more of the action, yet his body moved forward and continued the insane slaughter. Nuada's immense strength lay in his gathered mind; nonetheless it was his body that propelled onward as if an entity unto itself. He knew he could all but fall asleep and still his enemies would fall by the hundreds to his much-honoured sword.

On this very thought, Nuada bent to avoid a strike from an enemy's sword, even as he pulled a small dart from the leather pouch on his waist and threw it into the throat of another painted combatant advancing on him. He knew his deeds would be recorded by the bards, yet again, as those of the mighty king who stood his ground and made all those who opposed his family's rule weep.

Nuada swung his battle-axe at an approaching warrior and screwed his face up as the impact slapped him with sticky red flesh. The scream of his enemy's excruciating pain mixed then with a low gurgle of a man half-drowning in his own blood as death grasped his soul.

Nuada looked more closely at the dying man before him; perhaps the first time ever in battle he had done such a thing. He saw a committed warrior whose face might have been his own—but for the battle-axe that had been cleaved into his head. The warrior's hand reached forth and gripped Nuada's naked shoulder. In that moment, Nuada knew he himself sought peace, just as the dying man sought peace; each in his own way.

He pushed his short sword outward and upward into the weak body of the nameless man. The man's hopeless struggle ended in a dull, effortless slump. Nuada used his embedded blade to hold the man in place as he pulled his battle-axe from the skull it had brutalized. With the axe removed, Nuada used his foot to extract his short sword, while he swung once more the hatchet outward to keep off yet another enemy's attack.

To his side he saw a flying dash of colour. An unarmed man, bare as the day he was born, ran toward Nuada. The man turned his hand into a fist while he screamed a war cry. Nuada felt no fear. Though he did not know on which side the man fought, he relaxed as best one might in battle and sensed that the crier was no enemy. It was, after all, not the idea to give one's position away if one had not been noticed prior to a full assault.

Nuada watched the scrawny man running towards him. He knew it was the naked and unarmed ones that one should be most aware of. He readied himself for any possible impact and pulled his shield high against his face, as his head would surely be the man's first place to strike.

When the man stood only two steps away, a loud roar behind Nuada forced him to turn. He saw another man, as naked as the other and just as bare of weapons. Then Nuada knew exactly what was happening. Many years of training made the warrior certain on the battlefield. Nuada knew his friend and he knew his enemy, even when naked. Clearly, Nuada this new warrior did not have Nuada in mind as his target.

A leap, and the second charging man's body blackened, his eyes grew as large as the bottom of a drinking vessel. His form extended and inflated in a moment until it grew to the size of six men, with the teeth and face of a dog. The creature gnawed and growled as great white slides of mucus fell from its mouth.

"Changeling," Nuada breathed heavily, and ducked to allow his naked, now transformed, ally overhead clearance. He then straightened and observed in a strange silence as the two massive changelings fought on the ground directly in front of him. He did not move to aid one or the other, as it was near impossible to tell them apart. All around him the battlefield was calming, so he kept one eye on the field and the other on the fight.

Teeth gnashed as the changelings' flesh tore. Great cries of pain went up as each injury left deep grooves and blood began to flow. With his quick eye, Nuada surveyed the battlefield more thoroughly. Most of the fight had moved away from him, for the entire enemy around him had been killed or pushed down the slight incline toward the sea. The only fighters in the immediate area were the Dagda, who was battling a much-damaged challenger, and the warring changelings nearby. The Dagda dispatched his foe quickly and moved to stand by his king to watch the changelings in battle.

"It is done, oh king," the Dagda said. His gruff, deep voice matched his large physique as perfectly as ever a voice might match its man. The Dagda stood at the same height as Nuada. His muscles showed every string of strength as they laced across his body. His hair, greying in areas, and the beginnings of lines on his brow, proved him to be much older than Nuada—yet even these marks of age smoothed out and disappeared as he recovered from the battle.

"Yes," Nuada sighed. "It is done."

"The Firbolg will take their leave," the Dagda said, as he wiped entrails from his face.

Nuada knew it was true.   There was still the problem of a possible the traitor who had stirred the Firbolg to attack and had given details on the Queen's court away. He hoped there was no such thing anymore; that the battle had seen an end to the life of it all. Yet even as the thought went through his mind, he knew it was not so. Nuada pushed his tongue into a shallow cut in his mouth that had come from his teeth hitting upon the inside of his lip. He found no other wounds on his body as irritating as that which was in his mouth. And like this tiny, hidden wound, the matter of the traitor still stung and worried him.

One of the changelings screamed as its arm was torn away by the bite of the other changeling, who spat the arm to the side as if it were poison. The arm nearly landed on the Dagda, who jumped sideward to avoid impact.

Nuada stepped closer to the pair as they fought and called back to his friend, "For the life and death of it all. How can I vanquish? But for the manhood of a man, how do you tell which is which?"

It was the truth. The changelings were identical, except for their exposed genitals that had not changed from their human form. Both men could see that the damaged changeling was getting weak and failing the fight. They had to make a decision as quickly as they could, for if the victorious changeling turned out to be their enemy, it would be upon them next.

The Dagda caught himself in a quick leg stumble as he slipped on the loose flesh of the defeated beneath and around him. "Wait." He pointed to the changeling's severed limb, which was deflating and beginning to show its true shape. As the magnificent beasts continued to fight, Nuada watched the amputated arm and saw that it was clearly tattooed in the fashion of the brands their Firbolg enemies gave their cattle.

The Dagda nodded toward the wounded changeling. "Kill the bastard."

Nuada caught him. "You're wrong. You'll not kill the damaged changeling." He pointed. "We kill the other one."

The Dagda did not ask why. He nodded with a wink and charged, yelling out their battle cry, "Tuatha Dé Danann! Children of Danu!"

Nuada followed his old friend, his short sword drawn and pointed towards its enormous target. He screamed the same cry as the Dagda: "Tuatha Dé Danann!"

In seconds they were both on the back of the changeling dominating the fight. It growled, gnashed, and bit at Nuada and the Dagda while it swiped its opponent, digging its sharp claws into the gushing cavity where the opposing changeling's arm had been. The horrendous cry given in return for this wicked action was of such dreadful pain that Nuada's ears hurt and he could not hear for a moment.

"You taste nought of me this day, you child of a goat lover!" the Dagda howled in retort to the snap of the mighty creature's jaws, while his blade pushed into the exposed flesh of its slit eye.

The damnable creature screamed and reared high upon its back legs, throwing both Nuada and the Dagda to the stained ground. Winded for a brief moment, Nuada took a time to get to his feet, and he coughed as he recovered from the violent impact. The Dagda had landed well on his sturdy feet and stood over his king for the while it took for him to gather himself together.

"Should I dance with you, as well?" the Dagda offered a helping hand and a friendly jeer to Nuada as he gasped for air. The Dagda shook his head in mock dismay. "You lay with the ladies too much, you become one."

"Such you say to your king," Nuada replied as he took the presented hand of the Dagda and pulled himself to his feet.

"King?" the Dagda said. "Queen?!" He shrugged as he yelled to his back and, armed only with his spiked mace, took the fight to the winning changeling once more. As he approached the dominating creature, he stooped to the ground and retrieved a long spear from one of the many fallen warriors.

Nuada half smiled and propelled himself forward, determined he would beat the changeling enemy and not leave any opportunity for the Dagda to mock him. He could hear his own heavy breath as he stomped the sludgy ground beneath him. Nuada frowned and narrowed his focus upon the beast as he raised his battle-axe and sword together. He cried as loudly as his tenacious demigod body would let him: "Tuatha Dé Danann!"

Both the battle-hardy Dagda and the courageous king Nuada were on the beast at the same moment. They clung to the great creature only with the stubborn strength of their legs, allowing their hands to freely use their hefty weapons. The switch of a once-sharp blade and soiled axe, an oversized spear and penetrating teeth, fist and fury, created wound on wound. Still the changeling did not fall.

Nuada felt the alarming sting of teeth as they tried to sink into his leg, but he would not allow himself to slip from the beast. The decorative metal caps on Nuada's belt were all that stopped the teeth from ripping off his leg, as had befallen the torn changeling's arm.

It was a blessing for Nuada that the Dagda pushed the long spear in the slightly open mouth of the beast and half levered its jaws into a gape before driving the spear's metal tip up through its brains. It did not roar. It fell in silence and twitched in the death heave.

Both the Dagda and Nuada jumped to land on their feet, but slipped on the scattered corpses and innards that lay about. The Dagda landed heavily on a rock, his arm striking awkwardly, and the popping sound of breaking bone was heard.

Nuada wasted no time regaining his footing. He dropped his weaponry and grabbed under the Dagda. There was no time for him to think about what he would do as he pulled the bulk of the Dagda away from where the changeling was bound to fall. The dying creature distorted and deflated from its bestial form and merged itself back to its natural shape.

As the first changeling crashed to the ground, the other mutilated changeling fell sideward as well; but not in death. Both creatures completed their change back to human form in the same time, though one lay dead, and the other looked to be barely alive and in extraordinary pain. It seemed to be only a matter of time until it, too, would lie as dead as the blood-clotted ground underfoot.

"Get the boy," the Dagda nodded toward the wounded changeling, signalling Nuada to move quickly.

"He's as good as gone," Nuada said, detached of sympathy or emotion.

The Dagda grabbed his king by his discoloured hair and pulled Nuada directly into his face. "There is never a time to be heartless as a king." He released the king and gave him a good slap to the back of the head to send him on his way while he hauled himself back to his feet. "Find his arm." He clicked his tongue and pulled his own injured arm up against himself. "Changelings are not the same as we."

The young changeling bled fast and, by the time the injured Dagda reached his side, his blood flow had started to slow; though there was still enough pulse to expel more with each reducing heartbeat. The quiet, scarcely conscious being looked to the Dagda and tried to speak, but nothing came from his paling lips.

"Don't be talking now, boy," the Dagda said softly. "It's going to hurt a bit. Only for a moment." He did not wait for an acknowledgement from the changeling as to whether he had been heard or not. He immediately forced his open hand against the wound. The dying boy found his vocals and screamed with harrowing clarity.

"Settle yourself," the Dagda growled, clearly in pain himself as he used his injured arm to pull the changeling tightly against his opposite hand. Seconds later, the changeling had ceased all motion bar a slow, easy breath. The Dagda closed his eyes, fully concentrating on stopping the flow of life source from the boy's wound. The Dagda hummed softly his supernatural spell; soon the blood flow stopped. "Your story is not ended, boy, and your fate not decided yet."

Nuada, who had searched well where he had thought the arm to be, could not seem to find the missing appendage. It suddenly occurred to him that they had been continually turned around and moved several lengths to the right during the fight and that he was in fact on the wrong side of the fallen. "Shit eater!" he swore loudly. He spat saliva and scurried to where, indeed, the arm had fallen.

The Dagda did not move from the uncomfortable position of stanching the changeling's wound, and with his mind in such deep, peaceful concentration, he did not notice when Nuada finally brought the black-and-red limb to him. Nuada solidly tapped the Dagda upon the shoulder and he jarred to life once more.

"He's gone, Dagda." Nuada lazily pushed on the back of the big man with his knee.

"Not gone," snorted the Dagda in return. "Sleeping." He groaned. "Now I must wake him, and on doing so you must hold him as tightly as you can and not allow him to move. Do you understand?" the Dagda asked.

Nuada sounded a grunt to show that he did.

"Good. Let's get it done."

The intense focus of the Dagda changed and with a quick sweep he took the dead arm from Nuada. He abruptly swung the severed arm and he brought it to the unconscious changeling. He tried to press it into place. The young being awoke instantly, shuddering at his approaching demise. Unable to express his pain in sound and with eyes that sought death, the changeling shivered in limbo. The Dagda shifted the bloodied limb to the changeling's wound and pressed it in where his palm had held the clench on life for the lad.

Nuada dropped to his knees and leaned into the two of them. He threw his arms around the changeling in an embrace of power and immobility. Nuada locked the changeling's head back until his eyes were directly in front of the Dagda's.

"You are a changeling, boy, are you not?" the Dagda asked gruffly, his deep growl of a voice drawing energy from the air. The boy shook as he nodded his head. "You take this time and show me why the changelings are such a magnificent race. Take your limb back. Push out through your body and merge with it. Take your blood to blood and take your flesh to flesh. 'Tis yours."

The boy did not move at all, and this enraged the mighty Dagda. "Boy! You listen and do as you are bid. Take it back. Push your muscle into it and it will come back to you!"

The weakened boy hardly moved at first, then began to scream, cry, and wail in a horrifyingly high pitch. The bones in his arm crackled as though they would burst and the smell of rotten flesh filled Nuada's nostrils. His stomach heaved as the odour intensified, and he flexed himself against the struggle of the changeling. A grotesque wave of yellow pus exuded from the wound, and it fizzled as if it were being burnt.

"Push it, boy," the Dagda prompted the changeling to continue the agonizing merge. "Continue."

With more terrible screams and howls, the writhing changeling did as he had been firmly ordered. To Nuada, it seemed that with each long moment that passed, the once-doomed changeling grew in strength. "His fight returns," Nuada murmured. "I can feel the life growing in him."

"Indeed, it is true," the Dagda said with an absolute happiness in his gravelly voice. "But now he sleeps again." The Dagda had just spoken these few words when the changeling fell silent once more. The young warrior's breath was as even and calm as it would be in sleep. Nuada helped the Dagda carefully place the boy in a comfortable position on the battleground and then the two men stood, flexing their backs. The Dagda held his hurting arm bent and held close to his impressive chest.

"Why is it that you put so much trouble into this one being?" Nuada asked, rolling the words out like a slow thought.

"If it were you …?" the Dagda returned a question in order to answer.

Nuada deliberately inhaled and nodded that he understood. "Still," he said, "there is more. I have come to know you well enough to see when you have knowledge of another realm in your focus." Nuada gestured his head towards the battlefield, which still had some minimal combat upon it, with many fighters looking on from the side of the Tuatha Dé Danann. "There is a war and here you stop to aid the near dead. I have seen you walk past one begging for your help and further from the hallowed doors of death than this boy. Why this one?"

"Your highness," a loud boom of a voice caught their attention. They turned to see they were being joined by more of the Tuatha Dé Danann as the battle settled and their fight was no longer sought to save the field. It was getting late and the horns would be sounded soon enough if the battle were to continue on the following day. It seemed unlikely that the drone of the bloodshed horns would come as the Firbolg moved away and out to the darkening sea.

"To the side, victorious Tuatha," Nuada said. "I have words with the Dagda to finish without ear." The warriors nodded and the largest of them, Ronan by name, slapped his forearm backward onto the uncovered chest of a slightly smaller version of himself, their brotherhood of birth obvious. The other six warriors waiting to approach saw this action and halted.

"To mead. For drink is many to celebrate such a levelling." Ronan raised his much-damaged hand to present several bloody Firbolg heads swinging by their short plaits. The other men and women responded in a similar way, presenting many hideously distorted faces, which bobbed to the glee of their slaughterers. Having displayed their trophies, the men and women turned and walked away to allow their leader privacy in his conversation.

When the men were far enough away that they could not hear, the Dagda spoke. "You are tired of the fight and want no more of this death and warring. Of all the things that have made you the king you are; is it some of those things that, in the future, come to destroy you?"

Nuada squinted at the way the Dagda spoke. "I do not like it when you talk about the future as though it is done; much worse when it is in riddles as well."

"This, I know," the Dagda smiled with half his face. "This changeling is called Cian and it is for his survival that your people, our people, the Tuatha Dé Danann, will finally have peace ... until it is no longer their chosen path."

Nuada eyed the sleeping boy, who looked weak and unable to even stand beside a noble without knees that bent and knocked together. He could have been no older than fifteen. He had a slim, pale physique; even his skin looked thin. His hands were the keepers of long, delicate fingers that looked as though they had no real use for heavy labour. His face was best defined as pretty and his hair swept across his face like a boy of instrument: someone to be played with, rather than someone of power. "This boy?"

The Dagda nodded. "'Tis true." The Dagda continued, "He must survive. You may never see Cian again, yet he is the beginnings of peace." He stood taller, stretching his back farther, and drew a deep breath. "Now, for me, I will find my club here and take leave of this field, for my arm says it needs to be healed." He began to walk away with a slow, sluggish step and called behind him. "Send Cian to my tent. I will bathe him as well. Bring him before any of the other men come to me for healing."

Nuada stood still for a moment and looked at the hilt of his sword, which was in its sheath tucked into the top cord around his waist. He often spoke to his dirk as if it were a person; nevertheless, today he was not in the mood and he remained silent. He half shook his head, not sure if he should doubt what he had been told. How could he doubt when the Dagda had said it?

The Dagda was different to the Tuatha and not of their kind, yet he had taken to the Tuatha Dé Danann as though he were one of them. He had several children, and had adopted many that had been orphaned or unwanted. The Dagda had knowledge unlike any other and was thought to be of the Sidhe, the ancient race of powerful fairy folk.

"King Nuada," it was Ronan who spoke, having returned to see what delayed his king. "Except for those collecting heads, everyone has gone back to camp. The Dagda is obviously going to his tent; so why do you stand here alone as you do?"

Nuada, with a somewhat glazed expression, looked at his friend. "Not alone, Ronan. I stand here with he who, as the Dagda says, is the beginning of peace."

Ronan frowned at what he thought was only dead around him. "There are only the defeated; friends and enemies that are removed of this life."

Nuada pointed to Cian. "Not all. The Dagda says we must take him to his tent before any others arrive for the healing."

Ronan moved closer to have a better look at Cian. His frown furrows deepened. "This is a changeling, is he not?"

"Indeed," Nuada affirmed flatly, not at all surprised that the man had recognised Cian's clan.

Ronan pushed the boy with the blunt end of his unclean sword. "He is a bit more … beautiful than a warrior, I would think."

"Indeed."

"The Dagda knows. His magic is forever and he lives beyond life, so who am I to doubt him," Ronan said, as though all uncertainty were cleared by chanting these words.

Nuada nodded, though his uncertainty still remained. "Who are we to doubt, indeed."

Ronan pushed his blade into his belt. Without the slightest hesitation, he stooped to pick up the changeling and then he saw the wound on the being's arm. "Been blessed by a sword I see. Best swaddle him, then."

He stood upright once more and moved to the nearest corpse, a big warrior wearing a heavy cloak. Nuada had not moved. "Come, Nuada." He indicated the dead warrior, and, more specifically, the deceased's woollen cloak. "Help me take this fool's bratt." Ronan pointed unceremoniously and laughed at the dead man. "He may have been cold when the fight started, but now he chooses between the fire and the ice of hell."

Nuada laughed loudly with his friend at the unfortunate dead man, gesturing to the cloak. "Surely he'll need that where he's going."

With no reverence given to the deceased, the pair rolled the dead man from his cloak and unfolded it to use as a sling for the changeling. "The field hunters will be down soon to pick from the dead, and the dead sorters will be out to make sure that only the dead lie upon this ground. The sun is lowering in the sky, and I am sure the lights shining on the horizon come from those who seek to find something to salvage for their own victory this day."

"Let them," Nuada snorted. "Their treasure is no good to those who have fallen, and will be left like the dead on the ground if it is not picked up. It will rot away and be buried with time. Let their treasure do someone some good. Then let the air and the nights come have their pick as well, and return the demons whence they came."

Ronan stopped to study Nuada. "You are in an ill-humour for a man who stands as king in victory this day." He returned to preparing the wounded changeling to be moved and indicated to his friend to help him in the placement of the changeling onto the woollen bratt.

Nuada grunted as he aided his friend, picking up two corners of the large cloak as Ronan did the same on his side. It was obvious there was not going to be any further conversation in regard to the king's mood, so Ronan simply did as he had been bidden to do.

The Dagda's immense tent was one of the closest to the battlefield. This was for a reason. Inside the heavily curtained tent there was warmth, and when the oiled hide of entry was pushed aside, steam was expelled as if it were the breath of a dragon.

The Dagda wore a pair of closely fitted striped trousers held to the bottoms of his feet with soft ties that were comfortable to walk upon. He was just in the act of inserting his feet into a pair of pliant, brown leather shoes when Nuada and Ronan entered the tent. He looked up at those who had entered his shelter and nodded. "Into the pot with him."

The Dagda's loose trousers began to fall, but he caught and secured them by threading a woven belt through hoops that had been stitched around the waist. He further secured his trews by a circular buckle that ended the belt.

In the centre of the tent stood a large, blackened pot big enough for any man to bathe in. Under the massive cauldron, the remains of a fire still glowed its heat. Though the top of the tent had a smoke escape, the hot water within the pot gave off great clouds of steam that filled the tent with a wet heat.

The Dagda continued to dress himself as Nuada and Ronan made their way to the great pot and carefully placed Cian in it. They made sure his head remained on the curled edge of the cauldron, and Ronan kept a grip on the boy so he did not slip under the soothing waters.

"You are not taking heads, Ronan?" the Dagda asked, though still his voice had a flavour of non-care about it.

Ronan laughed in a nervous manner. "Would be, but I have been told there is to be the curing of meat or the curing of heads. There is no room for hanging both about the house."

Nuada laughed, clearly amused by Ronan's words. "The wife. Man gives and the woman takes."

"If there is to be a claim that I do not fight the battle well enough, bring it forth, and I will see that I might add one more head to the cure," Ronan replied. "As to your comment that man is the only one who gives, I am sure my wife Badb would hear your words with sword in hand and dagger at your throat, willing to give her sister, Macha, something to gnaw upon."

"Steadfast to your defence, Ronan." A woman's creamy voice interrupted the light-hearted conversation. To the side of the tent and from a narrow shadow stepped the Morrigu. Like Badb and Macha, the Morrigu was one of the Dagda's daughters. Here she was, with her hair as black as a starless night, her skin as pale as the moon. There were days where her hair appeared as red as blood or sometimes even purple like the bell-heather or the dog-violet, but always her skin, always, her skin was pale. She moved and breathed like battle itself; in seductive motion, essentially like Brigit, her most beauteous kin. The chill of terror, the rush of energy, and the sexual high separated the Morrigu from being like any other.

Nuada turned towards Ronan so that the Morrigu could not see his face, and he gave a gesture of horror at being caught in such a trite conversation by such a woman of power and sorcery. He stared at his friend, but found no look in return that might save him. All he saw was the dumbed expression of a man caught aghast at the sight of a beautiful woman.

"Come," the Dagda interrupted what undoubtedly would become a boast battle. He pulled a heavy jacket onto himself and then slapped several torn strips of yellowed linen down onto the side of the cauldron next to Cian. "Let us get this boy healed." He nodded his head at Nuada and Ronan. "You two can go and leave the Morrigu and me alone to deal with this."

Nuada felt the pang of shame at what the Morrigu had heard him say in regard to women and wives, and left more quickly than Ronan, who spent a moment longer to stare like a lovestruck child at the Morrigu. Nuada found it easy to convince himself that his quick retreat had more to do with having no wish to endure any more of anything that day. Ronan soon followed close to his heel.

Once the two men had left the tent, the Morrigu turned to speak to her noble father as she looked over the changeling sitting in her father's vat. "Why is it this boy?" Her dark eyes turned back to Cian and she stroked his sunburnt cheek with her index finger. The blackness of her eyes melted into the darkness of her hair as it fell forward over her face.

The Dagda dunked the linen to wet it in the cauldron and carefully placed it onto the changeling's sealed wound. "There is little one can do to change the future. I am not going to let Balor of the evil eye have his chance to try to change what is unchangeable by the senseless slaughter and destruction of the clan. Cian is the link to end Balor and lift up the Tuatha."

He put another piece of cloth in the hot water and snorted. "It will be soon seen who has betrayed the Tuatha, but I do not think that Nuada will understand for some time yet, if he ever does."

"I cannot feel the power of a champion in Cian, father. I do feel the power of a lover and poet that is growing in him." The Morrigu smiled a catty grin and lifted one of her neat eyebrows. "A real lover." She slowly kissed Cian's cheek in the way a mother might caress her child. "You are blessed, Cian."

"And," the Dagda said as he crossed the room to grab a small bottle of elixir that hung on one of the wooden uprights, "he will never know the greatness his loving will bring." He handed the bottle to his waiting daughter and said no more as he nodded his head at it and tapped her narrow wrist.

The Morrigu took the little bottle with one hand and raised her other hand to cup it. With one fingernail she pierced the pastel skin on her right wrist, and as the crimson blood droplets formed, she pulled the cork from the bottle with her sharp, white teeth. She lowered the lip of the flask to catch her lifeblood and watched as it mixed with the strangely coloured liquid within.

The Dagda tapped the bottle's light-green crystal side with his knotty finger and the combination of ingredients mixed as a minute whirlpool formed within the container. As the Morrigu's blood flow stopped, the Dagda took back the bottle, raised it to his lips, and spat in it. After a little further mixing, a grunt from the Dagda declared it done. This resulting liquid was given to Cian, who was roused just enough to drink the concoction.

The Morrigu watched with her eyes half shut as her father poured the liquid down the changeling's throat, and she smiled. It was done and the favour given to Cian, who, in turn, would pass the blessing on when the time was right.

She stood ready when the Dagda had finished and pulled back hard on the young man's hair as her father withdrew the bottle. She placed her mouth over the changeling's nose, exhaled long breaths into his body, and let go of him. Then she stepped back and stood with her father against the tent's wall.

Cian flexed his weak teen body and his face reddened while his eyes bulged as though pushed by a force within. His body inflated fast and the skin became so transparent that his internal workings could be clearly seen. His eyes burst from the sockets and his brains oozed out of his ears, nose and mouth. The gurgle of air whistling up from within breathed from his insides and bubbled out with blood. Within a moment his chest burst, and all of his organs flashed across the tent.

The Dagda and his most lovely daughter stood with no movement and waited. Neither stirred to clear anything from their faces, nor did they blink. They watched, and soon that which had been Cian began to move of its own accord, as if drawn back to the body that it belonged to. Like the flow of water from an oiled surface, blood and bits of being that had exploded forth, joined back together to form their master once more.

Cian was no longer a simple changeling; a strange creature that had become very few: He was a child of the Dagda; one of the Sidhe.

ᔐ

Nuada passed many of the warriors on his way to the table head where he would sit close to his mother, Danu. She was one of the elders and queen of the four wondrous islands and their four great cities. She was truly beautiful, even at her elevated age. Her splendid hair had not lost any of its colours of gold and near yellow that seemed to glow and pulse with perpetual life. When the rays of the sun truly shone upon the mighty queen, many of the court had to divert their eyes, as the pain it would cause would last for a time—as if staring at the sun itself.

Danu's skin remained fresh, only marred by the smallest of wrinkles near the eyes. Her forehead was broad, with her hair drawn back and braided in a way that allowed her tresses to curl down her neck and over her shoulders. From just behind her left ear a thin plait tied with red twine snaked through her woven locks. She sat with her back straight and her magnificence shining over those before her.

Danu's body was covered by glistening cloth, the best of silks woven with gold and silver. This thin veil did not conceal her physical strength. Her sleeves exposed forearms that bulged with power. Still, she shone with pure elegance and femininity. She was adored by her people.

Danu silently watched her son enter the feast and wondered as to his heavy-mood expression. She had seen such an expression before, usually in her own reflection when she had tired of a lover. It was the face of one who had decided to move on from whatever fields they had been grazing in to find something different and new; exciting.

None paid much heed to Nuada's actual mood as he passed by each warrior. The men and women who had fought that day each offered him a raised glass and thought nothing of his grunting rejection; instead they gave a slap on his back or a drunken kiss on his bloody cheek. The dried blood on their faces and arms cracked and began to flake off onto the food they were consuming, but in their victorious revelry, no one noticed.

Macha, as big as any man and as strong as twenty, intercepted Nuada and held him for a moment. She was as beautiful as Badb and the Morrigu, her sisters, and most deadly to any she frowned upon. She presented to Nuada a skull still red with grue. It looked as though it been scraped with sharp rocks to clear the flesh from it.

Nuada found it impossible not to smile at the devilish woman, even with such a macabre thing in her possession. She touched the skull to her clean cheek, as if nudging a lover, then placed it firmly into the hands of Nuada. Most of her body had been stained with the gore of the dead, yet her face, hair, and upper chest looked clean. It was as though she had stepped down into an ocean of blood and guts, walking through it until she stood near shoulder-high in the gory waters. She was called the "devourer of heads" of many who died in battle. At the feast that night, many young warriors would shun Macha in fear, for well they knew how she tore head from body and chewed the brains from within on the field of war. She kissed

Nuada on his cheek and moved aside for him so he could make his way to his mother's side.

Nuada paused a moment, viewing Macha with soft eyes. He found an innocent beauty in her, more loveliness than even Brigit was renowned for. When the brutality of battle receded and the corpses had been cleared away, Macha's childlike energy could fill an entire town with playfulness. Only in battle did the cutting edge of a woman, so strong and absolute in her being, thunder down terror. Her frenzy in killing was like no other. Many men would shun her as a result, this was true. But even more would be compelled to her.

Macha smiled at Nuada. Her sharp teeth looked like diamonds and her face like a child's. "I must go," she said over the noise. "I hear the music and wish to dance." She kissed him again and hurried off to play.

Nuada watched for a moment longer as Macha secured a ribbon to one of the tables and began to dance around in circles, smiling as she watched the ribbon twirl. She could have been, in moments like that, indeed the most fresh and beautiful maiden of all. Soon many men flocked around Macha, encouraging her in her dance. Alcohol suppressed any fear, and lust pulled them in and aroused their loins' desires.

Nuada saw his mother watching him from her seat at the head of the feast and could hear her thought of concern. He shook his head to tell her he was not ready to speak yet. She sighed in his mind and did not pursue further. He continued to his seat next to her and pulled some bread toward him.

"The meat is good," Danu remarked, pointing to the selection being cut from the fire as the warriors yelled at the servers for more.

Nuada nodded, and firmly said, "Not yet."

She did not press him. Danu raised her oak cup as two servants approached. One servant carried a wine vessel so large that he stooped over and carried the weight on his back, while the other servant poured drink from it into the cups that were raised. The hunched servants did not speak, nor did they make eye contact with any of the warriors. The sweat on them both, despite the chill of the encroaching evening, showed the strain of their labours as they took turns at holding the vessel.

"I saw you with Macha," Danu said, slowly. "She has your favour, doesn't she?"

Nuada bit into the warm bread as he signalled with a low-waving hand for the wine-bearing servants to come closer. However, he did not take the cup the servant offered to him. Instead he pulled the great wooden vessel to his mouth and drank, standing so as to get a better grip on the vessel. He drank from the jug so quickly that the much of the liquid spewed across his face and hydrated the clotted pieces of flesh that still clung to his skin, sweeping bits away down his neck onto his chest.

The wine spilt onto the head of the bent servant, and he could do nothing to save himself from being saturated. The cupbearer servant stood back and, avoiding any eye contact, waited for the king to be finished. This would not be until every last bit of the liquid had been emptied and Nuada had taken his seat properly again. The servants had only taken one step away from the king when Nuada quickly turned himself in his seat and vomited heavily on the ground.

"You drink too fast." Danu raised a well-shaped eyebrow at her son.

"He drinks like a man," the voice of Ogma interrupted any further words being said on this topic—and several others Danu wanted to speak about. "Best he drinks like a man so as not to battle like a wench."

Ogma sat next to Nuada and Danu on a stool that had been rushed before him by one of the other many servants at the feast. Immediately he started to speak on the subject Nuada believed he had successfully avoided. "Macha has given you her favour I see, and yet there are all those that near-fornicate with her as she dances." He leaned his gigantic body in and whispered into Nuada's ear. "Ceithlenn of the crooked teeth is watching. It is never good for a woman when she loses favour, especially when it is king she has given her flesh to."

Ogma tapped Nuada's shoulder and handed him a clean piece of polished, reflective metal. With it cupped in his hands, Nuada could see, in secret, that it was indeed true that his lover had seen the affections he'd shown toward Macha.

It was no curiosity to Nuada that he found he did not care. "She has no more claim over me than I do of her." Nuada shrugged and sat back, tipping the mirroring metal so that he could see Macha. Though Ceithlenn was beautiful in her own right, Macha had a beauty that outshone his old lover and Nuada felt entranced by her. He smiled, then handed the mirror back to his brother.

Ogma sat up straight as he tucked the piece back into a side pouch he wore. "Oh, brother, you give yourself to such bitter sorts that they will come to give you the lines of an old man." He pointed his finger and pressed it heavily onto the brow of Nuada, where a few slight wrinkles had begun to show whenever his eyebrows lifted.

Nuada snorted, pushing aside his brother's mocking hand. "Yes, that may be. We were not all born to have skin of a suckled babe, Ogma. Nor an indulged woman's, as it is with you."

Ogma signalled to one of the feast bearers to bring him meat. "Indulged woman's skin I may have, but an indulged woman's hand is what swings your sword." He smiled wickedly at his brother. "Twenty heads I bring this day to my wife, and you?"

Nuada laughed, beginning to feel the wine forming a strange, pacified happiness within his body. "You may rouse the warriors to battle and you may rouse words that calm, but it is sad that the only way you rouse your wife is by other men's heads."

He helped himself to some of the darker meat from the tray that had been brought to them by the servant and tore a mouthful from the large lump. "Perhaps," he said while he chewed, "you should take her a couple of the women's heads, just to give her interest and something to look at when you are making a woman of her. More man than you, they are, even as heads only."

"Enough!" Danu scolded in a low, rumbling voice. "You lads may be kings of your lands, but neither of you need act like owners of your subjects in such a way. Do you forget that you are of the Tuatha Dé Danann?"

Ogma and Nuada looked to their enraged mother and bowed their heads slightly, as they had been put in their place by no less than the great queen. "No, Mother." They spoke together like two naughty little boys.

Danu scowled at Nuada. It was the moments of her wrath that the crone within her arose and her features turned from beauteous into something more frightening. "You will take a queen. I will not have any more of this playing. What woman, or man, you have as concubine is not my concern. Your wife is." She frowned harder. "Now, you will decide. I will hear your decision when we meet in

Murias after the Dagda and I return from Falias." She sat with her back straight. "That will give you three days."

"The Dagda goes with you?" Ogma raised one eyebrow slightly at his queen.

Danu scowled. "Watch your cheek, boy."

"It seems many a lover you ..."

"I said, watch your cheek." She put a stop to all inquiry. "I am your queen. Queen of kings and Goddess of high." These final, few words carried throughout the many lands and, though not spoken loudly, caressed every ear in the kingdom. The trees stood tall to her voice and flowers glowed in recognition of spoken truth. The waves on the shores of all four islands halted their motion for a moment of salute.

All those at the feast, Nuada and Ogma included, turned to their queen, knelt, and repeated, "Queen of kings and Goddess of high."

The high queen stood, and an older servant woman moved forward to pin a rich blue and silver cloak around her. Danu watched those assembled as she pulled the dazzling cloak inward to encircle her body fully. Then, without another word, she shot into the night air and was gone. A moment later, her servant woman followed in the same way.

Nuada knew that the Dagda, his tent, and all that was in it had left with his mother. He found it impossible not to turn his head to see if Macha had gone with her adopted father. His smile returned as his eyes fell on her and she returned his gaze with her eyes as caressing as his.

It was not to be for long. Macha moved through those surrounding her with ease and a motion that was more of a hover than a step, until she stood at Nuada's side. She picked the skull from the table where Nuada had placed it, leaned into him until her forehead touched his, and whispered, "'Til then." Then she was gone. Disappearing into the night sky.

Nuada threw his head back to watch her for as long as he could, which was not long, because in his drunken state he began to fall to the side and had to catch himself. His attention was called back to the feast by the sounds of celebration and by the moist, red skull, which he held once more in his hands. He knew his pick for his wife, but looked at Ceithlenn to see if knew. From the way she scowled, there could be no doubt that she knew of his plans for a future that did not include her. As he stared at Ceithlenn she stood and wrung her hands, and Nuada all but felt those hands on his neck.

Ogma had stumbled off to where Manannan, son of Lir, sat. The king of the south did not drink any beverage that was ever placed before him. Manannan would simply say that drink that played with the mind had more control of a person than the person had control of the drink. It was not the way of his people. But because he refused drink of any kind, it was a mystery to the Tuatha as to what Manannan did to survive. It was rumoured that he was of the water people and had no need to drink of the land. But that rumour had never been answered as to so or not.

Manannan was by far the most powerful of the handful of kings at the victory feast, and all would be ready to gain his favour; the men in their way and the many women around him in theirs. His hair was thick and flared outward from his head like a fire with its many colours, from the brown at his skull to the sun-bleached pale yellow at the ends. Manannan's eyes were a piercing blue, his skin as tanned as a lion's, and his heart did match a lion's for valor.

Nuada saw that Manannan watched him with an unshifting stare, and he realised that he too had the work of king still to do. "As it is always at the end of a battle," Nuada said softly to himself, "the king must work." He stood upon his slightly wobbly legs and, as his brother Ogma had, he moved to pay honour to Manannan and praise him for his fight that day.

ᔑ

Balor stared with a flat, uncaring expression out at where the land would be—if he could see it through the mist, that is. The heavy mists and fogs never seemed to lift completely from the many islands of the Fomorian clans. The weather conditions made it nearly impossible to properly grow anything, what with the limited sunlight and chilled air. What did grow, though extremely good for the body, tasted bitter and proved difficult to cook in a way that made it pleasurable to eat.

The native animals, and the not-so-native animals that managed to survive, were as tough as the plants. Unlike the plants' disappointing flavour, the meat the animals provided was rich and good to taste. Aside from the insufficient forests that, where they existed, were dense and dangerous, there were few areas to farm and graze animals on; the rest of the islands consisted of grey rock. There was so much slate and other rock that the Fomorians used stone as their only building material.

It was his lover's harsh cough that brought Balor's wandering attention back to the cold room. This irritated him. He balled his fists reflexively and then attempted to relax a bit. When he could not, Balor pushed the woman from the bed. "Get out. I have no more need for you right now."

The woman landed, naked, on the stone floor. Her body, thin and sickly, had little strength, and she struggled to pull herself to her feet promptly enough so as not to enrage Balor. He swept his leg around through the fur covers of the bed and kicked the poor creature with the heel of his foot. "I told you. Now leave!" he screamed. His roar was a man's; however, the whining tantrum of a child could be heard between the syllables.

The two guards who stood across from each other outside his chamber entered the room and dragged the woman from Balor's presence, her body limp as though her life had transcended into another dimension. Neither of the guards looked to Balor. They kept their eyes down and away so as to not be demoted from the favour of the chamber-door guard to some unidentifiable something spiked on the foreshore as a warning to possible invaders. The door shut behind the guards, which left Balor as he wished to be—alone.

Balor's hair, nearly white, was knotted down his back; hardly much cover for the many scars across his torso and arms. His one visible eye was black as night. The other eye was covered by a leather patch with a silver shield embossed upon it and held in place by twine. His nose sat crooked on his face. Otherwise, he could nearly be called handsome.

He stood, naked against the chill in the room, and moved to the narrow window. The air he breathed formed into clouds that were as dense as any outside. The only heat that had been in the room had been extinguished earlier, as he believed that it toughened the body to feel the chill in the morning.

Balor stared out the window. He hated being so close to the sea without being upon it. He would take his clan on the morrow to the more fertile island in the south and find some cattle to bring to the slaughter, which would feed his people for the coming winter.

Why should he not? His clan needed food and he provided it. The islands that lay south had plenty; more than enough to spare. He knew he was not liked, but none defied him. His own tribe would cower as he walked the streets, and if they entered a room in which he sat, they would crawl. It was known by all that any who encountered Balor should remain well lower than he of the evil eye, or they would be made lower by the sword. Sometimes Balor would merely raise the leather covering his lifeless eye socket and view insolent subjects with the blearing white power that would cease any offender's life.

As a child, Balor had been cursed by his father's lover, who was a witch and great spell caster. Balor had been sneaking around the castle grounds of his maternal grandfather as he loved to do, playing and pretending in and around the collection of long stone buildings that was more of a fort than a castle. In this manner he had accidentally happened upon his father making love to his mistress. His father was enraged at being discovered, knowing that his father-in-law, of higher status than his breeding, would surely kill the pair of them should the young boy speak of what he'd seen.

The witch consoled Balor's father, and together they created a magical mixture and formed a curse over the child that he would have no sight from the eyes that had spied upon them in their lover's roll. He would have lost his ears, too, if they had known he had heard them speaking of their plan to dispose of the high king. They threw the magical mixture they had made together at the child.

The searing pain that followed, Balor never forgot.

The blinded child had run from his angry father; however, the spell had been cast and Balor's vision faded into nothing. He lost in one of Fomorian forests and the darkness of the trees made no difference to the darkness of his eyes. One of his mother's search parties found him, near dead, and took back to her father's castle, where he told everyone all that had happened.

His father denied the charges and accused his son of being delusional, confused from all that had happened to him.

None were sure whom to believe. Balor's father was a great warrior and had done a lot to aid the Fomorians in becoming a strong tribe. Balor was only a child with no standing in the tribe other than being the son of a great warrior. He was also a child loved dearly by his mother. Unlike most Fomorians, she was soft and kind and had a beauty that would be continuous; even beyond her death, the legend of her kindness and beauty would continue. She would not allow her son to suffer, alone in his darkness. She called the Dagda to her aid.

The Dagda was of the Nemed clan and had driven the Fomorians from the land they often invaded in the south. Still, by most, the Dagda was regarded as immortal and not of their world. A wizard, if you would. He had a power the people agreed could only have come from the Sidhe, and as such the Dagda was consulted in matters that baffled ordinary human skill. He arrived as quickly as he had been called to aid the young boy.

Balor's mother put to the Dagda all she knew, and he threw sticks, showing the people how they fell. This test showed Balor's father to be a liar, and both he and his lover were strung up with rope to high rocks lashed by the sea. As the people observed the execution, the high king called upon Nature, summoning a strong vibration, until all that could be heard was the rumble of the earth. When the vibration reached its peak frequency, the rock split, taking the lovers with it beneath the waves. Balor, though he saw nothing, experienced a vision of the drowning bodies of his father and the woman being attacked by sharks and creatures that had come to feast upon their meat.

The Dagda took pity on Balor and, with the mother's help, created a potion that to be poured into Balor's eyes to heal him. The boy was told that the potion took three days to boil and then it would be fine to use, but not before that time had passed. Balor became impatient and, in his youthful stupidity, tried to put the liquid in his eyes himself before the potion had matured. He put it in the left eye and it pained so much that he screamed. His scream brought the attentions of the entire house to the room. He was laid down, and it took the rest of the three days for him to recover from the horrendous injury caused by the elixir.

On the third day, the Dagda managed to restore Balor's sight in one eye. It could not be restored in the eye that the liquid had been poured in earlier, as it was too badly damaged. When he asked why, Balor was told that his left eye had been destroyed. What was left was a stone which was death to behold. He felt for his eye. It had been covered in a leather patch, decorated with a silver shield, as it would be the rest of his life.

Eventually his grandfather told him that when he had cried out in pain, the fastest feet to come to his aid— as was only natural—had been those of his loving mother. When Balor's dead eye turned to her, she died and fell to the ground in an instant.

In the years that had passed by since, Balor's hate for the Dagda and the Tuatha Dé Danann had grown. Balor hated the Dagda form his mother's death and for the state of his eye. He hated the Nemed clan and their descendants. The Nemed clan had gone, but those whose blood pulsed the same were none the different to him. The clan had split into two when the high king of the Nemed had died. Half of the clan went off to shores far away, and the other half remained as they were; they became the Tuatha Dé Danann.

As Balor saw it, the Tuatha were tainted as badly as their ally, the Dagda. When their distant brethren returned from across the waves where they had settled, they returned as the Firbolg and tried to take with force the lands they felt they had lost.

The Tuatha people did not take too well to the invasion, and beat the Firbolg, then took those who survived in as servants. The high queen, Danu, decreed that the Firbolg would be protected until they no longer were in need of it. Some of the Firbolg stole, were dishonest and lazy, and soon many wanted more than to be servants of the Tuatha clan. They plotted against Danu.

Danu, Balor liked. She was a warrior and a great beauty. He licked his lips at the thought. Danu was one of few Nemed descendants he would have wed, or at least bedded, given the opportunity. Recently, his fancy had also been taken by another Tuatha woman who shook his body with a vibration that could jolt the ground into a quake. Still, he thought, Danu. None could surpass her for creating desire.

He forced himself to put a stop to this heated arousal at the thought of the beautiful Danu, before his passion got to the point of his needing a woman to be brought so he might relieve himself. There was a heavy knock at the door of his room. A little impatient at this interruption of his thoughts, Balor yelled, "What is it?"

The door opened and a fat, middle-aged man entered. The large, tanned cloak that hung from him shivered with his waddle. His face was cleanshaven, yet still looked dirty, with stubble that shaded his jowls. The fat of his face jiggled as he began to speak. "There are three boats of the Firbolg that wish to enter the harbour. The people have been defeated by the Tuatha Dé Danann and have scattered. Should we receive them?"

Balor bent to take a shirt from the floor and pull it over his head. "What good would that do for us?" Balor asked, and moved then to get his trousers, which lay not far from the shirt. "We are a clan with limited food and water. We go to the lands beyond to take from those who have more. Why would we receive any here who are not of our own blood, much less those who carry the blood of Nemed?"

The fleshy messenger bowed his head and began to leave, but halted as Balor spoke further on the matter. The short, hefty man knew that the Firbolg and the Fomorians had not had any war between them for a long while. He was terrified to speak against his king, and he kept his mouth shut on his personal predictions of any possible problems that might arise from the actions his king was suggesting.

"Do you think that I choose wrong on this?" Balor asked, a muscle in his face flexing and his eye narrowing in on the man before him.

The portly man felt unsure as to what to say and picked his words carefully. "You are king. You have led our clan to survival and have made us strong. I am merely an advisor. An advisor to such a great king learns more from the king than the king might ever learn from the advisor."

Balor was pleased with the flattery and smiled as he tightened his belt around his middle. "You are my favourite for your manner of speech, clever man."

The advisor felt more at ease, yet still trod carefully. "It is the curse we must stop, good king." He turned his hand palm up, as if reasoning. "Nemed blood carried by any is Nemed blood." He watched, cautious with each word as he said it and watching the reaction of the king; making certain his agreement with the king would not go unnoticed.

Balor frowned and pulled his sword.

The advisor jumped, yet controlled his reaction enough to escape being called a coward.

"The curse will end!" Balor roared, though not at his advisor, simply at the air.

The advisor took this as a sign that he must be on the right path with his wording and went on. "Who is to say which clan this prophesied Cian will come from, when all we know is that he is to be of Nemed blood? And Cian may not be his name at all, but a pet name that his wife, lover, or mother calls him."

Balor's eye glowed red with the anger that grew inside his body. "I will tear apart all with this name, and any man or boy child so named that he may never be called Cian by any. I will allow the women with them to live, after they have been had by my Fomorian men as many times as they wish before we release them to tell all of my hate of the name Cian. May it be no more! The people will be told that if I hear of child or man with this name or called this name in any way, he will be quartered, but first he will watch the same done to each member of his family until they are no more."

Balor dashed passed the advisor, who turned as his king left the room and could only offer the words, "My king," behind him.

꒰

The Firbolg who had chosen to sail west rather than seek shelter with the Fomorians arrived on the shores of the least inhabited isle of the Tuatha Dé Danann late in the evening after being at sea for many days. As the only inhabitants of the island were hermits and lost souls, they knew that they would be safe. They stumbled from two of the boats. The women were weak, and some had died. Most of the females had given their share of the drinking water to their children. Women and children alike had been regarded as less important than the men. The men had not taken so much as a moment out of their days for those who died; they tipped the dead overboard and let them be taken by the water's depths. A few men had tried to use a fresh corpse or two to bring the sharks closer so that they could cut them with their swords and so secure extra food—this failed at every attempt.

It was only luck that brought the Firbolg to the land, as none at all were versed in seafaring skills. The few among the Firbolg with navigational knowledge had perished, but for one: Sreng. He had been given leadership until his people could meet with Sláine mac Dela—Sláine son of Dela: the rightful Firbolg king.

It was possible that Sreng would have been able to lead his people to land had the weather afforded him a fair chance. Storms and horrible lashings had buffered their boats on the first day at sea, and confusing mists had blown down from the Fomorians' lands on all other days. The day the Firbolg arrived on the isle was the first clear day before them since they had fled the wrath of the Tuatha Dé Danann. They had survived, barely, though they were sure that the curse of Danu or the Dagda followed them.

Sreng called the men of the Firbolg together and they—dirty, dressed in their furs and their tight underclothes—looked at least as much animal as human. Sreng presented a more pleasing picture. He wore his hair combed back against his skull, kept in place with the sweat and oil of his body. He looked virile and striking. He was most appealing to those who beheld him, a dark handsome man with strength that did not diminish.

When Sreng heard how badly some of his clan had behaved with their women and children on their individual boats, his first act was to punish the men involved. The leaders, instigators, and aiders were forced to turn their hands upwards on a huge rock, and their hands were beaten until they bled heavily. The beatings lasted until the bloodstained rock glowed in the dawn's light like a red warning. The men then were made to drag the rock with their bloodied hands, up the beach and onto the land where—it being as big as half a boat length and as deep again—they used it for Sreng to stand upon to cast his final punishment.

"Our women are our bones; our children our flesh. To cast death upon our bones and flesh is to doom the Firbolg. For this reason each of you will give bone and flesh to this, our place of being." Sreng frowned, but his face spoke nothing of anger, only of law and justice being served. "You may choose that which you give, a foot or a hand." He pointed his finger at the men who had dragged corpses behind their boat to entice the beasts of the deep. "And to you three, I speak to you with the knowledge of the Firbolg law, an arm and leg from you each. All your punishments will be carried out for the viewing of all you wronged. If you survive—by the gods, you will be made to survive! —you will carry this penalty as reminder of the laws of the clan that have survived since time of Nemed and are carried now to our king Sláine mac Dela."

The Firbolg had amongst them an old healer called Gaillimh who had been trained somewhat by the Tuatha Dé Danann's greatest healer, Dian Cecht. The healer sat and chanted poetry as the punishment was fulfilled. Gaillimh was gentle and kindly; easily she lit the night with her perfection, shining brighter than even the sun.

She then burnt the wounds of the punished men, sending howls across the land so loud that birds scattered for great distances. Gaillimh bandaged the wounds with herbs, binding them against the maimed limbs. All the time the healer worked she spoke her bardic words and never stopped. Her breath flowed as her speech did, the words on both her outward breath and her inhalations.

The Firbolgs were quick to find good water, and it was near a great spring that Sreng saw that the weakened women and children were given aid. It did not take them long to recover. The people started to build a shelter near the spring, which looked down over the rocks and small beach where they had brought their boats ashore. As their tradition demanded, they watched as their boats burned that evening a week and a day after they had arrived on the isle.

Gaillimh cast stones the Firbolgs had brought with them and told them that Sláine mac Dela had landed with most of the Firbolg on the eastern shores of the isle. To join the rest of the Firbolg clan, they would have to cut a straight path across the land. They would have to walk for many days to return to the rest of their kind, and there was no way of telling whether or not they would meet with trouble on the march across the land, nor what would be the condition of the terrain they had to traverse. Sreng knew that they had to wait to cross the miles until the weakened travelers and punished wrongdoers were strong again. All agreed.

Sreng looked down that night at the rocky shore as the boats of the Firbolg burned with flames whipped high into the air by the winds. He saw in the flames an image. Unsure if he had seen correctly, he closed his eyes for a moment and then opened them. It was still there. He glanced behind him to make sure the other Firbolg took no interest. He saw they had their own thoughts that evening, and as Sreng slipped away down over the boulders and to the burning vessels, he kept his eyes on the quivering image before him.

As he drew closer to the boats, he could see several beings in the heat of the fires. It appeared that they did not notice the flames surrounding them. They played out their history as if in their own land and in their own time. Sreng stood on a rock, seeing peace and then war and then peace played out before him. All a cycle repeated over and over. The characters changed, and he could feel their emotions. He felt their laughter, he felt joy and celebration, but he also felt every fear, doubt, anger, and betrayal.

Suddenly the many characters disappeared and a creature of great beauty stood shining in the light of the fire. She, a woman, stepped from the fire and stood firmly on the rock with Sreng. Her skin glowed as the fire reflected on her naked skin. She seemed unaware that she was naked, or did not care at all if she was. She reached to the ground and picked up a pebble, which she gave to Sreng.

Without a thought, Streng reached out his hand and took the small stone. It felt cold against the heat of the boats, which even from a distance made his skin red. As soon as the stone touched the palm of his hand, the woman disappeared back into the flames and there were no more images to see.

Sreng watched as the flames rolled and smashed together. He stood for some while with the little rock tightly held in his hand. At last he looked to the stone again. It was nothing spectacular to look at and, as far as he could tell, not comprised of any valuable metal or gem. However it might be perceived by others, he felt blessed for this token of his vision, and the stone would be Sreng's most precious possession for the rest of his life.

∽ 2 ∽

The battlefields had been silent for many years. The Tuatha Dé Danann had prospered and grown strong over thirty years of peace and good health. The attention on poetry, music, and goldsmithing had been a luxury focus during such times. Sparring and fighting was an amusement that often came about when the mead flowed and the boast battles turned into something more physical. Danu was praised and she, in returned, protected her people. Yet despite all her powers and agelessness, there were things she could not control.

Nuada entered the court of his mother just as Danu sat upon her throne. Nuada's face was felt tight and his mouth clenched against any words of discouragement he might hear. He was set on what he should do and he was sure that he was right. The Dagda had blessed him, and the great wizard's council had assured him ever the more. Danu looked at him as though she knew what he had come for.

"Mother." He did not wait for permission to speak. "The islands are slowly sinking and, from the signs that have been given, ours will surely be destroyed sooner than we had thought. You know the time is now. We must take the clan and move to the far isle of the kingdom. In the coming years we will have more shakes and shivers of the lands, and waters will cause us more troubles. How long must we wait?"

Danu reacted no differently than any mother to a child stating a point already well known. "I am not stupid, Nuada. I am goddess." She sighed with aggravation and turned her head to her left as she did so. She clenched her own jaw and spoke carefully, in the same way that Nuada had. "We know nothing of the far isle, and even less of its inhabits, if there are any. Our first scouts did not return, and neither has the second group. It is only proper that we should make sure our people will be safe. Our people have not been to that isle in many, many years. Even the poems and stories that were told about it have dried up and been forgotten."

"We have no time to worry about such things as scouts." Nuada stepped to the foot of his mother's throne. "The Dagda says it will be well, and of all the beings that we might trust, I do him. The Fomorians' king Balor has been married for twenty-five years to one of our own: Ceithlenn of the crooked teeth. It is said that he is bewitched by her and, knowing this, surely you do not fear any reprisals as we cross the water near their realm."

Danu laughed sarcastically. "You do not wonder why your old mistress would marry such a man as the Fomorian, Balor of the evil eye?"

"It has been nearly thirty years," Nuada replied, dismissing his mother's comment. "The past is all gone. I chose Macha to wed and no more was said."

Danu raised her eyebrows at her naïve son; however, she said nothing more on the subject. "We have argued on this before. Now I wish to speak to the Dagda without an audience. The words spoken between a queen and her subjects must sometimes be more quiet than silence." She waved her hand at her son in a gesture that sent him to retrieve the Dagda. "It is only after our meeting that I will announce what it is we are to do."

Nuada bowed, left the room, and shifted himself for flight. His motion sped up. He walked forward until he was moving as though running, but his legs did not match the distance travelled for he hovered slightly above the floor. His breath slowed, and soon he was propelled at speed through the hall and out the great doors. He lifted into the air and sought the wind in the direction of the island of Murias. The island was the farthest of four great islands of the Tuatha Dé Danann from the island of Falias, where the Tuatha de Danann lived and the queen presided.

Nuada did not breathe in or out for the flight, nor did he hold his breath. To be with the wind and the universe was to be between worlds and between dimensions. Here, there were no limitations, and nothing was impossible. A separation from any troubles and a sensation of peace had to be embraced in order that Nuada, or any other, could perform such a flight. It was that sensation of peace which Nuada had accepted as his own; the flow of all things. He could stay in that moment. The ocean passed by under him and clouds stroked his cheek with the soft chill of the winter as it approached. His hair whipped behind him and mingled with the material of his cloak as if in a dance.

Flying above the ocean with the warm sun upon his body was glorious. It was not long until he found the island of Murias, with its magnificent mountain peaks. Each island was named the same as the chief city upon it. The island of Murias shone in such a way that its diamond crowning reflected light and cast rainbows into the sea. Finias and Gorias were called the shining cities, for they both appeared to glisten without the aid of the sun. Murias was rich and called the city of rainbows. It lay to the south of the other islands, with Finias to the West, Gorias to the East, and Falias to the North.

Murias had the warmest climate and sweetest yields of fruit and vegetables. The soil was volcanic and produced wonderful crops which, in turn, fed the sheep, cattle, and pigs. The quality food made the animal meat prime and the horses and people powerful. It was by far the most beautiful of all cities to Nuada.

He shrugged his cloak from his shoulders and allowed it to fall around his throat behind him. He began to breathe in slowly and, as he did so, his meditation ceased. His feet landed firmly on the ground of Murias, at the door of a humble building that stood amongst great walls of houses that reflected their crystal-white brilliance. All the glare made it painful to look at any building directly in the midday sun. He knocked firmly on the plated wooden door and waited. There was no need to announce his presence; the Dagda would already know.

The sound of a snort came from within the abode. As Nuada entered saw the Dagda standing before him, but also he heard a door close as quietly as possible in the far room at the rear of the home. He guessed that the secretive other must be Boann, who was known by all to share the bed of the Dagda. All knew, that is, except her husband, Elcmar.

Elcmar was the Dagda's steward and known to be cruel and unkind to all women, not just his wife. He had been disciplined for this in the past. Even Danu had gotten involved. But Elcmar did not change the way he spoke of or treated women. If it were not for his warrior's ability, Elcmar would have been sent out of the Tuatha with his male companion.

"Queen Danu ..." Nuada began.

"I know," the Dagda said gruffly as he picked his club up from the day bed on which it lay. "I will give her answer soon enough."

He did not say any more and headed to the back of the house, where Nuada had heard the door close. There was a whispering conversation, the soft sounds of kissing, and finally, a hushed woman's voice saying, "Good day, Emrys, my love."

Nuada felt a little uncomfortable with the knowledge of Elcmar's wife in the next room with the Dagda. But he knew their love was right and good, and so he let the negative emotion slide away. The woman had no soft person in her life except for her lover; she was locked at all other times in her home and her husband took the key wherever he went. The only touch her husband gave her was his hard hand.

When the Dagda once again entered the front room he swung his club around his hand. The wooden device had metal pieces and long spikes which completely covered the bulbous end of it. It reflected light from the outside windows and bounced it back across the room.

Nuada waited.

"We'd best go, then," the Dagda said.

Nuada and the Dagda flew back together to Falias, to the great hall and his mother Danu. Neither man paid any attention to the other as the winds took them to their destination. When they arrived at the palace of Danu, she seemed a little impatient with the entire affair and frowned, as she clearly wanted a direction for her people's future. She wasted no time with formalities, or to discuss why they were meeting.

"What is it that we do, great Dagda," Danu stood from her throne and walked down to meet the wizard. "The islands are growing hot with the earth's rock that boils down inside of it."

"It is true, my Queen," the Dagda's words rolled slowly off his tongue. "The islands will be destroyed by that which moves below. There is no doubt that the islands will either sink or, like the great Falias, will burn. I would say we have only a few years left here as the Tuatha Dé Danann, holders of the between realms."

Danu sighed as she paced around Nuada and the Dagda. "What then?" She raised her hands and sought answers from the skies. "What of all the Tuatha Dé Danann—my children?" Like a mother in distress, her voice pleaded for the solution.

"You know that there is one thing that can be done, and the only thing that should be: journey to the far isle. It is of the people. It has not yet been explored. It has lain there and waited for us. It is fertile and has much to offer the Tuatha." The Dagda frowned at the queen, as if irritated by the obvious. "Your children will be safe. Nuada has spoken to you already on this subject; why do you need me?"

Danu was displeased by the Dagda's question. Her face screwed up like a child's in pout. "Why should I not call you when it pleases me?"

"And it pleases you, does it?" The Dagda's response was a snort.

Danu leaned into the Dagda's face and drew a breath. "Whatever it is, it is," she responded in turn.

There was a silence for a moment, a conversation that could not be heard by any other person in the great hall. It took place only in the minds of the Dagda and Queen Danu. They stared at each other for a time, and the Dagda's look grew bored while Danu's became the more enraged.

Nuada paced across the room and pulled his mother by the shoulder to face him. Her hand instantly came up to grab his, and with the other hand she secured his elbow. She shifted her feet and tripped her son to the floor. He stumbled, but did not fall completely. He caught himself with time enough to sweep himself and his cloak around with dramatic effect.

"Do not," Danu said angrily. "I am your queen."

"Queen." Nuada nodded. "Decide. Stop with this performance and decide." He stood straight. "You are no queen to any in death, or to the dead."

Danu's frown cut across the room and she swept herself around in irritation, with lightning speed, to retrieve a drink from a bone horn that was being held by a hall servant. She swallowed the liquid quickly, then motioned to the servant to pour some more drink into the horn from the pitcher that he had in his other hand.

"I do not know the land, and neither does any other of the Tuatha. You know of the scouts?" She shook her head. "Of course you do." She drank her second drink as quickly as she had the first. "If my warriors have gone, and they are the best at what they do ... if they are as invisible as they choose to be ... and yet they never return ... what are we to think?"

"You are to think what you should, yet know what you know," the Dagda said with a shrug. He raised his club up and struck the ground with it. The sound rang throughout the island as the metal crashed to the hall's marble tiled floor. The club echoed as if hollow, as if the island were a drum struck by the rhythm keeper of the cosmos.

"Do you hear that sound?" The Dagda did not wait for a response. "It is the sound of the deep, to the centre below, where the rock melts and a heavy rain of fire waits for the dragon to spit it out. It is as real as any of this dream; just as pain is." He touched the floor of the palace and pushed his hand through the marble tiles and into what lay beyond. When he pulled his hand back from the earth and into the room, it was covered in glowing colors of red and yellow. The smell was horrendous and what escaped his hand and fell to the floor melted the marble it fell upon.

"Touch it." He offered his hand to Danu. "Be as brave as you wish your children to be."

Danu, being not a coward and of a warrior's mind, did as she was told and touched the heat. She screamed as if stabbed. All doors to the hall burst open and guards rushed in with their weapons pulled. They kept their heads covered and their faces hidden as warriors of the Sidhe, the loyal friends of the Tuatha Dé Danann; it was their way. The servants dived out of the way from the melted rock flicked from the hand of the Dagda; then they rushed to protect the queen.

The Dagda raised his club with one hand in warning to the guards, and with the other he rested his glowing fingertips to his lips and blew out the blazing colour. The soft breeze extinguished the flame and returned his hand to normal. The guards were ever the more confused. They knew very well never to threaten the Dagda. Though he was of the Sidhe, he was of a different order to them, and fear of the unknown always had magnificent power.

Danu nursed her pain, but she stood tall against it. She was leader and represented her people in the way of strength. She shook her head at her guards and bit her lip in defeat. "You are right, great Dagda. I will give to the Tuatha the opportunity to escape destruction. I will give them a new life within this life."

She waved her hand at the guards. "You must go for now. The Dagda, my son, and I are in discussion."

The guards paused for a second, then, without even a glance at the others in the room, they left and closed the doors behind them.

Danu turned to the Dagda once more. "Is it that we are to lose in this? My strength and the Tuatha's are deeply connected to these islands."

"But the isle we travel to is one of the islands born of these. It is more firm of soil and water will neither sink, nor flame engulf, nor air blow death, nor the earth swallow." The Dagda wiped his hand on his cloak. He stepped forward and took Danu's bent and half-melted fingers into his cloak, wrapping the fabric around them as if for a bandage.

He viewed the woman's eyes in earnest and said calmly, "On the new isle you may feel weaker, and your mortality will begin to show. But you must only go there by choice. Take the time to remember that it was the decisions of those who went before you to make our islands as powerful as they are. The far isle may be unexplored, but it is cool and sheltered. It will grow wonderful crops and provide greatly for us and our animals, just as these lands have. Be it your own free choice, my queen."

Danu paused, as if uncertain what to say. She looked to her hand and pulled it from the material that had surrounded it. She knew she would be healed, and she was. To see the badly burnt hand whole again was a fascination. "We prepare then," she said as if to agree to something that was never an argument in the first place. "Our power and our wealth will not be entirely lost. We will take with us the treasures we have."

The Dagda said, "There will be those who will choose to stay, and that will be their fate to choose, not yours."

Danu nodded. "The stubborn is truly with the spirit of the Tuatha." She looked to her son. "Is it not, Nuada?"

Nuada forced a smile and thought that surely he was not the most stubborn of the people in the room that day. "Will all of the land be completely destroyed, or will there be safety for any that do stay?" he asked.

The Dagda shook his head. "It is hard to say. I do see the isles all resurfacing eventually. It may take many thousand years." He snorted and dazedly spoke to himself. "A haven for heaven."

Neither Danu nor her son questioned what was meant by the Dagda's words. They both motioned that it was time to leave. The conversation had been brief; nevertheless, their minds were made up, and they had much to do.

Danu flew from the room and landed softly outside. She mounted the colossal tower to the side of the great-hall building, raising her arms to call all the creatures of the lands to hear her words. The winds whipped around her, and her clothes blew behind her like wings. The dark steeple surmounting the tower beneath her blackened to match her mood and grave concerns. The seawater in the distance churned and smashed on itself. The sun peered through the clouds and illuminated the noble queen.

"It is to you, my people, that I speak," Danu started. "The king, Nuada, and I have spoken, and I will speak with the other kings. A decision concerning us all has been made in this instant, not because of one king, but because the great queen has said it is so."

She spun slightly on her apex. Every being in the lands heard and saw her in their mind's eye. She sighed a little and lifted her hands higher, which pulled power to her. "The islands are ill and need rest from us. It has been known to me for some while that there is destruction within the earth that burns its way forth. The Dagda has warned of immense dangers and likely death for all of the Tuatha Dé Danann if we remain.

"For this reason I have sought counsel from the Dagda and a solution to be found: a great isle for us is our aim. I would not tell my children to leave their homes if it were not needed, and I will not summon them forth, either. I do not say to rush, but to plan carefully. For the next few years we must gather ourselves and what we need to take with us. It is your choice. Falias, Finias, Gorias, and Murias, the most wonderful cities of the entire world, will sink and burn, and all that remains on them will be doomed."

She paused. The silence was reflected from all islands to which she addressed her speech. The winds shuddered around her; her hair and her garb lashed in its breath, the only other sound.

Danu's strength of voice grew. "We are a brilliant people that shine as bright as the sun, and our path is more golden than the light given from that magnificent orb. Are not our hearts as firm as the stars and the moons casting light in the darkest of nights? Is not our fire as blistering as the elements of the earth that threaten to burn and sink our homes? Where we go and what we do, ever the more the sun is there, the moon is present, and our hearts beat as the proud and strong and flaming, the Tuatha Dé Danann."

A cheer arose in response to her words. It was the sound of the world believing in Danu and all that she commanded. She stood atop the tower's height and viewed the people whom she led. The reflection of brilliance came from a tear she shed.

Nuada could feel his mother's sorrow at the knowledge that they both had—they would never see these islands again in the same way. There was a knowledge that loneliness would be in their bodies forever more, a craving for the carefree days. Only the Dagda spoke of time in a way that was infinite and unified. It was a lesson yet to be learned: The old days were gone.

Danu spoke further. Nuada decided to begin preparations even as his mother continued speaking. His mind stayed connected; however, his body moved its own way. He had to organise many people to help with the travel. The old and knowledgeable would have to choose. He was sure that there would be many who would stay, locked in their own understanding. Tradition said each person had the right to decide their own fate.

The corridors of the palace emptied as he marched along them. The slightest sound became an echo of great magnitude. Nuada's face softened. He believed the hardest part of the move had already taken place; that is, the conference with his mother. He would not be weighed down by facts and circumstances he could not change, only what would be done from that point forward.

Nuada rounded a corner and spied a figure sitting on the side of one of the small walls surrounding a terrace. He was shocked at first to see someone there, but he approached nonetheless. When he was nearly upon the woman, he felt certain it was Ceithlenn, his former lover. Then—he would have sworn to it—he saw the facial features change from Ceithlenn of the crooked teeth to those of another, younger woman. Still, he grabbed her shoulder. She jumped in fright. On seeing her king, fell to her knees.

"My king," the woman said softly.

Nuada looked to the tower where his mother still stood and saw that she had fallen silent in her speech. Her eyes were cast down upon him. The wind continued to whip and the sound of what might have been the ocean rushed Nuada's ears. His hands fell to his sides and his mind turned to his mother. *It was Ceithlenn*, he thought forward.

You are acting obsessed over something that never was, Danu scolded, mentally. *You have a wife. You have a child. Is it that you want something that no longer wants for you?*

Ceithlenn was no more than play, Nuada insisted, and meant it. *Macha would always …*

There is no more of this then, Danu stopped what she saw to be Nuada's whining. *Apologize to young Aoife. She is but a child.*

Nuada looked down at the young woman, who could have been no older than thirteen. She had not moved and stayed quiet as she waited for her king to speak to or bless her. He found it hard to put his hand on her head, having seen what he had seen. He worked against any negative emotion and placed his hand firmly on her head.

"Young Aoife," Nuada said to her so that only she might hear. "I apologize for the fright that I gave to you just now. I wished to bless you with good fortune for you and your family on this journey the Tuatha Dé Danann is now undertaking." He saw her smile, even with her bowed head, and he smiled at her sweetness. "That is all." He raised his arms in a grand gesture. "The Tuatha Dé Danann of power and glory," he raised his voice into a roar. "Let they who speak otherwise meet with Claiomh Solais. Light Sword. Great sword of Nuada."

"And the club of the Dagda smash down and shatter their heads from their bodies," the Dagda boomed from Nuada's side. The menace of his club waved in the air for all to behold. The people cheered.

"And my spear or dagger," Ronan resounded from the side of the palace wall. Again, the cheer went up.

"May my manhood make sluts of their women," Arias, the comic poet of Finias, added. The men particularly loved this riposte, and the reply of hundreds in thundering applause sounded across what seemed to be all the earth.

"You best watch yourself and the way you command yourself, boy." The Dagda had taken hold of Nuada's forearm and spun him away from the liveliness of the multitude. "I understand what you say. Still, you are king and must always carry yourself better." It was clear from the look in the Dagda's eyes that he was not happy at the way Nuada had reacted to the young woman on the terrace. "Now she knows that she has been seen."

The Dagda took flight. Nuada could not leave this statement as it was, so he too sprang into the air. It was hard to maintain the peace of meditation needed for flight, and Nuada sank twice, but recovered himself quickly. He knew that the Dagda returned to his home and to his lover.

They both landed as they had not long before at Danu's court, within moments of one another. They stood back at the door of the Dagda's home.

"What is it you want?" the Dagda grumbled.

"Surely you know," Nuada offered up sarcastically.

The Dagda viewed him with a blank look. There was no anger, and it was as if he had no comprehension of what Nuada was talking about. "You act so strong. Strength is the basis of nothing that is solid," the Dagda finally snorted, and continued to open the door to his home. The Dagda's groan was loud and clear as he and Nuada saw his steward, Elcmar, waiting.

"Master, we have heard of the travel, and it is to you that I come to arrange all that need be done." Elcmar bowed slightly.

The Dagda, with the roll of his eyes, gestured to Nuada. "I have others to entertain, too. The arrangements can wait for a while. Return on the morrow and take some time to organise the island's fleeing, first with the boats that we have and their capacity, before you simply hammer me with careless thoughts."

"I have thought already," Elcmar insisted with a laugh that said otherwise. "It should be that the men be aboard the newer boats with the whores of their choice, food, and drink. The wives, other women, animals, and children will follow behind in the older boats, as they should. We have twenty-five good boats, here, that are fit for sail, another fifteen in the harbours near finished, and twelve that can be repaired in a short time."

"And why should they be anything of the like?" the Dagda frowned. "You think as if you are bound only by your genitals, Elcmar, or the glory you believe you carry from battle. Each house is to be together, their animals included. I will not have, nor would the queen have, such sacrifices made of certain individual people and their lives be seen as less than by any of the rest of the clan." He grabbed Elcmar with one hand on his chin and squeezed hard. "Even in a joke. Is it to Danu you wish this conversation go?"

Elcmar's face reddened, not only from the weight of the Dagda's hand on his jaw, but also with his humiliation. He, so much bigger than his master; his bulk being at least twice that of the Dagda's, moaned like a dog in the crushing grip.

Nuada stepped forward, even though he knew it was not his fight. He patted the back of the Dagda and moved to sit on the bed with its scattered covers.

The wizard removed his hand from his steward and calmed himself enough to even force a laugh, which Nuada had a feeling was a very hard thing for the Dagda to do. "Get on with it, then." The Dagda shoved Elcmar.

Elcmar said no more, nodded his head, and humbly left the house.

The mood had changed in Nuada, and after Elcmar had left he noted to the Dagda, "You will have to watch your behaviour with him. Your obvious dislike of him gleams brighter than my sword and is louder than the great harp. If he found himself a degree more intelligent than the hound he is, he might wonder why it is you keep him about. A jealous man he is not generally: having been forced his wife to marry to please his family. He may be unkind to women and even dislike them in some ways, but he does not seem like one to take well to his woman's betrayal."

The Dagda snorted. "He would only find jealousy in his mirror being tampered with or the loss of his foreign lover."

Nuada returned to the subject he had pursued the Dagda to know. "What is going on? Why was Ceithlenn …" he paused to rephrase the question. "The witch, what is she doing?"

"The witch, Ceithlenn," the Dagda said as he put his club onto a holder he had made for it just above his cauldron, "has become traitor. She has been for a long time. You have not cared to notice. She needs information. You are seeing her face in that of the innocent, which was not a hard trick for her. She is simply using the eyes that can be led like a child's. She deserted Aoife as soon as she knew that she was discovered. Where she went from there, I don't know. It would have been more useful knowing exactly how much information she had received and how much we could deceive her and the Fomorians."

"Surely she would not destroy the Tuatha Dé Danann?" Nuada asked, a great uncertainty in his voice. "She has one of the largest families of the Tuatha."

"She has chosen her path," the Dagda said, "and her husband." He reached into the cauldron and pulled a ladle of soup from within it, which he instantly drank. "Balor of the evil eye hates the Tuatha."

"It doesn't make sense to take one of our people as his bride unless he is wishing for a more peaceful resolution." Nuada pulled his short knife and scraped some mud from his shoe bottom as he spoke.

"There is a bitterness that eats at some," the Dagda said as he sought a second helping of soup. "There are three great bitterments that torture souls until they are tainted like a waste pit. These are resentment, anger and scorn, all of which fill dear Ceithlenn. She loves the king she is married to, but for thirty years she has formented these bitterments in her until they have expelled her own senses. Her ability as a witch is strengthened by her desire to destroy you and all who celebrated your union with Macha. Be prepared that she is not an easy opponent and she, with the strength of a warrior, will not stop until Macha's head is pinned to the side of an ox cart."

Nuada stood. "We will be prepared, then." He grunted. "Ceithlenn knows Macha and by Danu, Macha will not be defeated by a mere witch."

The Dagda bubbled a grumble from his ladle as he finished his mouthful of soup. He placed the empty scoop on the side of the cauldron, where it hung securely. "You have still to learn."

He pointed to the sky outside his window. "You had best go. Your brothers are coming to talk to you about why they were not included in the decision-making between you and your mother. The islands, after all, are four kingdoms, not one. Ogma is enraged, as you can clearly see."

Nuada looked to the sky and indeed the gleam of a radiant red shadow showed forth in the clouds. Ogma was flying and, even in his meditation, he was unhappy. The shadow tracing the ground ahead of him glinted with tentacles of heat that caused the plants on the ground to bend out of his path. There was little that stood when a king was in such a mood. The people sheltered themselves in their homes, willing to stop their departure preparations for a time rather than risk the wrath of Ogma.

Nuada exited the Dagda's house and stepped into the street to meet his brother, who descended at great speed. The wind blew at his body and rolled leaves back up the street. Two steps, and the brothers stood face to face.

"Why is it that I am always chasing you?" Ogma angrily asked Nuada.

"What do you want me to do?" Nuada replied, just as firmly. "We all knew of the lands and peril that is to befall them. You," he pointed his finger in accusation, "You knew before we did. You read and you write, you study the stars and know more than all the Tuatha. You teach us, and still you said nothing. You fear Danu, and for that you would sit and say nought. Would you watch your people burn, drown, and die? What would your prohibition have been when all your people called to you to ease their suffering? You teach us!"

The great Neit landed beside Ogma and, at the same moment, Dian Cecht also touched his feet on the ground. Neit was the biggest of all the Tuatha Dé Danann. His hands were nearly as large as Nuada's arms, and his muscles bulged as great mountains across his body. His face was stony, however, and remained so even in the lightest of moments. Neit did not speak much. Instead, he chose to watch and observe the actions and reactions of others. He was fair and kind in daily life, but wrath and death on the battlefield.

Dian Cecht, though great in their tribe, spent much of his time devoted to healing and magic. He was clever at all he did and the Dagda found him of great use; thus they spent much time together. Dian Cecht, strangely for a healer, loved to scrap and would often be caught in common bar brawls. His personality often called on the concerns of Nuada, as Dian Cecht was known to flick between moods for no apparent reason.

"What is this?" Dian Cecht asked Ogma. "How long have you known of these events? Even a little more time would have given us a chance to do more than run around like rats scattered from a carcass. What right was it of yours to say nothing when there might have been other solutions?"

Ogma was further enraged and seized his brother's shirt. "There are no solutions that I have found. Do you not think I was trying to find one?"

"You did not say anything," Neit said, his deep voice resounding down the empty alley.

"You did not give us or our people the chance to help," Dian Cecht spoke over his much larger brother.

"What did you think would happen had I done so?" Ogma pushed his hair out of his face, where it was blown by heated winds.

"The people would panic and either abandon the islands with no real minds as to where or what their future would be, or they would still fall into panic, and then to madness and chaos. How many would remain calmly in their homes and lives when they know what the future here holds?" He pointed his finger between his brothers. "You would all have to defend yourselves and your families from your own people. All our enemies of the past would not have to do anything. They would simply watch as we tore each other apart."

Neit put his hand on Ogma's shoulder. "We are brothers. Family to our kind is all important, but I do understand what it is that you say." He looked to Nuada and nodded. His deep brown hair swept upward in a gust of air and crashed back down onto his back. "It is a good thing, then, that Nuada spoke freely when he did and a decision was made before any such thing could happen." He glared down at Ogma. "Is it not so?"

Ogma did not say anything. He tapped the hilt of his sword in thought.

It was Dian Cecht who spoke once more. "We have planning to do, and that will be done by four years' end. The Dagda will plan with the stewards to work our evacuation as best we can with the boats and equipment that we have or can build. We will take what we can, and if we have too much in the way of cattle or other animals"— he exhaled heavily—"we may have to leave some. Pray there is time to plan well enough for none to be left. We have seed to gather, crops, food, and otherwise. We don't have time for any stupidities. If you have desire to argue you will have to do it against a wall, for that will give you the same response you as will be given from any of us."

Ogma frowned and conceded. It was the right thing to do. He had found no way to stop the destruction, and despite his irritation he knew that leaving the isle was the only way. "I will comply."

"Brother," Nuada said, finally, "we need you and all your knowledge to help guide us. We need the strength and fight of Neit, the calm of Dian Cecht, and the wizardry of the Dagda. If in the years to come, before we leave, you find a way to stop the destruction, it would be good to save us from leaving. However, we must prepare in case you do not find an answer."

"Then it will be you who will lead us," Ogma said, flatly and honestly. "It is your understanding of the people that shows to be more complete than all of ours. There is no better person to lead those whose destination is as visual to them as the blind man's path than you, Nuada."

"This is true," Dian Cecht agreed.

"Agreed," Neit affirmed his league with his brothers.

Nuada nodded and accepted the responsibility. "Danu, great queen above kings, I answer to only."

"It is settled and this is good," the Dagda said as he walked calmly from his home's entrance. "There is little I could do if you four decided to have each other's heads. It all seems a bit stupid to be in this argument in the first place."

He looked to Ogma. "In the future, for the sake of the Tuatha and all that is right, do not hold back on what you learn. Teach. There is no doubt you were trying to find a way of stopping the very earth's temper. If the great Danu has no say, why would you?"

Nuada suddenly realised what it was that they would lose in leaving the islands. "We will be weaker in the new land. How weak will we be?"

The Dagda shrugged. "It is too hard to say. What we have and what we are is carried with us wherever we go. If it is weakness that one seeks, then that is what one will find, no question in that."

Neit asked what the others thought. "We do not seek to be weak, but what we are in strength and timelessness, how does that carry to other lands?"

The Dagda's answer was short, "It doesn't. We do. We carry."

ᕚ 3 ᕙ

The ship leaned to the side and nearly toppled. The Tuatha ships had been counted and they numbered evenly at three hundred, which is many to care for and keep together. The ships had been covered in magical fogs and mists to protect them from alerting the Fomorians to the Tuatha's evacuation. However, the clouds also made navigation difficult.

The queen stood at the fore of the ship, her arms spread and raised to hold their cover. She was tired, as she had stayed there for three days, unmoved and unfed. The water lashed her face and dried her skin. Her golden hair, stuck to her body, was soaked in salt water, which battered the scabs on her head and body. She wore a cloak that rattled at the bottom around her legs, as its sodden weight would not allow any further movement.

Nuada, with the other warriors, waited in turns to make sure there would be no more attacks. The water stayed silent, as it had for days. He thought of the islands they had left behind, when they were like an earthly paradise, with attributes as glorious as their names.

This happy thought turned to the memory of being awakened in the night to yet another rumble of the land, much worse than any of the others that had happened in the past. He thought of the fire that began to spit from within buildings and the screams of the dying. There had come a flow of fire rock that oozed from cracks and breaks in the streets as the very dwellings of the people crumbled and melted. The place they had called sanctum became their destroyer.

On the same day of this catastrophe, as the survivors gathered themselves together in Finias, the land rocked again, harder and heavier than before. The great city of Falias had been completely destroyed. The Tuatha watched the far island as the sky stained black and the island disappeared in a deep grey cloud. From the beach of Finias, the people hurried their preparations. They had already begun launching their boats when another quake came.

Nuada breathed heavily as he remembered how he and others had tried to haul as many boats as they could back ashore as all around them heaved and rolled. It had been too late for several of the vessels as the roll of a colossal wave washed over the boats. The suck of the wave then pulled the boats under and drowned all passengers aboard. Whirlpools appeared and disappeared. The ocean had become as much their enemy as the land had. Nuada saw Gorias in the distance alight with volcanic fire, and knew the people in Gorias were in as much peril as those who were with him. He found himself calling to Danu, with all her powers, to help them, but felt devastated to find no reprieve.

That night they fought on. The survivors of the disaster finally launched their boats into a heated sea where fish floated, dead, to the surface. They began a speedy row to hurry their evacuation. All rowed, even women with babes at the breast or those in the final pangs of birthing. Tuatha Dé Danann kept steadily on with the goal of reaching the island of Murias.

They arrived at Murias to see that the entire island had been blackened. However, three families had escaped the devastation: these, along with the Dagda, Elcmar, and Boann also. All their boats had been destroyed. They had no food except for that which was charred. They had no fresh water but for what the Dagda could produce. Many were ill, and some also injured. The land had set hard like a rock and offered nothing for any animal or plant in their need. Nuada took all these survivors on board the boats, and they managed to slip aside just as water shivered, showing more destruction was still to happen.

They travelled for two days, and all that time Nuada had thought his mother dead. In the early morning of the third day, they saw the first of the Fomorian boats approaching. The Fomorians were strong and had no lack for any comfort; the Tuatha Dé Danann were worn and tired from their ordeal. The Fomorians had seen the distress of the Tuatha and were going to offer no mercy.

Ceithlenn had told Balor of the evacuation of the islands. All the Fomorians had to do was to wait in the waters near a narrow strait that the Tuatha had to navigate through to get to their new home. Then the Fomorians could strike and conquer the Tuatha, the people they viewed as their greatest enemy.

Nuada suddenly heard a voice come to him across the waters: the voice of his mother. "I am here." The voice sounded weak, and at first Nuada could not be sure if it were really her or just a hope he had.

"I am here." The second call was stronger, and then Nuada saw Danu on the boat of the Fomorian king, Balor.

"Danu!" Nuada called to the Tuatha, who all stood at the ready to fight their enemy. At this distance Nuada could not see well enough to view his mother, yet he could hear her well. *Mother,* he thought to her. *What is this?*

The Dagda took Nuada's arm as the ship bearing Danu suddenly came into view and they both realised what seemed different in the great queen. She had been used for the pleasure of king Balor, who had always entertained strong desires for her. Balor had raped her several times, beaten her, and then had her tied to the mast of the Formorians' boat. The Fomorians men had jeered her. They had pulled her hair until several clumps had come out. Now they slept at her feet in a drunken state.

Danu's yellow hair was discoloured with clotting blood and she was clothed in nothing except a dirty blue shirt. Obviously, Balor had thought it inappropriate to allow his men to view the naked form of the queen. Her hands had turned red and blue at the wrists from the tight binds upon them. She stood against the boat's mast, but her weak knees were bent—she was only being held upright by strong ropes restraining her.

The Tuatha took advantage of the Fomorians' debauched sleep and boarded the vessel, killing all but one man—Balor. Balor had fought with a mighty hand. He saw that the Tuatha were too many and his that his other boats were not close enough to aid him. He had escaped by jumping from the boat and swimming to the land, which was not far off.

In Balor's absence, the Tuatha took the Fomorians' boat and nailed, by any means possible, the heads of each and every Fomorian to the side of it. They spread their enemies' entrails across the deck and impaled their bodies on their own weapons. They displayed the corpses as if in the throes of fornication with one another and prayed that their afterlife would be cursed. Finally, with a breath of wind offered from the weakened Danu, they sent the boat and its grisly cargo back to the Fomorian land for the Fomorian families to find.

The days had gone by quickly, and it was not that long until Balor had formed a plan for another Fomorian attack. The Tuatha were well aware that they were the weaker of the forces at that time and the decision had to be made as how they would get by such a strong seafaring nation as the Fomorians.

Nuada felt his only choice in this moment must be to employ magic or illusion to slip past the Fomorians without harm. The Dagda could use a spell to churn the ocean and thus slow the Fomorians' boats; however, that would delay the Tuatha's progress and could possibly capsize them.

The only choice that did not put them at unpredictable risk would be to create a fog or mist dense enough that the Fomorians would have trouble navigating. This might cause the Tuatha some inconvenience too, but both sides would be at the same level of control.

Danu had the power of such, and she volunteered herself. The Dagda formed cords between the Tuatha's fleet and they were bound together so that none would be lost. Tethering all the boats and keeping them on-course in the fog took a monumental effort. It was a relief when the navigators' trained birds flew out and returned with grass in their beaks, signalling that the new land was just in reach.

The travel through the mist had taken considerably longer than anyone had thought, and the Tuatha were exhausted. On their landing, and the clouds dispersing, they realized that they had travelled farther north than they intended where the sharp rising cliffs were difficult to climb. They returned to the boats, travelling south along the coast. Nuada was amazed at the beauty of the landscape displayed before him. Shades of green he had never seen before lightened his heart, and he thought of a fresh beginning for them all. The land looked to be deserted as far as they could see, and was protected by naturally carved great rock walls.

They sailed along the coast, trying to find a place where they might land. The rock walls seemed to go on and on. However, it was all a misperception, as the boats had been caught in a current that did not allow them to move very quickly forward.

It was a time of silence and all of the Tuatha Dé Danann stood in awe as they sailed. Children pointed out their amazement at caves that dotted the cliffs and at birds that were unusual and strangely shaped—even the smell of the birds' excretions was something to marvel at.

To the side of one of the boats, a black-and-white beast of a fish reared from the water. It slapped back down into the ocean and blew droplets upon them from the round hole in the top of its head. Three other similar creatures joined the first, but the children, far from being frightened, laughed at the fish as they looked to be playing. The animals grew bored with following Nuada and the Tuatha and they soon broke away and went farther out to sea.

This was also the moment that a landing spot was sighted. The boats made their way there. Nuada saw the frolicking sea beasts as an omen; a blessing of the water. He had seen his mother smile, in her reduced state, for the first time in a long while as she watched the creatures swim away.

He saw Macha approaching him, walking carefully on the boat's slippery deck. "We will have the land scented with our combined essence by the morrow, my king," she whispered teasingly in her ear.

"Scouts are first," Nuada replied, and his eyes followed the trail of his wife as she moved back to her place on the boat. Her body radiated sexual allure and her voice aroused him, even after so many years of being together. The nature of Macha seemed fickle to some, but to Nuada she was whimsical, and he enjoyed that she was not as predictable as any other woman.

She was the daughter of Ermas, one of the female warriors who believed that no man would wed her unless they best her in wrestling. No man ever won. Still, Ermas had had many lovers, including the Dagda. Nuada glanced at the boat behind and could see Ermas at that moment on the right gunwale of the vessel, prepared to act as one of his scouts, as she had in the past.

Nuada raised his hand and whistled. His great eagle flew to him and landed on his wrist. He felt that he would trust it to select the scouts. He had named the bird Dea after his mother, as the bird possessed similar strengths and intelligence. He made clicking sounds at Dea, and she appeared to nod her head in consideration at what he said. Nuada let the bird sit for a moment and then he sprung her into the air, away on her mission.

Dea returned quickly. She had picked three young warriors to scout, not Ermas, who conceded, but remained on the edge of the boat anyway. Nuada signalled for the scouts to head off. He did not question why the bird had chosen only three. He had faith in Dea: She had always been right in her choices.

He watched the men jump from their boats and swim to the shore, where they climbed many boulders and rocks to reach the land instead of walking along the beach. They did this to prevent their leaving tracks and alerting any inhabitants of the island to their presence. It was not long before the scouts had all disappeared, heading in different directions.

The Tuatha Dé Danann in the boats waited much of the day in the warm sun. Danu slept at the bow of the boat next to Brigit, who had been burnt terribly on the left side of her face during their evacuation. The two women were watched over by Badb, who prevented any word or sound entering the queen or her sister's hearing that might disturb their sleep. Brigit and Danu had been placed down on hide and furs to give a soft bed.

A soft bed was especially important for Danu, as the queen's body was so bruised, and her head so scored, that she would not be able to fulfil any other queenly task until she healed. She needed rest, and the Tuatha needed to find herbs to aid her recovery. The salt of the water had prevented any infection in her wounds. Still, her exertions to cloak the boats in mist had made her body was as weak as when they had first found her after Balor's brutal attack.

The scouts returned to the beach in the late afternoon. They all seemed confident enough about their safety that they waved to the boats from the sand instead of from the rocks. Nuada beckoned them come to him and they complied, swimming the distance with ease. They were aided aboard by the Dagda and Nuada himself.

"What have you seen?" Nuada asked he signalled for a skin of water to be brought for the men.

The warriors drank as the king and others waited for an answer. It did not take long, because the men did not seem to be very thirsty.

Then Luchtaine, the young brother of Goibniu the smith, spoke. "There is much this land has to offer. I speak for myself and all I saw. The land is rich and fertile. There are herbs in a field for the sick and injured. There is also a stream that is not that far and will provide us well. None of us have seen any trace of human life, enemy or ally. There are many tracks of animals, and many animals did we see. We are blessed to have arrived at such a haven."

Macha drew near. She leaned on Nuada's shoulder and felt the round of his bottom, slowly and with sexual assuredness, as she pushed her hips into his leg. The young warriors, observing Macha's actions, seemed uncertain as to how to react. Nuada kissed his wife on her forehead. He raised his arms and broke her movement to hail the other boats. "We shall take fish for our supper and go ashore."

A cheer went up from all quarters, even from the people the farthest boats who could not have heard Nuada's decree. Surely they had guessed that the Tuatha had found a home.

As tradition would beckon, four of the Tuatha's wise men—Arias, Senias, Morfessa, and Urias—brought treasure ashore representing each man's respective island. Urias of the noble nature, who hailed from Gorias, was given the sword of Nuada that none are to escape, which was to be passed from king to king, and he strode the beach first.

He was followed by Morfessa, sometimes called Morias, who was accompanied by seven warriors bringing the stone of virtue, the Lia Fáil, taken from Falias. This was the stone from which all kings would be identified and taken to on their coronation day. The sword was placed on the Lia Fáil, the sacred stone, after it had been taken and rested on top of the rocks of high cliffs with great effort.

Next came Arias the poet, who carried the spear of victory, so named because the person who carried it could not be harmed. The spear was rested against the Lia Fáil.

Last in line was Senias; he carried the Dagda's cauldron. This was placed at the foot of the sacred stone. This action signalled the people to drag the boats from the water and set them alight.

The boats burned with a fire high and hot. Soon an improvised spit had been set up to allow the roasting of a feast of newly caught fish by the fire.

Manannan, who had been staying in the great palace in Gorias, had his musicians begin their music, and the people began to dance as the food cooked. The wine and mead they had brought was given in small amounts at first. However, as the evening wore on, the drink flowed more freely. Rapidly all felt the warmth of the flames and of the food and wine in their bellies.

The three young priestesses, Fodla, Eire, and Banda, danced between and around all of the Tuatha until late in the evening. Each priestess pressed her hands into the stomach of each man and woman and touched the cheeks of all of the children. They threw chants at the sun where it had set and then to the east where it would rise. The priestesses then approached the animals, a plough, and what seed the Tuatha had brought, and lay their hands on each of these before they lay down to sleep.

After the blessing, the Tuatha listened to Eadon, the high bard and poet who knew all of their history, as he spoke of the events that had taken place, then told them of their Nemed ancestors and their stories of similar circumstance.

Nuada and Macha, like many other couples, made their way between the rocks to a more discreet area where they would bring their own celebration to a climax. Groans of lovers and the slap of skin on skin sounded around them. Figures and shadows with bodies joined could be easily seen, so the lovers became further aroused while also being in sight and protected in case any intruder should try to surprise them in the night.

The king and his woman chose a place near the Morrigu, who had taken a young warrior for her enjoyment. She screamed as she ran her hands down the warrior's muscular chest and she arched back over the rock she lay upon. Nuada hastened himself into his wife and felt a high greater than he had in some while.

When they returned to the beach to sleep, Nuada was greeted with a roar of approval by those still awake. The Tuatha had placed rugs on the beach for Nuada and Macha to sleep upon right next to the fire, a place of prime importance.

Nuada lay down, unwilling to continue reveling into the night as he'd hardly slept for many days, and the need to rest was suddenly upon him. He sat, as Macha did, and they curled into each other as the fire warmed their bodies and kissed the air with orange and red.

Nuada fell asleep quickly. All day his mind had been full of the things he and his people had to do the next day and further on. Now he found that he had not a thought to think as he touched the ground; his mind emptied. His dream was realistic and filled with images he thought he should understand, yet did not.

He saw a clan who lived on the island and their king who was portly and tall, strong and confident. He saw that messengers were going to that king and telling him of the Tuatha's arrival. The king immediately sought counsel from his advisors, and their decision was to send out a warrior to meet the Tuatha.

In his sleep Nuada shuddered, and the quiver brought about a new dream. In that dream he stood on large rock on the plain of a great valley. He wore white and held a staff, instead of his sword, in his right hand, and a sprig of mistletoe in his left. He looked to the east and saw birds flying away in fright and other animals stampede away from something. A range of mountains encased him and the sky looked as clear and blue as the ocean in Finias had been. From between two mountain peaks a snake slid. It was as big as any mountain, and its tongue seemed the size of three men lying end to end.

Suddenly the snake, which was near upon Nuada, reared up. The creature focused on something behind Nuada. He turned and saw an eagle, as big as two mountains, come to fight the snake. They battled together for some while, but neither won. For every injury one received, the other would receive a similar wound. Eventually both animals slowed and ultimately stopped their fight. They seemed to view each other, not with resentment or hate, but with mutual respect. The eagle and snake then merged and became a dragon that flew into the sky just as dawn broke.

Nuada woke refreshed, but nonetheless worried that his dream might have some unknown merit. He sought his mother to speak to before any others awoke. As he made his way to the side of the beach where his mother lay, he saw something move along the rocks. The shock stopped him from moving for a moment.

He called to the Tuatha to rise, as he knew that the little fellow was not one of their own. The image in the early dawn's light could not be fully seen, there was enough light that they could chase the character. Though it moved like a person, they could not be sure if it was a creature or a man.

The figure moved rapidly away from their camp. The Tuatha Dé Danann who had responded to Nuada's call followed. The figure was obviously used to climbing the rocks and was quick in its upward movement.

The light grew and the Tuatha slowed their pursuit, thinking that they had definitely lost capturing the stranger. At that instant, far above Nuada, on a tall cliff rock, the fellow showed himself to them.

"Oh, great king," he said mockingly.

Nuada was close to exploding with anger at the fur-clad little man. "What is it you want?"

"What is it you want?" the twisted little man repeated. With long front teeth that overhung his lip and all the furs covering his body, he looked like an upright rabbit.

Nuada was unsure if the man was simply repeating what he had said to taunt him, or if he indeed spoke the language of Nemed. He did not have the time to say anything else as the little man disappeared once more, this time for good.

Nuada and his people returned to the beach to those who had remained behind and had no idea what was going on. The children clung with fear to their mothers' legs and the women looked to their husbands for answers. The newcomer was not what they had expected. The scouts knew what to do, what to look for, and they had done a great search in the area, so where had this strange man come from? The Tuatha gathered, some naked against the chill of the early morning, and discussed what they were to do.

Nuada knew his path and told the Tuatha Dé Danann of his dreams. The people listened with care to what he said.

Having finished the story of his dreams, he went to the remains of the boats that they had burnt and picked a handful of charred wood. "We have nowhere else and these lands were, a long time ago, seen by our ancestors the Nemed people. What was their land is now ours. It is not a Tuatha to run. It is a Tuatha to fight. Is this land more for any that may have slipped in while we slept? It is as much our right as theirs. It is not good for us to fear living in a land that is ours by legacy."

Nuada punched the charcoal piece into the air. "This was ours. Planted by our ancestors were the trees that made these boats. Hazel was amongst these woods, sacred and pure. We chose to burn and, yet, was it not ours to burn?" He thumped his hand to ground and planted the charred piece into it with force. "This is our ancestors' land, and though it was not cultivated and tended, is it still not ours?"

He looked to his people as they began to murmur. "There is a crooked little beast on this land. Does that mean he pisses on our ancestors' stones and we walk to the side and nod our heads? No. We have slain Fomorians, sea beasts, and giants. Does one little man have the power to induce fear in my people, the children of Danu?"

The Tuatha's murmurs grew.

"Should even a multitude of bent, irrelevant beings induce fear into the Tuatha?"

The group responded more loudly with their voices now as they shook their heads.

"We are warriors, not scared whores who take any as they might. This is the Tuatha Dé Danann that we will show them!"

Nuada's people cheered.

"Then bring them forth!" he roared through his people's calls of optimism.

They ate breakfast upon the sand, and Nuada called for some of the more expert trackers he had to join him in trying to find out where the man had gone. Sixteen trackers climbed the rocks where they had seen the man last, and at the very top they searched the ground for clues.

Bres, a half-Fomorian and extremely skilled in his understanding of plants, found what it was they were looking for. The man had trod so lightly that only the tops of the grass were pressed downwards. This trail provided enough to follow until the trackers found a clearer track alongside a spring.

They continued along the spring for a while, and then the tracks disappeared. If the creature had gone into the water, where had he exited? This they did not find.

It was Ermas who suggested that they take different directions. Luchtaine and Bres insisted that because of their king's dream, most of them should track toward the east. This seemed the most sensible thing to do, and within a short time ten trackers pursued to the east, two went south, two went north, and two trailed back west toward the beach where the chase had started, just in case they had missed a sign.

Nuada and his men on the eastern path found nothing and had to admit that the young warrior scouts had every right to believe there were indeed no inhabitants on the new land. The trees stood unmarred, the animals were abundant, and the rivers nearly flowed over with salmon and other fish. It was as if the twisted being had been an apparition come to tease them. The trackers eventually conceded and returned to their people, who had begun to build shelters near one of the springs.

Soon all of the search parties had returned, and all shared the same view. Ermas was angered and felt bested by a strange man that had looked old and worn, but she was consoled in her bruised ego by her daughter. Macha hissed as any approached; her anger as dangerous as that of any wild animal.

"We will build and we will train," Nuada said to his closest man-at-arms. "We will train every day with all the Tuatha, even the children. We do not know our enemies, but if they wish to know us and declare curses upon us, then it is so—they will know us."

The days passed by and no one heard any more of the little man, nor did they see anything else that would make them believe that anyone else occupied the island. By a year's end, the Tuatha had prepared a small fort where they intended to live for the time, until they felt their forces were strong enough to branch out across the land. The fort did not offer much protection, but it would slow down any newcomers who might try to disturb their sleep, giving the Tuatha time to react.

Now that his clan had some defenses in place, Nuada knew he had to find out more about the mysterious and unseen inhabitants of the Tuatha's new home. One night, standing outside the fort, he decided he would go into the air to try and see any strangers on the land below. It had been a long time since he had been mentally prepared for the meditation that would allow his body to rise. He tried to slow his breathing so that he might find his way to the nearest mountain peak; however, he felt as grounded as any mortal.

He relaxed his thoughts as best he could and then tried to reach with his mind's eye as far as it could go. The soft voice of Danu aided his mind, but he could not rise, could not see. He started walking, memories of his dream still disturbing him.

At last he went to wake Macha. They would call upon the Morrigu for help. Nuada summoned the Morrigu to fort's large, central hut. It had been quickly built with wood and reeds, and had long logs to sit upon, with a central fire for warmth.

Before Nuada, his close men and his wife stood the Morrigu, as pale as the moon, her hair as dark as the night itself and shining as if it had the very stars from the sky in it. "What is it you wish, my king?" she asked with a shallow breath.

"You are of the Sidhe, the Aos-Si clan. I know this. I can tell. We have known for a long while. Your people are of the fairy sort that is immune to that which weathers the rest of us. Tell me, what it is that you see?" Nuada asked flatly. "What is here on this island other than the animals, plants, and the Tuatha?"

"What I see is change for the Tuatha clan, and battles will bring about this change," the Morrigu said.

"Tell us further, sister," Macha insisted.

The Morrigu smiled at Macha's words and sighed. "It will be done for you, Macha." She sat the ground and bent her legs in a way that the right leg, bent, was flat against the ground with the heel just under the left leg's hip, the left leg with the knee pointed to the sky and the foot placed near the knee of the right leg.

In this position she began to whisper softly to herself, words that no other in the room heard nor would understand if they could. Her black hair draped around her body and grew longer as Nuada and Macha watched. The hair shone ever more as it grew, and eventually, as her hair covered her completely, the Morrigu appeared to be the night sky brought down to the ground. There was no resemblance of a woman left to be seen. The night sky image shuddered as she spoke the words directly to their ears, as though her voice stood apart from her body. "Ask now what you wish."

Nuada spoke. "Are they enemies who approached us on the beach when we arrived here?"

"Enemies?" the Morrigu cackled. "The old fool you saw is hardly an enemy to any. Much more than one of his kind would be needed to make enemies." She sounded derisive in the way she corrected Nuada's language. Then she continued. "I can tell you that he is hardy, but nonetheless weak, and his bowed legs have carried much in his years. He served the Tuatha Dé Danann and suffered his deformity at our hands."

Nuada was surprised by what she said. "I do not know him, nor any like him."

"Ah," the Morrigu disagreed. "But you do."

"Tell me ..."

The Morrigu knew the question and did not wish to answer, so she continued. "There are people in the east. There is a king who has created a kingdom on this island, be it mostly in the east. Some of his tribe walk the land like nomads. Eochaid mac Eirc stands as king. He is fair and good to his people. He has brought peace to the land and united the four brothers divided. His face is regarded as beauteous, yet is plain to look at. His wife is quiet and weeps in her heart for her lost children. He brings justice. There is no rain. Still, the harvest is good … yet his mind is beginning to suffer and his thoughts are slowly eating into his soul."

She exhaled heavily. The darkness that the Morrigu had become lurched and rolled slightly to one side, then moved upright once more. "He had a dream, did Eochaid, very much like yours, and he has called his advisors to see what they believe he should do next. They have all agreed to send their greatest champion to see the Tuatha and ask what it is that we are here for."

Nuada leaned in closer to the Morrigu. "Do we fight?"

The Morrigu laughed. "That is your decision and theirs." She shook herself and her hair retreated back to where it always had been, revealing her form once more. Her face peered through the dark threads of hair and her eyes locked with the king's. She nodded her head slowly, a signal to say that she was finished giving insight, and then she untwisted her legs and stood. "Is that all, my king?"

Nuada looked across at Bres, who had entered the circle, watching on in silence. "Yes, I suppose." Then a thought came to him. "Where is your father?"

"The Dagda has gone to help the great Danu, and then will seek farther for herbs and the guidance of the stars for the Tuatha's sake."

"Where is he now?"

"I would say, by now" the Morrigu smiled, "he is somewhere in a tree or floating above the ground."

Nuada did not ask any more. He could tell that there would be no straight answer from the woman, so he dismissed her.

He then turned to Bres. "What is it that you have found?"

"I climbed the highest hill near our people and I could not see any fires or signals that may be a settlement or camp of any sort. It would appear we are still alone. If there is any creature out there, then it is being very careful about being found or seen."

Nuada considered. "There are watchers set on the perimeter of the Tuatha fort. From the words of the Morrigu, I feel uneasy leaving as few watchers as I have. We will double the watch, and tomorrow night we will set a triple watch, and so on, until we know exactly what it is that we are to do." Nuada sat straight on his log seat. "We will hear from this Eochaid mac Eirc soon enough, I understand."

An uneasy sleep was had by the Tuatha that night and for several nights after that, but they did not see the strange little man again, or any strange men at all for a while after that night. The days were filled with building shelters and creating new homes.

The four wise men planted hazel trees and chose areas where seed would take best. The animals were pampered and indulged, as they were the people's only familiar source of food. The smaller animals and the cattle seemed not to mind living on a different island. The goats, sheep, and horses, though, acted uneasy and took longer to settle on the land.

The Tuatha had not been as well prepared as they had hoped when they had fled the islands of old; they had brought relatively few numbers of each animal. This made them worry about future supply and want to seek fresh stock.

On an early morning of the second year after the little man had appeared, a great warrior was seen coming toward the Tuatha. The warrior sat upon a beautiful steed. Oddly, the sight of the horse gave some of the Tuatha Dé Danann happiness. It meant that, most likely, there would be more horses on the island and even, perhaps, other such animals that the Tuatha were used to.

Nuada was called for, and he met with the other Tuatha who had gathered on top of the hill where Bres had set a watch. Nuada saw a tall warrior coming forth. The horse he rode looked small under him. On either side of the steed, fastened to with leather to the saddle, was a great spear. The rider carried a shield on his left arm. On his right side, pushed into his belt, was a sword. The man was well-armed. Nuada sensed that he approached to enquire; however, the rider might very well be an emissary of war.

The Dagda joined the men at that moment and Nuada spoke, sideward, to him, not taking his eyes from the rider before him. "We should send out our own rider before he comes upon us and gives fear to the women and children. There has been enough fright for them, and we are not prepared for full combat."

"A wise choice," the Dagda agreed sombrely.

Nuada looked at the warriors of the Tuatha Dé Danann who had gathered on the hill. He had a choice of which man to send. He knew that some could speak other languages; of course, there was Morfessa, who could speak many tongues. However, Morfessa was no warrior and would be useless if the approaching man sought trouble. Nuada's choice was Bres. Being half-Fomorian meant that Bres had greater skills in understanding differences in culture. He was also a great warrior, and the women found him very beautiful to behold.

"Bres." Nuada beckoned to the tall man, who looked to be much the same build as the oncoming warrior. It was obvious why Bres was a favourite for the women in the Tuatha Dé Danann, and even Danu had shown interest in the half-Fomorian. His face was perfect and unblemished, and his blonde hair was partly in plaits and partly loose.

When Bres was a child, Nuada had met him and been astounded to learn that his age was only six or seven, for at that time he was tall as any fourteen-year-old. He had been trained as a warrior since that first day Nuada had seen him.

"Yes, my king," Bres said as he stepped forward.

"You are the one that must go forward to meet this warrior. You alone have the skills and understanding. I trust that no matter what it is the warrior wants, you will be able to negotiate."

Nuada placed his hand on his sword. "But let him know that we are prepared for whatever fight his people might wish for, and we will not slide back into the sea. We can share the land in the west where we are and will be friendly to one another and live in peace."

He spoke to the others on the hill. "I want Bres fitted out with the same weaponry as the rider has. He has his shield and his sword. I want two spears brought. We will meet them with equal power. We will not appear weak for that reason, nor will we appear threatening."

Two spears were brought; then Bres bowed and rode away as quickly as he might. He started his horse down the hill, making sure to go at a reasonable pace so his horse would not arrive puffing for breath, for that would show weakness on the Tuatha's behalf. To meet the warrior head-on, Bres went through several lines of bushes and some of their thorns scratched his legs. He did not slow his pace; nor did he rush.

Nuada stared down from the hill at Bres and the unnamed warrior as they approached each other. Those on the hill could easily see details of the encounter from where they stood. The rider dismounted and tied his horse to a tree. Bres mimicked the action. The two men moved towards each other at the same rate—neither wished to appear hostile. They were as two dogs, each seeking to determine the standing of the other.

Within ten steps of each other, both warriors stopped and stared for a while at one another. The strange warrior pulled his shield from his arm and pushed it into the ground before him. Bres copied all the warrior did and then spoke to the stranger. From the hill, certain words carried to the Tuatha on the wind every so often; however, they were not sure which man said what.

The men talked, and they looked like they were beginning to enjoy their conversation. Nuada felt sure both men were speaking the same language, that of the Nemed; that is, the language of the Tuatha Dé Danann.

He continued to watch as the men stepped away from their shields completely and moved towards each other as if old friends. They each pointed to the other's spears, and Bres laughed as he was given one of the stranger's spears to hold. Bres, in turn, gave over one of his spears. Nuada was confused. Did this mean peace or war? However, he was quickly made more at ease by the sound of his Tuatha warrior's chortle.

The two men spoke for some while longer and seemed to be quite friendly. Nuada was relieved, as he wanted peace. He had found he no longer could abide war.

By the time Bres returned to the hill as the other warrior rode back to the east, it was getting late. Bres brought with him the spear the warrior had given him, having given one of his in return.

"Who is it that the warrior represents?" Nuada asked.

"His name is Sreng and he is warrior to Eochaid son of Eirc, king of the Firbolg. They have been here for many years and have had several kings since arriving. He told me of some of their history and of their life here. They have had several kings, as I have said, because they seem to argue with their own family. Such a thing I do not understand."

The warrior Ronan looked sour as he spoke of his own knowledge of the Firbolg. "The Firbolg were driven from the shores of our lands for being ill-willed toward each other and the Tuatha. There were few that were noble. They are mostly taught to steal and be lazy from very young."

The king was not sure whether to take this information of the Firbolg as being a good or bad thing. The Firbolg were, in many ways, their kin, though both clans had also grown to be very different. As in any sibling relationship, there are always views that are not the same and sometimes could cause fighting; or in this case, warring. Nuada was well done with war. He looked once more to where the rider had gone and wondered. But he wanted to hear more.

"What of this?" he asked as he pointed to the spear Bres held.

"These spears are called Craisech. They are designed to go through armour and shield and even the bones of any man that they are buried in. The size of them and the shape would cause such that there would be no surviving an attack. He took one of my spears to show his king, that he may see how such a thing of finery and so cleverly made must of be of a clan that has great strength.

We spoke, and I said to him that we could share this island in peace and that the west side, where we are, is not inhabited, and we would be glad to settle here. If they have no wish for us to be on the west, we will go east or south. If they have no interest in any solution, then we will fight to stay, as we have nowhere else but the sea."

Nuada thought for a moment and decided that he was pleased by the events of the day. He believed that surely it was not such an impossible request that they be peaceful neighbours. "It is good." He grabbed the shoulder of Bres. "Let us celebrate. This is a good day. Yes?"

He looked to the Dagda, who stared into the distance towards the east. Nuada could see he would not get an answer, and so he called to the warriors on the hill. He regarded Bres, who looked uncertain as to what to do, and he saw also that Ronan seemed equally unsure.

"Watch will stay. All others, let us eat and drink. We look to the possibilities of a good outcome for us all. The Firbolg may have been a problem to us in the past. I hope for something better. It has been many a year since we sighted the hide of them. Pray Danu for blessing on these events." His last words trailed away as he started to leave the hill and march back down to the camp.

Nuada was well gone. The Dagda stayed in the dark by himself, watching to the east and frowning. The Morrigu soon stood at his side; she came on a gust of wind and appeared out of the darkening sky. "What is it?"

"We need to see what is to come." He continued to stare eastward. "We need to prepare."

↬ 4 ↬

The Tuatha Dé Danann had been given a night to relax before Nuada held council with the Dagda. A decision was made to create a better fort against the Firbolg in case king Eochaid did not receive the news of their arrival well, or would not accept their terms for staying in the new land. The Tuatha leaders, including Nuada, saw no harm in such a precaution and set the Tuatha to work.

Nuada's dream had caused him to be more nervous than he cared to be. He wished for the people of Danu to be protected and safe in their new home. To assure this, Nuada decided that his people would move to a new location. From the hill where Bres had first spotted Sreng, the Tuatha could see that the land stretched farther to the west, and that in the distance there was a great mountain across from what looked to be a large plain. Nuada set the far place to be his people's destiny, and immediately began to move the Tuatha.

The clan moved as quickly as they could towards the mountain that Nuada had chosen. They encountered some wild horses on their path, and the warriors tracked the herd. The herd was so large that it took some time for the warriors to pick the leader.

Once they did identify the lead, they trapped it quickly, which drew the other horses in to follow. Now every warrior could have a steed. As the Tuatha migrated, they found that food was far easier to come by than they had expected, which gave the people more confidence in the new land.

They arrived at the plain, and Nuada was pleased to see that his choice had been correct; this was a much better place for them to settle. The water ran clear and plenty, with purer areas of land to farm. Many trees had to be cleared first. From the top of the great mountain nearby, a watch could be set that would be able to see any friend or foe approaching from at least half a day's march away. The timber on the plains would provide for the clan's houses and for their fortification. There was also much in the way of rock and stone to further strengthen their buildings.

The Tuatha set to work immediately, and they had long days of labor even after the sun had set. They lit their paths in the night with heavy torches that burnt high so the work they did would be without fault. They named the plain Magh Nia, the plain of the champions, which encouraged the Tuatha again, as this was a form of blessing to them.

They took rocks from the mountain and, with the wood they had cut from the forest, they built walls around their settlement. They dug a deep ditch outside the wall, and spears were forced into the ground at the base of the ditch at an angle, so that if any enemies got close enough to enter the ditch, they would have to do so with precision and care, which would slow any onslaught considerably. The dirt from inside the ditch was used to aid in the building of their houses and to help keep out any chill from the air; for this they also added dung to the clay soil and pushed it into a lattice of woven saplings.

The bases of their homes were made of rock, and on this rock base they stood the frameworks for the rest of the walls, putting in an occasional window. A cone-shaped roof would be constructed on top of the walls and covered in long grass, leaving a small hole in the centre of the roof for any smoke from a fire to escape, while any lingering smoke would seep through the long grass roof. Chalk and lime were gathered and made into a wash that was painted across the walls to stop any wear from weather. The largest of these houses was constructed for any gathering called by Nuada or the any other members of the Tuatha, as all the Tuatha had a voice in their tradition.

After many weeks of working, building, and training, Nuada called to him the Morrigu again. He knew that the Firbolg would probably prepare their defences in a similar manner, and he wanted to know exactly what it was that his people were to fight against if that were really to be.

The Morrigu came to the meeting house as soon as she could and presented herself before the king. Danu, who was rarely seen by the Tuatha Dé Danann anymore, sat on the right side of Nuada, and Macha sat to his left.

"What is it you summon me for, my king?" the Morrigu asked with a half-smile.

"The Tuatha need to know what the Firbolgs are doing. Are they preparing for war, or have they settled back into their lives and are prepared to ignore us?" Nuada asked.

The Morrigu thought for a moment and then sighed. "This moment you will see." She turned and pointed to the entrance of the big meeting house. In that instant, as if by magic, the warrior smith Goibniu came in.

"King Nuada," Goibniu said, his words hurried from his lips, "we have a messenger arrived this moment from the Firbolgs."

Nuada, unable to contain himself, stood. "Bring him."

A tall, thin man was brought before Nuada. The Firbolg man seemed to have no strength in his arms, and he looked to have the muscles of a five-year-old child. Hiss dark hair was tossed over his shoulder, and his cloak exposed a soft body. He carried no sword, and his shoes turned up at the ends. When he spoke, it was with a voice of a woman. "My name is Aibhne. I bring to you word from my king in Teamhair. It is his reply to you for your request of sanctum, given to our warrior Sreng. My king, Eochaid mac Eirc, says he will not concede any land, as you will grow and breed at great rate and you will suck the life of the land. My king says that it will take you no while at all to cover the whole country, and the Firbolg will be pushed into the sea."

"This is not so," Nuada insisted, still in the hope that war could be avoided.

"The old ones say that you take many lovers and that you spread your seed as the weeds," the messenger said.

Nuada was surprised that such a feeble-looking man would be so brave as to speak such words to the very king of his now-declared enemy. "You speak like a much bigger man than you are. You speak to me as if the Tuatha are an illness upon the land, rather than granting us the respect due to the great warriors we are."

Aibhne shrugged. "It is as it is, and what was said was said. I tell you the truth, for that is my vow this life."

Nuada considered this. "What is it then that your king is prepared to do? We are not to walk off into the water and ride the backs of whales to far ends of the earth to please your king."

"Eochaid will see it as a declaration of war if you stay and will wage war upon you. He prepares now for that attack, and has vowed that the Tuatha Dé Danann leave or he will turn the waters red and brown with your blood and excrement. If it is battle you wish, to the plains of the mid is he prepared to meet you. He says they will be fields of death for you. If you do not march, then he sees that you are cowards and he will arrive here and burn you in your beds."

The words the messenger spoke enraged all in the room, Nuada being no exception. "You will tell your king that you were received well by the Tuatha Dé Danann and that you were fed and given all you needed for yourself and your horse. You will then tell your king these words that I say. Your king will have the waters stained as he wishes, but it will be the Firbolgs who will fall. Their heads will be our tokens, and their women sheaths for our men's lust."

The warriors in the room applauded loudly at what their own king had said. They all sensed their blood pumping as they felt their energy increase at the excitement of a coming battle.

Nuada signalled to two of the young women who stood at the side of the meeting house holding flat-bottomed pitchers, to take the messenger on his way and do as he had said. With the women he sent Ronan and Bres to accompany Aibhne to the edge of the village when their hospitality concluded.

When the messenger had gone and Nuada was all but alone in the house with his wife, his mother, and the Morrigu, he spoke again to the Morrigu. "What can you do to slow the beginnings of this war that we might have more time for our preparations?"

The Morrigu sat on the floor barefooted and pointed at the chair of the king. "There was a spell I was taught a long while ago. A spell that can be done with the aid of my sisters. Though they are not both of the Sidhe, it is possible. Badb, Macha, and I can go to Teamhair, and we will make trouble of our own upon the Firbolg. It will not stop them. It will only slow them for a while until their own druids work a solution."

Nuada looked to Macha as she sat on her chair. He knew that she would go to Teamhair to work the spell, and probably would even if such were against his wishes. She was not one to back away from a fight. "It is so, then."

The three women did not wait until morning to follow Aibhne on his trail back to the Firbolg's city, but shadowed him from the moment he left the Tuatha's territory. In the forest close to Magh Nia, the messenger met with six other Firbolg warriors. Three of the warriors had bowed legs, but regardless, they were tall, strong, and well-armed. The other three looked younger, yet stood as tall as their older counterparts and carried twice the weapons. All of the Firbolg had dark hair tied back in a knot to keep it from their faces. They had skinned four rabbits and were cooking them on the fire they had built. They joked and boasted just as any good friends might.

On hearing what Nuada had said to Aibhne, the warriors quickly ate their food and packed their things. They brought their horses around and were upon them as fast as they could be. They hurried off east to their city and their king. The three women followed on horses also, far enough behind that they were not seen or heard by those they followed, yet close enough that they always had eyes on the Firbolg.

They arrived in Teamhair twelve days after leaving Magh Nia. The women had eaten berries and raw meats during their travel, and were careful enough that no trace of them would be found. As they drew closer to Teamhair, their caution heightened. More and more Firbolg were to be found in the forests and on the grassy hills.

They left their horses in a place they could remember where the animals would be safe, and then took to foot. There were stages where they crawled upon their bellies through a pig's hole, and where they briefly took the guise of Firbolg women. Their arrival in the city brought them relief that their travel away from their kin had finished.

When the evening came on the first night in the city, the Morrigu found the Firbolgs' main water source and made it the target. The three women pooled together herbs they had collected together in a bowl and stirred them with a branch of hazel wood. They breathed words and winds across the mixture, and it ignited briefly. The bowl's contents were then tipped into the water, and the women hurried to their next destination.

Along the way, they listened, ears to the ground, for sounds of the old islands that they had left behind. It was Badb who found the first sound and tapped the ground where she had found it. The Morrigu held her two sisters' hands, pushing her feet into the ground until her body was immersed in the soil up to her chest. From within the earth a rumble came. The Morrigu was pulled from the hole she had made and the women dashed sideward; they cackled as they did so. Then they ran with all their might back into the forest and watched to see if their spell had worked.

It did. The earth split and, from the hole the split made, smoke and gas came forth. The women blew winds at the explosion so that the toxic fog would cover Teamhair. On finishing their work, the sisters immediately set out to return to the Tuatha Dé Danann, happy they had fulfilled what it was that they had set out to do. As they started back, four watchers on a hill saw them. Three of the four watchers gave pursuit, and the fourth went to tell the king what they had seen.

It was a well-lit night as the women made their way along toward the forest. It did not take them long to realise they were being followed. This did not worry them terribly. On reaching the forest, the sisters spoke about what they should do about the Firbolg men who followed them.

"We will not run as swine being chased for the slaughter. We are Tuatha and we are warriors," the Morrigu said to her younger sisters. "You are called the goddess of war, dear sister," she said to Badb. "The battleground is so named for you. And you," she told Macha, "place fear into the hearts of our own when in the rage of battle. What do we have to run for?"

In the moonlight, Badb looked pleased at her sister's words. She was a very beautiful woman and resembled a lover more so than a warrior. She was slim and tall, with long deep-red hair that appeared almost black on occasion and at other times as bright as glowing copper. "We do as you say, sister."

They continued into the forest. Rather than being quiet and careful, they made noises that confused the men who followed. The Firbolg pursued with weapons raised, and they cursed and swore at the women. The women had climbed trees and were leaping from limb to limb, calling out as they did so. The forest filled with their echoes of crow and raven calls. The Firbolg came to a halt, confused and disoriented. The sound of a scared horse whinnied through the trees, followed by sound of dogs attacking the horse and ripping into its hide. The men no longer knew which direction was which.

The women cackled and continued to taunt the Firbolg. They blew fog amongst the trees, which forced the men to stop moving in any direction. Back-to-back the men stood and again cursed the women, daring them to come upon them so they could rape them, cut their breasts off, and leave them to bleed to death. The sisters laughed at the men's boldness, for they knew that it was fear prompting them to speak, not courage.

Badb was first to drop down from the trees and show herself. With a quick hand she pulled her dagger from her hip and slashed the Firbolg leader's face. The man called out, more from shock than from pain. As swiftly as she had descended, Badb leapt back into the shadows of the tree branches.

At the same instant, the Morrigu and Macha dropped down from the trees where they had been patiently waiting. Macha ripped at the leg of one man with a hook, and the Morrigu landed on the back of the other, knocking him to the ground. She pulled his hair and cut his throat. The other two men, despite their pain, made to attack the Morrigu. She hissed at them and bounded upward into the trees.

Badb came through the fog and ran between the two men; she tripped them as she did so. Both men stumbled; neither fell. It mattered not, as their lives were taken from them with swords drawn by Badb's two sisters. The Firbolg fell directly onto the pointed shafts. The last of their lives departed from them as the sisters pulled the blades upward, tearing greater wounds and ceasing the men's struggles.

"We must hurry back," the Morrigu said. "I believe it will only take days for the Firbolg to work a way of breaking the curse we have set upon them this night. They will pursue us with the lust for our blood. We will take whatever we can on the way back that they will know we are not in fear of them."

The sisters did as the Morrigu suggested. On their path homeward, they came across farms. There they spared the farmers' lives, but stole some of the cattle. The women drove the cows hard and constantly. They followed the rivers, which made their path harder to track, and soon they arrived at Magh Nia. The Tuatha Dé Danann cheered as they saw the warrior women returning with such strong beasts. The sisters went immediately to the king.

Nuada embraced his wife, for he had missed her and found it hard to be apart from her. He caressed her hair and rolled his fingers across her face. The lead warriors of the Tuatha assembled and they came to the meeting house, where Nuada sat with his mother and his wife.

"We have done what we could to ensure the Tuatha have time for preparations," the Morrigu told the assembly. "We found places of weakness in the earth, with heat under the ground, just as our great cities had, for I remembered that my father, the Dagda, had said that this island had such things.

"We struck the ground, and from the hole we tore in the earth, great clouds of gloom and darkness came. As we ran from the field where we had struck the ground, fire began to be expelled from the earth's wound. Soon rock and fire rained down on the Firbolg. Blood and pain they suffered for three days until the clouds abated, and the druids found a solution with their spells and herbs. The Firbolg recover quickly, and the strongest will be ready to march upon the Tuatha soon enough."

"They will wait until they have full strength and they will gather as many as they might from far and wide to join them," Nuada said gravely, knowing that war was directly upon them. He nodded to Ronan, who knew exactly what to do, and Ronan left the house to warn all of the Tuatha that they must prepare themselves for the upcoming battle.

Nuada turned his attention back to the sisters. "We thank you for bringing the cattle. It is needed stock, and the strength of those who survived your hard hand will breed with ours that they will be strong and built as giants."

Nuada's insights proved correct. It did not take the Firbolg king long to gather all his warriors together and march on the Tuatha. The spies Nuada sent out returned to tell their king that they had counted eleven well-armed battalions of Firbolg. Nuada prepared the Tuatha warriors and they went out to the mid plains, which the Firbolg king had said would be the end battleground.

The Tuatha arrived quickly on the plains. They set themselves a close-knit camp and went about getting all they would need for the coming battle. Even looking across the plain at the Firbolg forces, Nuada still believed it was possible to end their conflict without war. Since the Firbolg had sent a poet to his people as a messenger, he chose to do the same. He had his poets Eadon, Arias, and their young apprentices brought to him.

He pointed to other side of the field and showed the poets the Firbolg camp. The Firbolg were still in the process of organising themselves, and Nuada did not want to give them time to cross the field before he had sent the poets to deliver his message.

"Tell their king, Eochaid mac Eirc, my offer for us to live in peace on our side of the island is still there for him to take. I don't wish for war if we can create a friendship and have trade between our people," Nuada told the four poets. "We are all of Nemed blood, and once more may we live together as such."

The poets left. They took only spears with them, including the spear of victory. This was to show that the poets were not warriors and had safe passage. Caution was needed, for their every move and spoken word was being assessed.

The Firbolg admitted the poets into their camp and took them to Eochaid. The Firbolg king received them with disdain, and he laughed because they looked like they were carrying spears too big for them.

"These are the spears of our warriors," Arias told the king. "We are not warriors; we are poets—the bards of the Tuatha. We speak of their adventures and their battles. Also, we know the battles of the Nemed people, for they are our fathers and our mothers."

Eochaid stared at the four thin men. The man who had spoken, Arias, was handsome, and like the rest of the poets, not of warrior stature. He eyed them for a moment. "What is it that your king says to us this day?"

Eadon came before the other poets and held the spear of victory diagonally so that the point touched the ground at his right foot and the shaft touched his left shoulder. "King Nuada of the Tuatha Dé Danann has said the same offer as before. That we might stay on the west side of the land. That we, of the same Nemed blood, might share this country and be brothers who trade and have great friendship."

King Eochaid smirked to himself. He felt there was no need for such a thing and that the Tuatha were acting as cowards. As he studied the bards before him, he felt sure that Sreng must have been exaggerating about the size and strength of the warriors the Firbolg would be up against.

His advisor saw his face and knew what his king was thinking. The advisor leaned into Eochaid and whispered. "You'd best please your people, or they will take to you as they have your brothers. Do you want to be torn to pieces by the people and left for the birds, as they were?"

Eochaid nodded at his advisor, then addressed the poets. "I have considered what it is that Nuada has said, but I will not speak for all my people. You will take yourselves down to where the Firbolg warriors are training. There you will see my chief, Gann, son of Gann, and you will ask him and the warriors surrounding him what he chooses."

Though the poets thought the request unusual, none of them asked why so they would not be seen as frightened or simple-minded. As they approached the warriors, Arias whispered quietly to Eadon, "Is this a good thing that we are being led to where many men practice tearing the Tuatha apart?"

"If we do not do as we are bid, we would appear to be cowards, and the entire Tuatha Dé Danann would be seen as such. This would fuel the idea within the Firbolg that they have power over us and our clan. Would you have that?" Eadon spoke firmly as he walked in the most powerful manner he could muster.

Arias did not reply, becoming quiet as they approached the training Firbolg warriors. The warriors towered well over the poets, who tried to stand tall in the midst of their enemies, yet still looked feeble against their much bigger opponents.

The arms and legs of the Firbolg men were clad in fur taken from the backs of wild boars. Their trews were nearly completely hidden by the fur, which gave the appearance of their legs being those of goats or swine. Their hair was tied in knots, and the muscles on their stomachs showed through their long shirts. The bards looked small next to these men and, as children would, they waited until they were asked to speak.

"What is this that you bring to us?" the oldest warrior asked of the Firbolg who had escorted the poets to them. "Targets for our spears?" At that moment the spears the poets carried caught his eye. He moved to secure one; however, Eadon pulled it from his grasp.

"This is Gann, son of Gann," the Firbolg man said. "Ask of him what the king told you to."

Once more Eadon stepped ahead of the other poets and relayed the question that he had put before the king. To show he would not be bullied or made fearful of the Firbolg, he added. "The spears we carry are small, for our warriors are so strong that the greatest spears of the land are usable by their hands. The swords our warriors carry are so heavy and tall that they are like the bulk of a horse. Our shields resemble the very wall of a house. Do not be confused by our small size. We are bards—poets—and we watch the battles and learn the stories that we, by mouth, might relay down the centuries all that transpires between king and king, warrior and warrior, hero and hero."

Gann eyed the poets and wondered to himself for a while; then he turned to ask his men their thoughts on the matter. He moved off to discuss with several of his warriors what they should do. The poets stood and waited in silence.

When Gann returned, he seemed confident in their decision. "We are not going accept your king's terms, but we are of the same blood and we are reasonable. Eochaid knows that we cannot rule over him, for he will put us to death. But we can arrange his decree for the better.

"I have spoken to Sreng, a great friend and noble warrior. We will delay the battle for a year. You have travelled long, and you have fewer defences than we ourselves. Though our king may sometimes be unreasonable, we are not. We allow time for ourselves and for you to train and be ready with the best equipment. We like your spears, and I understand you like ours. The delay will give you time to make such things. It will give you time to ready your armour and us time to have ours as perfect as it might be."

Eadon nodded and Gann stated, "It is decided, then."

Both groups left it at that. The poets walked back across what would be the battlefield in a year's time. All felt the daunting understanding that there would be many who would colour the field with their inner workings in the war to come. As bards, the poets felt the sadness of loss in a different way to what a warrior would feel. They had to watch the battles and walk among those who fought, observing but not participating, like shadows. They lived without the rage and the sword. Nevertheless, they still lived with the grief.

Nuada received the poets as soon as they arrived back in the Tuatha's territory. He was eager to hear what had happened. As tradition dictated, he had to wait until at least three of the Tuatha's lead warriors were called as well, to act as witnesses. Ronan, Bres, and the Dagda came to their king's house, where Nuada sat once more with his mother and Macha. The Morrigu and Badb stood to one side and listened.

"The Firbolg appear to want our differences resolved in a peaceful way. Their king does not, and has ruled he will consider no offers from the Tuatha. Even so, sure in decision, he sent us—instead of answering the offer himself—he sent us to his warriors to ask what they thought of peace between us. They left us for a time and spoke to Sreng. When they returned—the warriors—they said were not taken by the thought of war. Still, they conceded that if they go against their king they will be known as enemies themselves."

"To war it is, then," Nuada said under his breath, yet loudly enough that they all heard.

"No," Eadon said. "The warriors believe an immediate battle would be unfair and, having the same blood, we should, therein, have the same armoury and defences.

"They have said the battle will take place in a year. In the time between now and the war, we will share knowledge of our weapons and teach them to make spears such as ours. They will, in turn, teach us to make their spears."

Nuada, a little confused, looked to the Dagda and waited for him to say something. The Dagda noticed this and spoke. "It appears that they hope for something to happen in the time between that might change the king's mind, or, perhaps, the king himself."

"If we cannot stop war from being upon us, then we cannot stop it," Nuada said. "It is already written in our destiny. It would be best for us all to know whether or not we will have battle. I asked, Morrigu, what is it?"

The Morrigu leaned her head to one side. Her dark hair slid across her shoulder and trailed down to her hip. "There is no doubt of war. I have seen it."

"I have seen, also," Badb stepped ahead of the Morrigu.

"Victory?" Nuada asked.

"Victory will be ours. There will be a great cost. Cost to them and to us, but then the Fomorians will come—and then ..." Badb stared at Macha with a dark message in her eyes, cautioning Macha. She said nothing more.

Macha shook off her sister's warning and stood. "I create my own destiny," she said. "None, not even the stars, will take that from me." She approached Badb and embraced her. "Do not fear. Nuada will be with me. It is only a worry you have, not a vision."

"It is a vision, sister," Badb insisted.

"Shh," Macha cooed to her younger sister. "All will be well."

The Dagda wondered what the truth of the matter would be, for he had visions, but his visions were never as clear as those of his daughters. He would have relied on Brigit to enlighten him, however, because of the burn she had suffered, she was now unable to see the future clearly. Knowing what was to happen would normally be the Morrigu's best strength. But the strongest of all his children for predicting death was Badb ... and she was never wrong.

Nuada stood and joined his wife. "We will do as the warriors have given us allowance to do. We will convey all our knowledge to them, and they, in turn, will do so for us. Brigit will teach them of her death rain by arrows, as she is known as the "fiery arrowed one." She will teach them of the smiths' work with Goibniu. She will even show them how to make the whistle that calls one to another through the night. So great a poet she is, she will always keep peace. Her heart so pure she will still any lust for our women, and the Firbolg will respect us more so."

The Dagda, Ronan, and Bres agreed on this course of action, and they left immediately to start all that needed to be done. Nuada waited with his wife. The Morrigu and Badb left to do what they could, and the house once more stood nearly empty, save for Nuada, Macha, Danu, and their servants.

"We have come here, a long way," Danu observed in a whisper. "It has cost us much already. There has been a change in you over the last few years. I have noticed it."

She spoke to Nuada, and he knew it. He could not tell her the cause of the change in him because he did not know himself. He went to the fire burning in the centre of the room. He picked up a wooden bowl that had been placed near the blaze and scooped a bowl of broth from the pot still on the heat. He pointed around the room as he drank a little of the hot soup.

"We came from a place where we were superior and all around us shone like the sun. We had buildings of great height and of astounding beauty." He tapped his head with the fingers of his free hand. "Our minds created amazing things, and we could do most anything. We bounded from land to land, and we sported ourselves with the best." He pointed to the camp outside. "And yet we are reduced to this."

He walked to his chair and sat heavily. "I am tired, and for the first time, I feel aged."

"We are a strong clan and we have as much as we need," Danu answered her son. "We are not so proud that some of us being grounded means the end of us. Our minds created great things before, and we will again. No matter what happens, we will not lose ourselves." Danu spoke calmly, her soft voice sighing across the room. "The land is beautiful and, if I may say so, it could be seen as even more lovely than the lands where we are from. We have been shifted, but we do not have to be lost."

Nuada looked at his mother who sat in the shadows. The front of her hair hid much of the damage that had been done by the Fomorian king's attack, and the bruising on her neck had long-since faded. Still, Nuada swore that some days he could still see the terrible marks. Even now Danu moved with a slight limp; she had not healed as well had been hoped.

The healing abilities of the Dagda and Brigit had not found a way to properly heal a wound inside Danu, a wound more terrible than any the eyes could see. Brigit had been led by magic to a natural spring, where she performed spells with her sisters and her father. Brigit, without any sleep, stayed by the spring day and night, chanting incantations over it.

No one had really seen Brigit aside from her sisters and her father since they had arrived at Magh Nia. Only Danu was given that right. Brigit often now kept her face covered. She appeared and disappeared as if she were an apparition. And it seemed her once-great magic had been baffled when it came to healing Danu.

"We defend our existence," Danu said. "This is not for us, but for those who we leave behind. They will be the ones who will create all the beauty of our old cities and bring that beauty alive here." She shook her head and arose to leave. "I do not worry about that. It will be as it will be."

Nuada and Macha watched her go. Neither said a word as they stood in the room by themselves. Nuada looked to his wife, and he knew that Badb was right in her dire, hinted-at prediction. His heart hurt at the thought.

✺ 5 ✺

The Tuatha spent the year in anticipation of the upcoming war. Always, on the other side of the would-be battlefield, the Firbolg were camped. They had begun to make their own houses and built their fort much in the same way that the Tuatha Dé Danann had built theirs. The fort walls were no higher than the Tuatha's. The Firbolg gates were made of same material and the same size and their ditch, no deeper.

The camps sat across from one another on the long flat plain, surrounded by green mountains and, on the northern side, a river from which they all used the same water. Knowledge on weaponry was shared, and friendships formed. But neither side could forget there was a battle looming.

Brigit's burn finally healed. However, the scarring on the left side of her face was permanent, and she chose not to hide it anymore. Her skill with the arrow was envied by the Firbolg, but none of them gained as much competence as Brigit possessed. When she lit an arrow and fired it, it was sure to bring a slow and painful death to anyone unfortunate enough to be struck. She shared her knowledge with the Firbolg and taught them how to forge. The Firbolg were taken by her. Yet, even with all of all this sharing of Tuatha knowledge in the spirit of friendship, Eochaid refused to change his decision to go ahead with a war.

The Firbolg king had many days of meetings with his advisers on the lead-up to the date he had set for battle. His biggest concern was that his Firbolg warriors were no longer of the mind to fight the Tuatha. It would not work for him if his soldiers did not cross the battlefield on the day they were needed.

"I have seen what you mean about their friendships," Eochaid's oldest adviser and bard, Cesarn, said. "I would suggest that peace now would be the best way for us to advance forward."

"Peace?" the youngest of the Firbolg king's advisers scoffed at Cesarn's advice. "You are old and foolish. If Eochaid retreats from the challenge and his word to his people to drive the Tuatha into the sea, will he not look weak to the Firbolg and like no more than malleable metal to the Tuatha?"

Cesarn, angered, jabbed his finger into the chest of his counterpart. "The people will be not pleased to lose their men and women who fight on the field where there is knowledge that their lives could be spared, with a plan, also, for peace and trade. A brotherhood, even, against the Fomorians who attack and take whatever it is they will, killing our Firbolg without scruple."

The two men faced each other, neither wishing to concede to the other. They had received word that the Fomorians had already done exactly as Cesarn had said, conducting raids along the eastern coast. None, in these attacks by the other-landers, had been spared, with even the children taken by the Fomorians to rear as slaves. Farms had been laid to waste, and even the great city of Teamhair had been attacked. The Firbolg people had gathered together and fought as hard as they could. Eventually a large tribute was paid to the Fomorians to stop the attacks. The aggressors left, leaving a warning that they would return soon—for more.

Eochaid waved his hand to dismiss Cesarn. "I think you are wrong, old man. A battle won against the Tuatha will show the Fomorians that we are as strong as they are. How could they not fear us? The Fomorians have never won in battle against the Tuatha, so if we have bested their foe, they will fall at our feet. Midsummer is in two days, and it is a blessed day for us. The sun will be in the right position for our victory, so all of the signs say."

Cesarn looked to his king with disgust. "Your pride is your problem. You make it your people's downfall." Lugubriously he shook his head. "Who will save them?"

Eochaid snorted at the bard. "Get out of here, you stupid old man." He laughed. "Go and join your lovers. Perhaps you will be better bent over for them than standing straight for us."

The bard began to leave. For some reason this action enraged king Eochaid. "You leave here now! No longer of our clan, are you, and if you are still in the camp by the time my message is received on the ears of the warriors at the gate, then you will be struck down and your head displayed on the highest point of our wall."

Cesarn hurried from the king's presence; he knew his path. He rushed through the great gates the Firbolg had built on their side of the battlefield, straight to the gates of the Tuatha Dé Danann.

He had hardly exited the Firbolg camp when an arrow whistled past his ear. It was a deliberate miss from one of the posts, who had just received word from the king that he now considered Cesarn an enemy. To the Firbolg, as with the Tuatha, it was wrong to kill one's own bard, and all of the heavens cursed those who did. Even so, Cesarn was not going to take the time to tarry, and he rushed on his mission of warning.

The gates of the Tuatha Dé Danann stood open, as they had for the entire year. Cesarn called to the Tuatha as he entered their village. "I need audience with your king. Nuada! Come to me, Nuada!"

The alarm of the old bard caused many of the Tuatha to come out of their houses and stop any work they were doing. The Morrigu latched onto the arm of the old man and whistled as she spoke to him. "I will take you."

His terrified look brought fear to people as he walked past them. Warriors who had been training, smithing, or doing other such tasks, followed him and the Morrigu. They found Nuada on the other side of the village cutting saplings down. These would be used for a fence to keep in a young litter of pigs. He was surprised to the see the group heading his way.

"What is all this about?" Nuada asked, pointing with his sickle at the masses.

"I am Cesarn, the bard and once adviser to Eochaid mac Eirc," Cesarn said, nervously.

"And what of it?" Nuada asked, confused as to where the conversation was going.

"This moment, I have been exiled from my clan, and I have been told I will be struck down if I return."

Cesarn rubbed his hand across his nose as the worry swelled up in him. "I told the king it would be best to accept peace, as the Fomorians attack us often and the Tuatha would be good allies to drive them out of our lands. The king insists I am a fool. He has taken the word of a younger adviser and he will be bringing the Firbolg warriors to the battlefield in two days, for it is Midsummer, and he believes this day to be blessed in his favour."

Nuada threw down the sickle. "The men have become more friends to us than foes. How will they take up arms?"

Cesarn wrung his hands. "From my knowledge of the Firbolg king, I will tell you." He gathered himself and then went on. "He will spread rumours and untruths amongst the warriors. He will confuse them, and he will make sure they are told that there is a reason the Firbolgs have been attacked by the Fomorians—and you have not. He will tell them such things as to make them believe you are in league with the Fomorians. Lies and such, until the Firbolg will seek someone to blame—and he will point to the Tuatha."

Nuada looked at the Firbolg bard accusingly. "You seem to have a lot to say on this."

Cesarn raised his hands with his palms out and began to beg. "Please. Please. Do not blame me. I have to warn you. That is all I can do. I wish for peace, just as you do. Please. I am not ... I am a bard and I am old and have not gone to arms in many years. Just a poet who knows herbs and old spells that don't even seem to work most of the time. Please. What I do know I have told you. I have assumed some of what I've said, yet it is the way of the king that I know. I have been with him since his third year. Please, great king Nuada. Please."

Nuada walked past the bard and laid his hand on the old man's shoulder.

Cesarn jumped, as he had his eyes shut by that stage for fear of his head being struck off.

"I understand. You will be safe in our village for as long as you wish to stay. You, not of my enemy and acting as brother to the Tuatha, shall be taken in as one of us."

Nuada may not have taken such a trusting approach toward Cesarn were it not for the nod of the Dagda signifying that the terrified little man was telling the truth. The Dagda stepped up to Nuada. "It would appear that we are to arms then in two days."

Nuada nodded and blew a deep breath out as he hurried to advise the rest of the Tuatha Dé Danann; that is, those who had not followed the Morrigu and Cesarn to Nuada. "We will watch the other side of the plain. We will not assemble until we see them assemble, for it will now be on our misled brothers who seek to battle as to when we fight."

The camp, which had become very much like a village, was tense. Nuada had the women not fit for fighting, and children, along with Cesarn, sneak out of the encampment in the night. They would take shelter on the mountain they called Belgatta located behind the village they had built near Magh Nia. The height of the mountain would give them the ability to see whether or not they should take further flight north and hide amongst either the bogs or the area known as the Ros and its stony landscape, scattered with lakes and bays of the sea.

As Cesarn had said: On the Midsummer morning, king Eochaid assembled his men at one end of the battlefield. He had his favourite man ride out. Nuada chose Ronan to go to meet the Firbolg warrior. The two men spoke briefly and then rode back to their respective camps.

Ronan pulled himself high and spoke to Nuada. "They will be sending three times nine hurlers, unarmed with exception of their slings and shields. It will be battle; blood to blood. Eochaid's man said that they will keep the heads taken for later use."

Nuada turned on his horse and looked around him, deciding who would be the match to the Firbolg. It was tradition to stage an even fight, one warrior to another. Only the break of this tradition, and what would be regarded as cowardly behaviour, would place one warrior against many.

"The hurlers are being sent," Nuada called to his men behind him. "Three times nine. Who will be the Tuatha's fighters this day?"

A field of warriors soon lined up. There were women hurlers amongst them, even though the men had stronger arms for the act of throwing the stones and the occasional human head. Both men and women would go to the fight to get their trophies of heads or hands.

Of those warriors who volunteered, the oldest of all were chosen. Nuada hoped that this would show the Firbolg that the Tuatha did not wish to fight. One hurler even had grey hair and a hump upon his back. Quicklime was brought out to the hurlers, and they marched forward as the Firbolg moved towards them.

Nuada sat and watched as the Tuatha strode ahead. The hurlers he'd sent were not the strongest of all the fighters, and they were definitely not of the warrior standing of he or any of the Tuatha warband. Nuada knew that the Firbolg, like the Tuatha, respected the elderly. He still hoped that arms would be put down and the Firbolg king displaced. He could do nothing to inspire the Tuatha warriors, as fighting the Firbolg was to them like going against their own kind, so the hurlers approached the fight in sombre silence.

The line of men and women on both sides looked at each other. The Firbolg had more fire in their hearts, as, true to Cesarn's guess, they had been told things about the Tuatha that were not true. They stared at the line before them and their anger grew; however, the Tuatha warriors felt no such hatred. The Firbolg saw the aged line before them as an insult, and it flamed the untruths and ignited a hate which had not been there only days before.

The first to strike was a tall Firbolg who stood at the battlefield's farthest end, to the north. His stone was met with a shield and, though aged, the Tuatha man struck back, hitting his opponent on the shoulder.

The Firbolg advanced over the line of the Tuatha Dé Danann. The Tuatha fought back hard. They still did not wish to kill any Firbolg, and stood only in their own defence.

The hurler named Máel Sechlainn of the Tuatha line was first to fall. The old warrior had his leg dashed from under him and his bone broke. His scream of his pain was muffled by the grass he fell upon. The Firbolg hurried upon him with heavy rocks. He pushed his shield up and smashed the jaw of a Firbolg warrior, then was crushed by the blows of the many rocks that flew at him. The Firbolg hurler could not look to the old man he slaughtered as he struck the life from him with the heel of his foot. He turned away to aid his fellow clan members.

Late afternoon came, and the horns sounded for the end of the day's battle. All of the Tuatha hurlers lay dead, and the Firbolg were cutting the heads from the defeated bodies. They held them up first so that Nuada and the Tuatha Dé Danann could see, and then they turned and showed the Firbolg, who cheered so loudly that the trees seemed to shake. The cheer echoed across the plain, to the hills, and to those who had fled to Belgatta, so that the women and children of the Tuatha, too, could hear.

"This is to show there is no possibility of peace now," Bres growled. "They took the lives of our oldest warriors. Without mercy they struck their heads from their bodies and we know they will be used against us. Their hate for us was always there, and they tricked us into believing it could be any other way. They were always a bad sort, and their words were untruths. They were a lot of bow-legged bag carriers who stole more than they earned even as far back as when the Nemed people were one. They would slip in bed with the Tuatha's wives at night, pretending to be their husbands." He spat at the ground. "We will fight as they do and suckle their children as our slaves."

Nuada stopped Bres from speaking any further. "They are under the influence of a prideful king. They do not know the truth; only what they have been told. They have not eaten but for what they have been fed. As the pips grow in their stomachs there will be more wars. This field will be the end of this grievance between the Tuatha and the Firbolg, regardless of how many days must pass."

"Rider!" Dian Cecht called the alert.

From the Firbolg king a messenger approached. Dian Cecht gave ample warning of the horse and its rider, which gave Nuada time to select a return rider. The warrior who rode toward the Tuatha was patched in leather and wore a leather cap, with a horse tail waving behind, on his head. It was something unusual to see, and the Tuatha Dé Danann watched in curiosity as he drew closer.

On arriving in the middle of the field, the rider waited for a Tuatha member to meet him. Nuada sent Bres out to meet the messenger. Bres rode out to speak, but had not the opportunity to say a word.

The rider thumped his shield and spoke without even identifying himself. "To Nuada, king of the Tuatha Dé Danann, my king, Eochaid mac Eirc, has sent me to ask a question."

"Yes," Bres said. "That is?"

"Having seen the slaughter that the Firbolg brought to your fighters today, do you wish there to be a daily slaughter, or every second day should our own take their pick and cut you down? In the future, my king will not give you the opportunity of an even battle. Our numbers are twice yours, so says he."

Nuada grew angry when Bres rode back and repeated Eochaid's jeering comment. He felt hate for the king and thought how stupid the bulging man was. He was careful not to express the anger he felt, and he was even more cautious in picking the words he said back to the enemy king.

To Bres, Nuada said, "If he feels he needs an uneven fight, so be it. It is the way of the Nemed, of which we both have blood, to have even beginnings for each day. So, I will not send forth any more than he sends, and if any warrior breaks such a bond then it will be their undoing. We will fight day upon day. We will end this war as soon as possible and not delay another year."

Bres rode back to the middle of the field and told the Firbolg warrior what Nuada had said. The messenger nodded. A small smile even slipped to the side of his face, as the return message pleased him.

He turned his horse and returned to his own line. The Firbolg king had already left the field and was putting his horse to water—not the act of a king, as seen by his clan, to leave the field early.

On hearing Nuada's reply, Eochaid wanted to throw all of the Firbolg warriors into the battle at that very moment. His adviser stopped his words and dismissed all from their presence so that he could have words with the king without any others hearing.

"If you do try to rally all the warriors now, especially after such a day of slaughter, they will not do your bidding. They will find the request of an even battle honourable, and anything against that will make them question whether all we have told them in the past days is really so. They can be tricked into believing that the part-Fomorian Bres is in fact a Fomorian brother that they aid along with other Fomorians in order to take all from the Firbolg. But if you step wrong, they will question whether all you say and do is honourable."

Eochaid thought about what his adviser had said. "You are right. The Firbolg may believe for now that the Fomorians have allied with the Tuatha. I want them to remember me as the powerful Firbolg leader, loved for his greatness."

"For that you will be, my king." The adviser bowed and summoned the messenger back, telling him to relay the message that the Firbolg king accepted the terms of sending equal numbers of warriors from each side to fight, every day, until the battle was won.

On the second day of the war, the same number of warriors went forward as the day before, this time consisting of spearmen and women and hurlers. The Tuatha could see the line of heads that the hurlers had collected from the day before, covered in the white of quicklime and impaled on spikes, at the Firbolg end of the field. They did not fear; nevertheless, they did not feel the enthusiasm for the battlefield they had in the past, either.

Both sides went at each other and they came together with a loud roar. Immediately two of the Tuatha were struck down, and the hurlers quickly removed their heads. Sreng fought amongst the spearmen of the Firbolg, as did Bres for the side of the Tuatha. When Bres and Sreng had opportunity to fight one another, they avoided it, and instead turned away to deal with someone else. The fight went on for the entire day, until the evening, which was the signal of the new day to their kind. Those who walked away from the field had the feeling that nothing had been gained, only lost.

The third day saw twice as many on the field, and once more the number of Tuatha fighters matched that of the Firbolg. Ogma and Manannan mac Lir were forced to fight for their lives back-to-back, as Eochaid had discovered a way of sneaking more of his fighters onto the battlefield in such a way that neither side knew the king was no longer honouring his word to stage an evenly matched fight.

Ogma was cut several times and then saved by Manannan's quick moves, and in turn Ogma saved Manannan. Nuada had taken the field, and Bres stood by his side. The crush of Firbolg had descended fully upon them when the great queen Danu appeared on her horse and dismounted by jumping onto the back of a Firbolg. With her spear she drove a wound deep into the neck of a man who would attack her son, then raised her dagger and smashed it into his face. She slithered between the legs of her son and rolled to stab upward into the groin of another fighter, allowing Nuada to take the Firbolg's head.

Badb appeared from overhead, her legs in a crouching pose and her arms outward wielding a short sword in one hand and a shield in the other. She looked like a great, dark bird, and the Firbolg warriors did not know where she had come from. Her red hair flamed against the sun, and the death she brought made them fear that she had powers they could not possibly win against.

Both the Morrigu and Macha had taken to the field, also. The Morrigu insisted on pushing her sister Macha back to the edge of the field to exclude her from the fight. Macha knew that the warning Badb had given a year ago worried the Morrigu. Though Badb had not specifically described her vision, Macha sensed she could very well be part of the "great price" the Tuatha would pay for victory. Yet she refused to let her people down and committed herself to fight as well. She reminded herself that it was Firbolg she fought, not the Fomorians, and she felt more powerful for the thought.

By the end of the day, more dead warriors lay on the ground than had entered the field in the first place. Surveying the carnage,

Nuada's anger grew heated, and he gnashed his teeth as he spoke to the Dagda. "It is hard for me not to want to storm their camp and eliminate their supposed king with my own hands. His trickery and deception, his lies … all lies!"

The Morrigu spoke firmly. "Calm yourself and think more clearly."

"I agree, calm yourself." The Dagda spoke quietly. "If you attack in the night you will be as dishonourable as he is, and your people, and his, will say as such." He thought for a moment. "I do believe I have another way."

Nuada pinched his moustache. "What would you do?"

"I will prepare a potion with my daughters. That is all you need to know." The Dagda left the field and called to his daughters to follow as he did so.

Later that night, the Morrigu set out by herself into the dark and carried a small vessel containing some liquid with her. The long neck of the vessel had been stopped with a little beeswax. The Morrigu crept along in the shadows, where her dark hair and clothing made her nearly impossible to spot. She slinked along the shrubbery and merged with each bush as she made her way to the Firbolg camp.

When she arrived, she saw that the camp was well-lit. She knew the layout well enough to be able to slither in and make her way to the king's hut. The king was playing with some whores he had brought out from Teamhair. His heavy stomach heaved over one woman, and the other prostitute stood rubbing her breasts along his back.

The Morrigu smiled, as she could not have asked for a better distraction; the room had been emptied so he could have his fun in privacy. Through the hut's back window slit, the Morrigu slid into the room like a flow of water and tipped the contents of the vessel she carried into the king's drinking horn. With as much ease, she slid back out.

As the Morrigu exited the camp, she heard Eochaid's men talking about the Tuatha's supposed alliance with the Fomorians. The men said there had been raids on Teamhair, and that there had been lives lost, with children taken away to be raised as slaves. For all this, the men blamed the Tuatha just as much as they faulted the Fomorians, all because of king Eochaid's lies.

The Morrigu felt saddened by what had happened and angered that Eochaid would flap such an evil tongue. She resisted returning to the king to slit his throat. Instead, she took the news back to Nuada.

Nuada frowned. "We were warned by the bard, Cesarn, that Eochaid would say such things. Still, it gives me hope that when the fighting is done, and all is revealed, that there will be a brotherhood made between our clans." Then of the mission that the Morrigu had just fulfilled, Nuada asked, "What is it that you took to Eochaid this night?"

"I slipped into his drink a liquid that will make his thirst unquenchable. It is a slow potion, taking time to work on the body. He will feel its effects by midday tomorrow. He will seek out water, and he will call for some to be brought to him. We must strike down any who bring water or any other drink to him, for that leaves only one way to go. He will away to the strand and try to drink from the stream. If the Tuatha know of this, we have ways of making sure that it is a fairer fight this day: I will ambush him."

Nuada thought this was a good plan, and they rested that night. Dian Cecht and the Dagda went around to the Tuatha to make sure any injuries and wounds were tended to before they, too, laid down to sleep.

In the morning, Brigit called the Tuatha to arms. The Firbolg had begun their march, and she had seen Eochaid and all the warriors intending to fight that day. The Tuatha were outnumbered, for king Eochaid had abandoned any pretence of fighting fairly. Yet still, to arms the Tuatha went. Their hands steady, they did not feel any fear at being overwhelmed, and they laced themselves into their war attire with quick fingers.

Nuada, Ogma, Brigit, and Bres were first across the field and into the encounter. Nuada wore only his trousers, sword, and shield to show he was not afraid. He knew if he was to be killed that day, then it did not matter how many clothes and armour he donned. His fate had been chosen by a force well above him.

The Firbolg pressed upon the Tuatha, so intensely that wherever Nuada pushed his sword, he was bound to make contact with one warrior or more. The heat of their bodies and the rise of pressure from within sent Nuada into a frenzy, and he sought out blood for his sword and shield. As he fought, his breath slowed, and the motion around him seemed to slow down also, yet he continued to move at the same speed. Others observing him noted that he moved at extreme speed, with deadly accuracy. His face was relaxed, his muscles flexed and engorged with power.

To his side Bres fought, and to his other side fought Macha, sticking her tongue out, as she always did when in a fit of rage. Her face pulled many expressions as she lashed the Firbolgs with her sword.

Brigit, who sat on her horse in the rear of the field, shot at the Firbolg fiery arrows coated in a tar mixture. The Firbolg hurlers had returned to the fields—Nuada and the other warriors had to avoid the devastating blows from the quicklime-covered heads their enemies had taken earlier.

The Tuatha were so greatly outnumbered that several Tuatha warriors had to fight two or three of the Firbolg at the same time, yet they kept fighting and stayed upright. They were all aware of the potion the Morrigu had slipped to Eochaid, and they knew they had to keep up the fight until its effects kicked in.

Midday came, and the Firbolg king did not seem to lust for water as the Morrigu had stated. The Tuatha warriors had been keeping any liquid from being brought to him, and they did not understand why the king had not been overcome with thirst. Then Badb noticed, while slicing the arm from a female foe, that there was a pouch on Eochaid's side. A bladder of water.

She moved towards the king. Badb could cause confusion in battle by using her warrior skills combined with mystical flashes and her overall speed. She found it easy to duck and weave, even sliding along the ground or using the backs of standing men or women to launch herself into the air with such speed that none of her enemies knew they had been mortally wounded—until they saw her blade extending from their guts.

Badb noted that the Firbolg warrior Sreng stayed close to Eochaid, and though Sreng was a giant compared to her, this did not stop her. She shifted to Sreng's side and struck his buttock with her sword, which cut through his clothes and wounded him deeply. His attention turned to her. Nuada stepped forward and pushed the Firbolg back. The two of them fought hard while Badb reached through the wall of warriors protecting Eochaid and sliced the bladder so all the water ran from it.

The battle continued, and soon the thirst did come upon the Firbolg king. As the Morrigu had foretold, he began to seek out water. Fifty men stayed to aid him, and if one dropped, another rushed in to try and replace the fallen. The Tuatha pushed their own king toward Eochaid, so that he might be able to take the enemy leader's head.

The Firbolg king called for his horse, which he had dismounted when he had reached the fray. A horse was brought covered in leather for protection, but it was struck down by one of the Tuatha before it could reach him. The thirst had come over Eochaid so heavily that the king stumbled on the ground and moved from ditch to ditch, even trying to find mud that he might drink. He clutched his neck and swallowed. His throat met with no moisture. The water bearers had fled the field, and he scurried to find any with water.

Sreng continued to fight Nuada as he tried to follow the king. Nuada struck the Firbolg's left shoulder at the same moment that Sreng's sword slashed out and cut Nuada's hand all but off. The shield Nuada held fell to the ground. He continued to fight, despite the agony of the wound and his hand flapping on the end of his arm as it clung on by smallest amount of flesh.

Ogma saw his brother's distress and tried to move to help him, but attacked by three Firbolg men. He called to the Tuatha warriors, "To the king! He is wounded!"

The Dagda heard Ogma and looked to Nuada. "To the king!" he called to his men, and the Tuatha moved in. The Dagda came between Nuada and Sreng, and held his sword up to stop a death-blow. He pushed Nuada back into the Tuatha men, who quickly surrounded their king, while six men in the middle of the throng picked Nuada up onto their shoulders and hurried to the edge of the field.

The Morrigu saw a chance to slip aside from the field and make her way to the shore of the stream. Several Firbolg men followed her, and soon she was once more in the fight. Six men stood against her alone, and she knew if she did not play the battle well it would be death for her. She slowed her breath and let a flow of energy overtake her. Her eyes rolled back in her head briefly, so she could see a vision of the actions she need take to beat the six Firbolg.

She snapped to attention as the first Firbolg made his play, and all others came in to dispatch her and tear her to pieces. They all had seen her fight, and knew she was a formidable foe.

The Morrigu grasped the spear the Firbolg brandished at her. She pulled upon its shaft and flexed her arm behind and away from her as she snapped her leg in a kick forward. Her arm's thrust saw the spear lodge into the stomach of the warrior to her rear-left.

She dipped as the Firbolg holding the spear came struck at her with his other hand, which held a small axe. She swung her leg behind as she pushed, in a blocking move, the spear-wielding Firbolg into the sword of his ally to the fore.

Her rear-swinging leg kicked the knee of one of the upcoming Firbolg, and then she spun on the ball of her foot to push her sword into the leg of another. Instantly she pulled her weapon free and slashed upward into the face of the Firbolg she had kicked.

She forward-flipped over the shield of the Firbolg she had slashed in the face and used his back to launch herself as she slit his throat. To avoid the weapons of the Firbolg, she pulled her legs up close to her chest while still in the air and then grasped hold of a branch, snapping it clean off. In one quick motion, she drove the branch down into the throat of one of the Firbolg to the fore, and with her other hand she stayed a sword attack from another. On impact with the ground, her legs bent, and she rolled away from her attackers. She then stood and viewed those who were left.

On the ground rolled a warrior with a spear protruding from his gut. He hastily clawed his way to a tree, and with shaking hands, tried to break the spear's shaft. The spear was one of Firbolg's Craisech spears and was nearly impossible for the weak hand to break.

Two men were left standing for the Morrigu to fight; one was severely wounded on his

upper thigh and was likely to die. The look in his eye said that he would try to take her with him.

The second warrior left standing was much bigger than the other five. He grunted at the Morrigu, "You fight well, but you are too beautiful, and these fools were too distracted by that. I think such a pretty head will look good with my manhood in its mouth as it hangs from my belt."

The Morrigu gave a half-smile at the strange compliment as the two surviving warriors moved in to attack her. She leaped and dashed to the side of the injured man, slashing at his side as she went past him. From the corners of her eyes she had caught sight of Eochaid as he made his way to the stream. At his back he still had at least fifty men all fighting and aware of those surrounding their king; however, they had not seen the Morrigu. She had to get to the Firbolg king.

She hastened herself along the soil, still pursued by the big Firbolg warrior. The Morrigu ran a lot faster and knew that she had only one chance of reaching the Firbolg king. She dashed closer to the trees, unseen by all other Firbolg; only the one behind her knew her position. He called to his brothers, but they could not hear him above the clash of war. It was her chance, and she bounded to the branch of a tree near where the king stumbled in his thirst and confusion.

As Eochaid touched the water with his lips, the Morrigu threw her full weight down, with her sword brandished. She drove the point of her blade through Eochaid's exposed neck and into his skull. He fell dead.

The Morrigu, from the back of the fallen king, saw she was surrounded by Firbolg men and though she was a strong warrior, she recognized fighting them all off would not be possible for her alone. The water was at her back by then and she knew only one way to go, so she took to the water and moved as quickly as she could to the grass plain beyond.

The Firbolg snapped at her feet at first, but she hid in a shallow ditch, and the grass bent around her as cover. The Firbolg ran in all directions. They did not know where she had gone. Soon they stopped their pursuit and returned to their fallen king to claim his body and bury him.

The warring continued on the battlefield. The Dagda raged against Sreng, but neither of them was the stronger, and so neither yielded to the other. Both men struck out and were blocked again and again. They danced around each other, yet neither got the advantage. On both sides of them, men fell.

Suddenly, the Dagda noticed a weak spot in the warriors surrounding Nuada, so he backed away from the fight with Sreng and ran to protect his king. Sreng followed, but was stopped by Aengaba of Norway, a foreigner who had been saved twice by the Dagda and saw his chance to return the favour.

The Firbolg were being cut down quickly. Corpses lay across the feet of those who stood, and the dying were immediately trampled upon and crushed to death. Horses lay amongst the dead, and crows and other scavenging animals began to gather as the afternoon wore on.

Aengaba and Sreng fought bravely, but were both worn and making mistakes that cost them. In a blow that nearly took his head, Sreng was struck against his ear. The ear hung by the side of his neck and flapped with every movement he made, like a dancing woman's earring.

Aengaba struck Sreng's face with his shield, and the impact forced the Firbolg warrior to step back several times; his nose and his cheekbone had been broken. With an opportunity to do away with the Firbolg, Aengaba stabbed forward; however, he did not protect himself with his shield properly. Sreng, even in his stunned state, saw his own opportunity, and pushed his sword into the side of Aengaba. The warrior fell, and then it was Ogma who took to Sreng, while Aengaba was carried from the field.

By evening, when the finals of battle were called, only three hundred of the Firbolg men had survived; the Tuatha had lost many as well. They did not leave the field immediately. They moved in silence and dragged their dead away. Nuada was still being tended to by Dian Cecht, who had stopped Nuada's bleeding, yet could not save the king's injured hand and was forced to remove the king's hand completely.

"I can no longer be king," Nuada said, panting through the pain that even the healing herbs had not completely removed. "Even surviving this, I cannot be king. It is our law that the king has to be perfect." His voice quivered with pain, as nearly hysterically he spoke. "What is it that I can do? The Tuatha Dé Danann must be led, and there is no leader." He cringed as Dian Cecht applied packing to the stump at the end of Nuada's arm, followed by the strapping of material to bind the packing in place.

"The Tuatha do not know yet you have lost your hand." Dian Cecht spoke softly in the ear of the king, his brother. "Only I and the Dagda have knowledge of your loss, and for now it will stay as such until this war is done. Then you will select a new king when there is peace and you are strong enough to do so."

"Rider!" a voice alerted them.

"It is Sreng." Bres had rushed to tell Nuada of the rider's approach.

"I cannot ..." Nuada started to say.

Dian Cecht cut his sentence short. "He will come."

Bres watched his king for a moment and looked at the bandage on the end of his arm. Dian Cecht had fashioned it in such a way that it looked like the king's hand had been merely covered up. Bres left without saying any more.

"No one will know," Dian Cecht reassured Nuada. "They need their king now. The Firbolg have lost theirs. What are we without ours?"

Nuada stared at the healer and nodded. He stood to his feet; however, he was woozy and nearly fell back down. Dian Cecht waved a cluster of smoking weeds in front of Nuada's nose to help revive him, and continued to waft the smoke they moved to the field's edge. Dian Cecht helped the king onto his horse, where he sat, wet with sweat.

"Their king has fallen. What is it now that they wish to do?" Nuada grumbled loudly.

Dian Cecht stayed on one side of the king, while the Dagda took his place on the other side. They believed, if they stayed close enough, that even if Nuada fainted, they would be able to make their enemies believe that their king had only sustained a flesh wound. So, they stayed close, holding him upright.

Bres rode out to meet with Sreng, and they spoke for a short while. When Bres returned, Nuada did not want to hear what had been said. In his dazed state, he waved his good hand and spoke. "I will ride out to Sreng and we will speak. No more of this."

The Dagda and Dian Cecht looked at each other and went to stop their king. It was too late, as Nuada took the field and moved to Sreng by himself. They could do nothing, only watch.

"Kings do not ride out to meet on the field," the Dagda yelled behind Nuada.

"He is unafraid and will not be taken by the Firbolg. Nuada is showing the Tuatha that we are strong and proud and that a king will not cower on the side!" Dian Cecht called to the Tuatha so that they would not wonder at the odd behaviour of Nuada.

Nuada allowed his horse to make its own way to Sreng. He did not try to sit tall on the horse; nonetheless he looked stable and in control. Luckily, his horse was so well-trained and such a calm beast that it counteracted any unusual movement Nuada made that might have led to him falling off. To the Tuatha, Nuada rode slowly, and they saw this as making a proud statement that the Tuatha would not hurry themselves for the sake of any other clan.

Sreng waited with patience at the centre of the field and did not react to the change of messenger. "You come to me with no men?"

"Yes," Nuada said with a slack jaw, "and what of it?"

Sreng let the topic drop and he moved to speak of the war. "We have had four days of fight, and our king lies dead on the strand. We have buried him, and we piled many stones upon his grave. We mourn a king who was just and did right by the Firbolg for ten years.

"We of the Firbolg saw that our king was starting to act differently. This war was to do with his pride, and it became something that controlled him. This is useless bloodshed, and the calling to one another across the field … when it was only a week gone that we were brothers."

"Your king had deceived you into believing that we are brothers to the Fomorians, whom we scorn and loathe." Nuada spat to his side and wobbled heavily. He gathered himself and sat tall again. "I present to you this option: to leave this land or to share it."

Sreng looked at the back of his horse's head and considered. "Eochaid would have me fight, but to you, I say this. If we had been allowed to continue our fight on the field, it might have been you who lay dead and not my king. It is fair that, for that reason, we determine whether the gods have favour on you or whether your death was always meant to be. We will fight, you and me, and put an end to this. If I win, I will be fairer than Eochaid, and put the options you give to me, back to you."

Nuada was quick to respond. "I will fight you as you ask, but only if you tie up one hand for an even fight."

"It is not as it would have been if we were left to fight on the field. So, I say no to your request."

"Then we will go to arms again tomorrow and the morrow after until all of the Firbolg or all the Tuatha warriors lay dead. Let the one left standing claim victory." Nuada intended to ride off with his words, yet he found himself unable to move, and his stomach felt sick. The herb mixtures that Dian Cecht had given him made him sleepy, and he had to battle to stay awake and on his steed.

Sreng did not notice. He thought Nuada had not moved in order to see if there might be a change in the Firbolg warrior's decision. Finally, after a time, Nuada did move to leave.

He was stopped by Sreng. "I do not want any more death; there has been enough of that. I would give myself, but the Firbolg need to

see a new leader who will teach them mercy and peace. Now I say …
we will leave in peace. We have nowhere else to go, just as your clan
has nowhere else."

Nuada sat higher. "There are five provinces of this land. Of these
five provinces, I give you the choice of wherever you wish your people
to live."

Sreng thought for a moment and then nodded. "I will choose to
walk for now. Our battle was here, and if any ask as to the battle, I
will say that the battle of Magh Tuireadh has ended, and we walk to
our freedom and peace."

Nuada reached down to the sword at his side and cut a small
wound on his remaining hand. "It is done, brother," he said as he
reached his hand out.

Sreng mimicked the king's movements and placed his hand on
Nuada's.

Nuada smiled. "You will walk your Firbolg clan away from
the field for five days and five nights, then stop. Whatever land lies
beyond will be your land. A nobler warrior of the Firbolg, there is
none. May your life be long, and your only lack, that of misfortunes."

With that, Nuada turned his horse and rode back to the Tuatha
Dé Danann, while Sreng rode back to the Firbolg. The Tuatha waited
as Dian Cecht and the Dagda helped the king from his horse. The
Dagda spoke in a whisper to Dian Cecht. "We had better get him to
shelter and away from all these eyes as soon as we can."

"I have words to say first." Nuada pulled himself from the
handling of his two men and moved near his horse, where he took
his sword and raised it aloft. "We this day have ended the battle of
Magh Tuireadh and claim for us a victory!" He walked toward his
people with an unwavering step as a tall warrior and king. With all
of his strength he shook his sword. "From this day the Firbolg are
no longer our enemies, but our allies! I gave choice of any of the five
provinces, and they chose to walk! We, this day, have gained their
city of Teamhair of the Beautiful Ridge! It is in this moment that I
say, because of the Fomorians who raid the land from the north, we
will make ourselves stronger in Teamhair! We will not cower from
them! We are the Tuatha Dé Danann!

"We will take the stone Lia Fáil, our stone of destiny, and build
our fort there! It will be measured a thousand troighid long and will
be on the summit of a hill! It will have an inside ditch and a high

bank on the outside! We will call it Ráith na Ríogh, for it is our fort of kings! We will create the seat of all kings and let the stone scream out our victory across all the land with every king that rules! Let any who want our blood see that we cannot be squeezed like rotten fruit for it!"

Dian Cecht and the Dagda cheered with the rest of the Tuatha Dé Danann, but their applause only masked their worry. While what their king had said was reasonable, the discovery of his missing hand would lead to trouble, so once more they took positions on either side of Nuada.

"Come now, my king," the Dagda said, loudly enough that the Tuatha would hear, yet quietly enough that his words did not sound strange. "We must bind your hand again, or the wound may get sick and you may lose it."

"Come, Nuada," Dian Cecht took the king's arm firmly.

They moved off, and none of the Tuatha bothered to note any difference. Injuries happened and were dealt with. In most circumstances, kings were never treated in the same space as any other warrior. The king was given privacy and a place where he would be able to gather his thoughts better than if he were placed in a row of men writhing in agony, with the smell of death and rot in his nose.

In the king's house, Macha rearranged some hides and furs that had been on the floor for use as a bed. She then went to get some water, as she had been requested to by the Dagda. Once she had left, Ronan and Ogma came and tried to enter the house, but were stopped at the door.

"He has lost a lot of blood, and he needs to be rested if we are to leave as soon as we can. None is to enter this place, and all who insist should be stopped," the Dagda urged. "Do you understand?"

They both answered that they did understand, and offered to stand guard at the door. The Dagda saw that this arrangement would benefit them all, and agreed.

"Ogma is very inquisitive," Dian Cecht whispered to the Dagda when he returned to his side.

"Ogma must learn not to be," the Dagda replied.

Dian Cecht nodded. "We must have Nuada think carefully over the next seven days about who will replace him as king. We can hide the loss of hand until then. We will not tell the people when it was removed, and they will not ask."

For the next two days, Nuada was kept in a state of constant sleep, and was only awaked to eat some broth and sip some drink. Macha stayed by her husband's side, while Danu walked to the mountain to fetch the women and children who had remained hidden.

By the third day, Dian Cecht and the Dagda agreed that Nuada was strong enough for the business of choosing a successor, and they spoke to him in private, at length, about which warrior among them would be best fit for king.

Nuada considered this. It had been several years since the Tuatha had first declared him the high king. Years since they had begun the preparations for leaving their islands and had come here to this new place. Nuada looked at the back of his undamaged hand. The blue streaks of his flowing blood under his skin made his hand look knotted and worn. The calluses on his knuckles looked like the foot of a dog, and the cuts upon them were scabbed and ugly. He felt he was no longer of use, and questioned what it was he could do.

Suddenly, on the seventh day, it came to him. "Bres," he said to the Dagda.

The Dagda was not pleased with Nuada's pick, and Dian Cecht felt equally unsure. "If we place Bres with the high kingship on his head, what will that make of the other kings?"

Nuada stayed set in his decision. "His father is rumoured to be Prince Elatha of the Fomorian clan. His mother is Eri, daughter of Delbaith. He has been raised by the Tuatha Dé Danann, and has often come to my aid, and your aid too."

He pointed to the Dagda and Dian Cecht. "The Fomorians often attack any part of the coast they choose. Most often, they come from the north. If there is a half-Fomorian as high king for the Tuatha Dé Danann, then there will be peace made between all. The Fomorians will not attack, for they will see us as their own kind."

"Fomorians attack their own," Dian Cecht said, doubtful of his brother's plans. "Who is to say they will not want a king of their own choosing?"

"Bres is seen by all as the most beautiful of us. He is strong, and has a pure enough mind that he keeps his word. It was his promise to Sreng from their first meeting that regardless of what happened, they would be friends and like brothers. They had opportunity on the battle field to slay one another, as we all saw. Yet they did not. He is a man whose word is truth. I will follow him," Nuada stated, and moved toward the door of the hut.

"I can see your decision is made and that is all," the Dagda said with a sorrowful glance down. "Some of our lessons in this life take longer to learn and must come from knowing the future."

"Alas," Nuada said to the Dagda, "I do not have that ability, nor do I have the patience or time to learn. If I sat with your daughters to see the future ..." he stopped and shook his head. "They only see the future that is when the stones of destiny have already been cast."

He looked to the Dagda. "Badb predicted that Macha would die at the hands of the Fomorians, as they will battle us next. This may be the only way to stop that war from happening. I cannot lose her, for I will cease to be if she dies."

The Dagda was not convinced. But he was forced to leave the decision of the king as it was. It was decided later that day that a council of warriors would be called in the morning. The Dagda spent an uneasy night unease, filled with bad dreams. Again, in the morning, he beseeched the king to change his mind and pick another warrior as king. Perhaps even Danu herself could be called upon to serve until a son was given to Nuada. He went as far as suggesting that Nuada take a child as his own; the Dagda had on occasion adopted a child when an orphan was presented.

Nuada, however he was begged, simply stated that for his love he would endure what was needed. The Dagda swore and cursed softly to himself as he opened the doors to king's round house.

When the group was assembled, and the room crowded, Nuada sat at the front of the assembly on his chair, which had been raised above those in the area. There were no other chairs—they all had been moved to the side or taken from the house. The Dagda called for the assembly to hush, and he presented the king.

Nuada looked around the room, and at first found it difficult to speak. Then the words came. "I have been ill for days now and there have even been rumours of my death. I am here, obviously, to stop all the gossip. There is truth in one thing." He held his injured arm up. "My hand was damaged, and Dian Cecht and the Dagda gathered all the knowledge they could together, and they saved my life"—he paused—"but they did not save my hand."

The crowd made no sound, and they watched their king to see what he would say next.

Ogma called, "You do not have the right to go against our tradition of being physically perfect to be king, but I, for one, will walk the street and point to you as a complete man. Rule us, Nuada."

"I have not the right," Nuada said.

"You are king," another warrior declared. "God on the earth. Let not history decide your path, but take us into the future."

The group applauded and raised their fists in approval.

Nuada hushed them. "If I break with tradition, another will, and further on. What law will not be broken, and who will be the one able to control any?"

"I will see you as whole," cried another voice.

"I will, too, see you only as being complete," Ronan called at his king's feet.

The people in the room continued trying to convince Nuada to remain king. After a long while, he quieted them. "I have decided that Bres would be the best to lead the Tuatha forward. His half-Fomorian blood makes him more likely an ally to the Fomorians who raid this land from the north. We will live in peace."

The room stayed quiet, and Bres did not move.

"If it is physical perfection that is needed for the kingship, who am I to go against law? Bres is the most handsome of all our warriors. Is it not true that many have used his name when talking of something else of great beauty? Is it so that even the great ridge and the lead stallion are both said to be as beautiful as Bres himself?

"Come, if we do not know whether the rumour that his father is the Prince Elatha is true, then we do know that Bres is half Fomorian and half of the Tuatha. If it is true that his parent is Prince Elatha, then we know that Prince Elatha is at least fairer than the wicked Balor of the evil eye."

The room was still silent, and still no one moved.

Nuada stood on his chair and pointed down at the warriors. "Then who of you would you have? Who? Point such a man out and make him known now." He viewed the room, and still no one said anything. "There is no answer, then, and I stand by my choosing."

"Bres is liked amongst the Tuatha," Dian Cecht observed. "We have all called him brother." He looked down at his feet for a moment, and then up again. "I will follow Bres."

"He helps with all and he protected us with his might. I will follow Bres," Miach, son of Dian Cecht, said.

The Dagda raised his fist to the roof. "I will follow Bres."

The room roared into life once more with the Dagda's calling, and the Tuatha hailed their new king. They carried Bres to the front of the room and pushed him upward into the chair as Nuada vacated it. As Nuada dismounted the seat, he kissed the head of the new king, a gesture that showed he gave his blessing to the reign of Bres.

The new king looked a little shaken and uncomfortable with his position. He tried to cover it by the thrust of his fist towards the roof, and he shouted, "The Tuatha Dé Danann!"

A cry went up, and the room began to empty to make way for the chair to be carried around the settlement to display the new king for all to see. Four warriors picked the chair up from its stand and moved to the door. Bres ducked to stop his head from being hit on the door arch, even though the chair had been dropped nearly completely to the ground.

Once outside, the warriors hoisted the chair and then, with the call of the people, Bres was taken around to all the Tuatha. They raised their hands to show their approval as the warriors lifted the chair up and down as it floated on waves. The raising and lowering of the chair was symbolic, showing that Bres was their king on land and on water. As they held the chair they stepped over fire to show there was no fear in his leadership, and then the feast began.

ᔆ 6 ᔆ

As according to tradition, The Tuatha Dé Danann clan had a year and a day from the end of the battle of Magh Tuireadh to leave their old village. Within days of becoming king, Bres, having taken counsel with the Dagda and Nuada, led most of the clan away from the village on the battle plain and all the death that had occurred there.

Some of the Tuatha had already gone to Teamhair with Lia Fáil, the sacred stone, to begin work on the Ráith na Ríogh, the fort of the kings, as Nuada had decreed as his last command. At last, the rest of the Tuatha went to Teamhair, where the Firbolg clan had had its stronghold. Nuada loved the area very much. It was beautiful.

The Firbolg had cleared the land around Teamhair for farming. As they left their city, the Firbolg people told Bres that there was land to the east that one might see from the northeast side of the coast, but only on clear days. On hearing this, Bres was intrigued, like any young warrior, and wanted to see what they were talking about.

So, after the Tuatha settled themselves, Bres and several warriors, including the Dagda and Ronan— who had already decided to head in the direction indicated by the Firbolg—set off to see. By that time, the winter had finished, and spring was once more upon the land.

The Dagda and his daughters, including Brigit, accompanied the warriors. Bres had been taken by Brigit's intelligence, and he rode with her often. The Dagda saw this as a good thing, as he had been concerned that such a young king would easily make irrational decisions. Brigit's wisdom could help steady him.

As it was, Bres felt very uncomfortable with making decisions alone and would often seek advice from others as what to do in any given situation. He knew how to be a warrior, and never had questions about how to strap a horse or take care of an enemy. With the responsibility of the Tuatha on his shoulders, though, he was lost.

The terrain they rode through consisted of a lot of forests with paths cut through them. To Bres, these forests were not dense and horrid and smelly, but pleasant, with the scent of freshness and wonder within them. He rode his stallion and spoke poetry so beautifully and wondrously that the warriors with him followed in silence and listened, mesmerized.

At night he sat with his people by the fires and ate, drank, and played music on a harp, while the Dagda played his harp or his pipes, and Ogma played the horn. All the warriors were uplifted by the sounds. Within these eastern forests, Bres took Brigit as his wife, and said his happiness could not be greater. The Dagda was more than happy with the union and became further relaxed with the idea of Bres being king.

They travelled along the coast and waited for a fine day so that they could see the lands that they had been told of to the east. Sure enough, on a fine day as they looked to the east, the cry of wonder went up as they all saw the land. Bres seemed impressed at first; then the Dagda saw something in his mood change. He took Ronan and followed Bres as he made his way back into the forest by himself.

Bres sat on a fallen log and put his hands to his face. Ronan and the Dagda stepped to his side. They both could see that his face had filled with fear and that he was trying to erase the emotion with his hands as he wiped them across his brow over and over again.

"Why do you retreat and sit here by yourself, my king?" Ronan asked.

Bres bade Ronan sit next to him. Ronan complied, as did the Dagda, sitting on his other side. "I have a kingdom, so I am told, that I must protect, and all those within the boundaries. I must be friendly and aid those we share the land with, the Firbolgs. I must make sure we are all fed, watered, wined, given mead and ale, and pleased. There are protected borders, and word of these borders is known to all. Still, here I am, and I do not know the lay of this land very well. I did not know, until this moment, how close are those that might encroach upon us. I am only one man." He shook his head. "I am not a god. I am not of the Sidhe. I am not ... I just am not."

"You are king, and all kings have concerns, and all kings have the weight they carry," the Dagda reassured him. "We will leave and make our way to where the Lia Fáil has been taken. We will go to where Nuada, as past king, has seen it placed by those who went before us from Magh Tuireadh. They surely have begun work on the fort of the kings by this time. You will feel better in yourself once you have touched the rock and it cries out for all of this land to hear."

Bres nodded his head. But the Dagda caught a look in the young man's eyes that said he would not do any such thing. For the first time since Bres had become king, the Dagda saw the rise of something that made his concern grow again.

"I think," said Bres, "we should remain here for a little while. Just until I get used to the idea of such a close land to this and knowing that there may come a day when we meet those on the other side."

The Dagda nodded, as did Ronan. They all stood at once and were about to leave the log where it was, when Brigit appeared from between the trees. "I thought you were off fetching mushrooms or something the like, but here I find you sitting and talking like old women," she teased.

Bres was not impressed. "Old women should be doing their work, just as kings must do theirs."

Brigit was taken aback by her new husband's words. "I am sorry to have offended you. There was no intention to do so."

Bres sighed and moved to his wife. He took her hands up in his. "I am sorry. You are right. I am being foolish." He kissed her hands and cupped them to his lips as he spoke. "To offend you, or to make you feel you have done something unjust when it is not so, is my folly. I have many new things I have to learn. I am willing to learn."

Brigit, pleased by her husband's affections, kissed him on his head. "I could not understand what it is like to be king. I will always be by your side as your wife."

Bres kissed Brigit with such passion that the Dagda and Ronan felt it was time they should rejoin the rest of their company. When they reached the edge of the forest, they looked out at the marvellous waters before them, and they began to talk about the Tuatha islands before they were destroyed. The Dagda pointed into the distance and spoke to the younger warriors—who were beginning to forget where they had come from—about the islands. Wood for a fire was brought, and soon supper was being cooked. They were happy for that time as they sat there, reminiscing about the old days.

They stayed at the same spot for several weeks and no one complained; instead they ventured during the day away from the area in different directions, but always returned at night to the same spot.

One day, those in the camp awakened to strange sounds on the water and noticed the thick fog that lay around. The fog made it hard to see anything, even with the glow of the fire, until they were upon it.

"What is this?" Bres asked the Dagda.

"It is cloud, my king," the Dagda answered. "I do not feel any magic, but I do feel the presence of others who are coming. We must return to our people. I feel there are those who are coming to do us harm."

Bres felt excited at this news. Battle was something he knew well, and he could handle himself on the field. "Who is it, do you know?"

"I believe the Fomorians approach," the Dagda said. "It is time to see how you fit in the position of king, Bres."

Bres frowned. "I will do what is best for the Tuatha Dé Danann, this I have promised."

Ronan and the Dagda stared at the back of their new king as he mounted his horse. Neither knew quite how to take his behaviour. Eventually, they decided to shrug off the entire thing and they, too, prepared to leave.

When they returned to the Tuatha, they could see immediately that the work had indeed begun on the fort of kings. They rode by the workers, and some of the Tuatha warriors nodded to those workers they knew. Others sat in their saddles and paid no heed.

As soon as they got closer to the main house, a large man whom they had never seen before greeted them. The man was bearded and had many tattoos decorating his arms and chest. He had only one hand, and his face bore a scar that was not completely hidden by the hair upon it. Next to him came another man, very handsome, whose hair was nearly white. His eyes shone a blue that reflected the sky. But he, too, was damaged, using a crutch to help him walk.

"I am Conand of the Fomorians," the large bearded man said. "We have come to you because we have heard word on the winds that there is a Fomorian boy who has become king among you, and here I stand to see that it is truth."

"And who are you, Conand, to approach us like this?" Bres said, his youthful anger clear.

Conand gave a crooked smile to the Tuatha king. "I guess I could ask the same of you."

Bres flew from his horse and directed himself at the Fomorian. He was checked by the Dagda's hand on his shoulder. "A king …" was all the Dagda said, leaving the rest for Bres to think about.

Bres inhaled. "What are you here for? War? Peace?"

The two men laughed and stomped their feet into the ground. "You see, it has been many years since we've come to these shores, and we take from the land what we need. This land you have inherited is our garden, and we pick from it as we choose."

"What if we choose you to leave?" Bres asked.

"We choose our own path, and are not to be told which way we face," Conand said firmly. Then he smiled again. "However, it is understood that your father might be Prince Elatha of our clan. We came to put to rest any rumours or confirm if truth."

"My mother is my concern, and with her any truths can stay. So, your truth, you will never have," Bres grunted.

"Not so," Conand said and he walked closer to Bres. "I see you are Fomorian, and your father is as like you as a twin. He, like you, has not a scar upon his face, and what wounds he has had, have healed so well that they make his muscles look twice the size, for they underscore his strength. Tell me the story of your father that your mother has told you?"

Bres complied. "My father came on a dark night; my mother thought he was a lost god. He arrived in a beautiful boat that looked to be silver, and he wore clothes that were threaded with gold. On his neck he wore five gold torcs, and on his hands he had several rings, of which he gave one to my mother. I wear it to this day. His hair was yellow, with many touches of silver through it, but it was not grey like an old man's; he was very young. My mother had never loved any Tuatha, but only loved him, and she was broken when he left."

This time Conand grunted. "Much more like Elatha than not." He then livened up. "Still, I do come all this way to hear a story that might be as much from a horse's paddock as it is the truth."

"You call my mother a liar, now?" Bres pressed himself forward.

"Boy," Conand pushed back, "if every story is to be believed, then there would be more children born to princes, kings, and gods than walk this very earth."

He laughed at the anger he could see he was causing Bres and thumped his open hand on the king's chest. "I have simply come to take you back to Prince Elatha, so he can say himself. As for a ring—

" he laughed again, "—trinkets and bits come from everywhere, for we are Fomorians. There is nothing to find in that ring other than someone's loss, our gain, and then a gift, or perhaps, payment."

He winked at Bres, who found it hard to control himself at his mother being called a whore.

"By whom," Conand shrugged, "well, that is for Prince Elatha to say."

"My mother's word is enough." Bres took Conand's hand and threw it back at him.

The Dagda came to his king's side. "Let it be, Bres," he whispered to the king. The Dagda pulled Bres to the side and spoke to him quietly. "Let us sort this, for there is Fomorian blood in you, even he says as such. I know your mother well. She is no liar. She has never been with any except whoever your father is. You must remember, though she would not lie, that whoever your father is, may have lied. No matter what is revealed, she need not know anything except what she has always known, if that makes it easier."

Bres thought for moment, and then turned back to Conand. "It is so. I will travel with you to the lands of the Fomorian clan and I will meet with Prince Elatha." He paused. "And my mother will come with us." He turned and eyed the Dagda with anger for suggesting that his parentage may have been at all questionable … on either side.

The Dagda shook his head as he watched the king enter his round house. Ronan slipped from his horse and stood before the Dagda. "What do we do now?" Ronan asked.

"We prepare boats to sail to the land of the north. Prince Elatha has summoned our king, and our king intends to bow to the summoning."

Ronan stared at the back of Conand and his companions as they entered the round house behind Bres. "We will talk to him and tell him that to bow at the bidding of any other is to show that we are no more than their peasants who work their fields. It might well be a play for killing the king. The prince, if he questions Bres's legacy, should bring himself to these shores, not send his men to fetch him like some dog's catch."

"Who would Bres listen to?" the Dagda asked.

"You have always been the closest to him, and you are respected as if our father," Ronan said.

"I saw his eyes say otherwise," the Dagda responded, "yet, you are right. There are no others close to Bres like a father, for his mother isolated herself so completely."

Later that evening, the Dagda spoke to Bres and told him of the Tuatha's concerns.

Bres was less than impressed. "Here I sit being told I should be king and not do any other's bidding, and yet you have come to me to tell me to do your bidding," Bres glowered. "I stand, and you still convict me of being in the service of another, and tell me to sit. I listen to what you say, and it is all contradictory. If I were any other king," he flung his hand in a bold gesture, "traveling to visit his father, wherever that may be, would you question it if his father had asked for his attendance?"

"This is very different," the Dagda said.

"I see no difference," Bres argued. He softened his tone and went on, "I am trying to create the peace wished for by the Tuatha clan. If I go and my father recognises me as his, I can make peace between our clan and theirs. They will leave our country alone."

The Dagda did not go on with the argument. "What will you have us do? How many men will attend you and your mother?"

"I will have my mother choose." Bres frowned again at the Dagda to accent his point. "I trust her."

Sixteen men were chosen to accompany Bres and his mother to the northern islands; the land of Fomorian kings. While they were gone, the Dagda did most of the work expected from a king. It was not his idea to be chosen for this task, but the Tuatha clan stated they needed him while there was no other.

By the time Bres returned, the winter had passed twice and the summer was coming in again. Bres had been king for nearly three years, but the Tuatha clan was losing interest in its king. The people felt he had abandoned them.

In Bres's absence, The Tuatha Dé Danann had spread out across the land. They had planted crops and they had bred their cattle. The crop that year was good, and the birthing of their calves were many. They were very happy the land they had come to was proving to be so generous towards them, and they celebrated and thanked the earth and the sun.

King Bres entered the waters of the Tuatha Dé Danann, bringing six extra boats filled with people of the Fomorian clan. He came ashore and greeted the Tuatha with a quick word, then went immediately to his round house. All the Fomorians followed him.

The Tuatha clan stared as the men went by; many had discoloured skin and looked ill. Their flesh looked damaged, bearing many scars that had not healed properly. Some of the Fomorians had no feet, and some had no hands. Among the many who arrived was Balor of the evil eye.

The Tuatha Dé Danann snarled quietly their hate at Balor as he walked past them. He drew himself up higher and smiled wickedly at them. Bres called all head warriors to his round house so he could speak to them about the future between the Fomorians and the Tuatha Dé Danann. Nuada, the former king, stood amongst the warriors. Balor of the evil eye sat next to the king, as though he were Bres's right-hand man.

Bres addressed the assembled people. "My father, who has greeted me as such, and the other leaders of the Fomorians met with me, and we had many words between us as to how we may live in peace. I refused many requests. Eventually, we came to a decision. The Firbolgs and the Fomorians had negotiated peace many times, but peace failed when the Firbolgs did not keep their end of the deal. I intend to be unlike them and to do as I have promised. We will pay tribute to the Fomorians that we may be in peace. A tax will be levied on all. A third part of all we gain will be paid."

"A third!" Nuada shouted, his rage uncontainable. "What are we to do with ourselves by losing a third of all we have? What of a harsh winter or a failed crop? We are Tuatha and we do not pay money to any just to be their whore."

The other warriors sounded behind him to show they agreed. Ogma said to Ronan, "We should have followed our instinct and kept Nuada as king, or even the Dagda, until another suitable Tuatha came forward. Look now at what has happened."

Bres, who heard Ogma, became angry, and he knew exactly how to state that he was king and no other. "The Dagda, I feel, is best to spend his time for the Tuatha Dé Danann building the fort of kings and other such forts, so we will be a strong clan with many forts and seen as such from as far away as the other land. He is a good builder and has done a lot of work using stone, so all forts will be made of stone. Then, ditches he will dig around the forts and to the sky they will press. You claim to have flown, great Dagda—then face to the sky you love. Of course," he said with an evil smile at the Dagda, "I do this so the Tuatha will be a stronger clan and so all will know we are the greatest clan.

"Nuada, you," he then eyed Nuada, "being such a wonderful soldier in the past and once king for the Tuatha, and with your keen eye ..."

"Nuada is still ill," Dian Cecht said from near the door. "I have been treating him with the herbs I find, picking them with the dew still on them. I have been breaking them down and grinding them all together. It has been this long, and his arm still gets boils and sores on it." Dian Cecht had the look of half-madness for lack of sleep and for being baffled by Nuada's arm, which never seemed to fully heal.

"Are not your children healers as well?" Bres asked.

"Yes," Dian Cecht said, "They are apprentices, and we are all learning because the herbs are very different to us here than in the lands we are from. We are all ..." He pounded his fist to his head repeatedly, as if trying to hammer a solution out of his skull.

"In all these, you still find difficulties in locating the herbs you need. You have spent much of that time in caves and hidden on the land in forests and such, and still you do not know?" Bres asked sarcastically.

When it was obvious Dian Cecht was not going to say anything in his own defence, the king continued. "Well, I think you can spend time all together and resolve this. Don't you think that is a good idea?"

Dian Cecht nodded.

"Good," said Bres. "And when he is well, Nuada will carry sticks for the building of round houses and fences in the day, and he will have the latest watch on the fort with Ronan at night. If your bird Dea only serves you, Nuada, then we will see you also each morning take to the highest peak, and you will send your bird forth to scout the seas and the land around."

Nuada remained silent and nodded; the king had the right to place such an order. It was Ogma who said, "Nuada was good to you and believed in you when there were those who did not. Why is it you wish to treat him like a slave?"

Bres glared at Ogma, "He is merely making the Tuatha clan stronger and working with the Tuatha people to do so. Would you disagree with that?"

Ogma retreated. "No."

"I think it best that you learn to do for the Tuatha, as does the rest of your clan. I will see you carry firewood for the smiths and the bakers and any others who need the wood for their work, bringing us as a clan to a greater strength," Bres sneered.

"Will not the Fomorians want a third of that?" Ogma asked sarcastically.

Bres could hardly contain his anger as he rose off his chair. "If what I choose is law, all, including you, will succumb to that law."

The room felt tense as Ogma stood with his chest out and his face set. He was as big as Bres, and a far more experienced swordsman. It was not a question of whether he could cut Bres down where he stood, but whether he would do it. He stood his ground against the king and did not move.

The Dagda grabbed his arm and pulled him aside. "Do you think that the many Fomorians who have entered our Tuatha clan this day will tolerate you rising up? Balor is amongst them. We must tread carefully." The Dagda said these words and then let the arm of Ogma go.

Ogma turned back to the king and with a sigh he said, "I concede, and will do as you command."

Bres sat back down. His face showed he was pleased he had control of the room and, therefore, the clan. "I will concede also," he said. "Nuada need not do menial chores. He will present himself as the lookout and guard to the fort." He looked to the side, where Balor sat, and studied the Fomorian king's face to see if he agreed; Balor gave a nod in reply.

Bres spoke again. "I have also the mind for many a contest for the warriors of the Tuatha. This will provide amusement for our guests, and the reward to the winners will be worth the anguish they endure."

The idea of contests that would cause anguish silenced the entire room, and the Tuatha warriors did not even turn to look at one another. They thought their own thoughts on the matter. They saw Balor at the fore of these new events and they did not know what to do. They left the round house feeling defeated by their own king. The Dagda beckoned a few of the warriors, indicating they should meet him in the woods outside the settlement later that evening.

Several warriors came to the woods that night, and they spoke. The Dagda told them how he had tried to help Balor when he was young by making a potion to cure his blindness, and of all the trouble his intervention caused.

"Yet," The Dagda said, "it is only a false story about his eye being able to turn to stone any who sees it. His mother's heart stopped with shock on seeing her son in such a terrible state; that is true. He has convinced himself over all the years that there is power in his eye. This is not so. Those who fall dead at his feet do so from fear and the expectation that it is to happen." He tapped his head. "It is here that he bests them and destroys their bodies. His eye has no command over any but those foolish enough to give command over to it."

The warriors were not convinced, and Dian Cecht spoke. "I have heard stories of him lifting that cap that he has over his eye, causing fifty men to fall by the wayside at a time."

"I, too," Neit added, "have heard this, and that when he grows weary, he sits on the back of his horse and summons his men. It takes the strength of many warriors to lift his eyelid by pulling on ropes he attaches to those iron rings that hang from his eyelid. The eye itself turns blearily, looking to the enemies, and then they are struck down."

The Dagda tried to calm the warriors, "It is not true. It is rumour that aids the Fomorians. I am as old as the mountains and I still stand, so says rumour, but my age is my age and I do not have to justify that I exist."

The Tuatha warriors agreed.

"However, has any Tuatha seen the feats of Balor that are spoken of? No, we have not. Many of the Tuatha are to suffer for the word of a Fomorian. We must rise and place Nuada back as king."

"Nuada is not whole and will not be king, those are his own words and his own choosing," Ogma said with the shake of his head. "And the people will not aid us until there is proof that Balor's eye is no more than a blind rock in his head."

"That," Dian Cecht said, "or the Fomorians' hold gets too painful."

The Dagda sighed and shook his head. "So be it. We will wait until the time is right. Until then, we will work towards that right time. Dian Cecht will heal Nuada and then, by your own skills, you will create a hand made of silver for our once and future king. There will be no question of his purity if his hand is made of such a pure metal."

This was agreed upon, and the warriors spoke for a little longer before they left and went back to their homes. As the year continued, more Fomorians arrived, and Balor returned back to the country of the Fomorian clan. He left one order spread throughout the land: Any Tuatha refusing to pay the tax would have their nose cut off.

This order was told from one Tuatha to another. In the case that any did not hear, Fomorian men were sent to find all the homes and farms and settlements and make sure the people there were well aware of all that was expected.

By riding through the land, the Fomorians noted every house, home, farm, and village. Nechtan, one of the tax collectors for the Fomorians, noted the cattle and the crops of wheat and barley, all the mutton, goats, pork, and different types of game birds and their eggs. He went back to his king and told him that the Tuatha had so much more than the Fomorians had known, and they ate a wonderful stirabout broth with butter or milk and honey. Balor received the first round of taxes brought to him, and on hearing what Nechtan had said, he thought the Tuatha could give even more.

The next year the taxes became heavier, though Bres said they remained at the same rate: a third of everything. The Tuatha king declared that the Tuatha had been given a good deal, and that he had been generous in letting them keep so much. Bres said he found the people's complaints unjustified.

To prove that he had not taken so much from them in the years prior, and that it all could be so much harder for them, in the third year of the Tuatha tribute requirement to the Fomorians, the Tuatha also had to give a third of their children. To lose their children pained the Tuatha, yet no matter their protests, their children were still taken.

Nuada stood on the fort of kings when he saw Tuatha children being led to the Fomorian boats and taken away. He hurried to hide Macha, who had become pregnant with their child. The child she carried was their fifth child; however, only two of the other four children had lived—a son and a daughter. Nuada would not risk losing any more. When he arrived home, he found Macha sitting on the floor with their little son cuddled in her arms, her large stomach heaving with sorrow as she sobbed. Their thirteen-year-old daughter had disappeared; nor did it require much guessing to know where she had gone. Nuada bowed to Macha on the floor, scraping his knees as he did so.

"I will bring our daughter back," Nuada promised, and he rose to his feet and rushed to the door. With his good hand he gathered up his weapons and rushed to the shore. By the time he arrived on the beach, the boats had left, and he could see just the dots of them as they rowed into the distance. His daughter was gone, stolen from him and Macha. To his knees he dropped again, and tears ran down his cheeks. His child's sweet face and laugh were not his to see or hear anymore.

The goldsmith, Creidhne, heard the sobbing of the Tuatha's past king and put down his work. He went to the beach to find Nuada and tried to speak comfort to him. "You must think she will be well. Such a pretty girl they will not use as a slave for long. She will eventually be taken as a bride by one of the nobles, and she will live on, having many children and a long life. You are blessed that she is so beautiful and not an ugly child that would look better in dirt and cinders. Even as she was led away, she did not cry like the others, and the Fomorians commented on how she was the most noble of all the children. You will see." He gripped Nuada's shoulder. "She will be a high queen of the Fomorian clan one day, and she will call them by another name and they will be strong. This I can tell you."

The words of the goldsmith settled Nuada, and he nodded. There was something in what Creidhne said that he felt was truth. He embraced his old friend as a brother and thanked him for his prophecy.

"It is time we do something," Creidhne said. "Dian Cecht has been working hard, and I am helping him create a replacement hand for you. It will be ready by next spring."

Other Tuatha gathered on the beach and looked to the distance where their children had gone. The silence was peaceful and strangely soothing. An older woman saw Nuada and went to him. She knelt before him. "I will always see you as our finest king, great Nuada."

"I am no longer king," Nuada said, emotionlessly.

"You will be again," Creidhne declared. Nuada said nothing and continued to stare into the distance.

"I had to pay in tax for cattle that do not even exist. The Fomorian tax collector Nechtan deceives by making decoys and lying, so that what Bres believes is real, is not," a farmer complained.

"I, too, have felt these lies at the expense of my harvest," a peasant remarked.

"I have been to Bres's round house," said Creidhne, "and so have my brothers, and none of us have been fed. We received no drink of mead, nor were we given any hospitality. There is no music there, and we of the Tuatha Dé Danann love music. There are no poets allowed in the villages, and singers and other musicians must stay hushed.

"Bres has even hushed Brigit, who sits alone and speaks to no one. She goes to the caves in the day when Bres is away and talks to the animals and trees. Their son is all she has to love, as any love that she has cast at the king seems to have fallen away from his favour. She, in silence, takes in those who are ill and helps to heal them. Bres cannot know these things, or she fears he will punish her."

"Of poetry," said a peasant woman, "Etain's son, Corpre, came to the fort looking for shelter and hospitality. Bres gave him a hole in the ground to sleep in with no bed or fire, or any light of any sort. He gave him a few small cakes to eat that were dry and tasteless. When Corpre woke in the morning, everyone was gone, and there was no food, drink, or anything given to him.

"He came to the people and asked for food and drink, which we gave, and then he began to speak poetry of the misery of the reign of Bres. It was the first poem of such mockery and ridicule that I have ever heard. We laughed. Then he thought he was better to walk in another direction to find hospitality, and he left."

"Ogma," the peasant man said, "I see Ogma on the beach bringing the firewood he has been ordered to collect. He is weak and has to walk against the tide, and sometimes through it. Still, he does not stop, or show Bres that he is weak."

"The Dagda is weak, also," another said. "I have seen him stumble in his tasks, yet he does not ever fall. He has grown thin and looks starved."

"He has a son by his old mistress, doesn't he?" Nuada asked.

"Yes, that is true," another Tuatha man said. "His name is Aengus mac Og, and he has all of the signs of being a powerful warrior—he has been raised by Midhir in the far-off forest, close to the Firbolgs' land."

"Perhaps it is time to summon this son," Nuada suggested.

The Tuatha took what Nuada said as a command from their king, and they sent for Aengus mac Og to come. When he arrived, he was sent to his father, who was still carrying the stones and building, as he had been ordered to do. Aengus was horrified to find that his father looked like a sick man, and that his bones showed through his skin. His muscles were taut and his skin thin, so much so that Aengus could see every vein within the Dagda's body.

"This is the great Dagda, my father?" Aengus asked. "What has become of you? You are the immortal, and here you have allowed yourself to be treated in such a way and let your body all but dissolve."

"It is the path I have chosen to follow," the Dagda said. "I am waiting for something to change in Nuada and the Tuatha."

"That may be so," Aengus said, "but you look as though you are never fed. Why would you allow yourself to become so weak?"

The Dagda snorted. "Not by choice. The Fomorian called Cridenbel comes to me every night. He is blind, and he is cruel. He swears and screams horrible things at the Tuatha people, so much so that they cringe at his name. Every day he comes to me and says I should give to him my three biggest portions of food. With everyone in the Tuatha Dé Danann suffering and giving the best of theirs, I feel I am no different, and so I oblige and give to him my best and biggest portions."

Aengus looked at his father and understood his sacrifice. He then had an idea. "Why do you not put three pieces of gold into his food? If he slows his eating he will notice the coins and be happy that you have blessed him with the reward, but if he does not eat slowly he will choke on the gold."

The Dagda eyed his son and considered what the young warrior was saying. He nodded. "I have gold that I will use, and I will do what it is you suggest."

That evening Cridenbel came down to the Dagda where he sat to supper, and as usual he demanded the three biggest bits of food. The Dagda was ready and had prepared the food, placing coins in the three best portions. Cridenbel selected the pieces of food he wanted and ate as quickly as his fat little stomach could tolerate swallowing. The first coin did not catch, and neither did the second. By the third portion of food, the Fomorian had become more disgusting in his eating, and the coin caught in his throat. The Dagda stood over the bulging Fomorian and smiled as his tormentor died slowly.

A Fomorian warrior came to fetch Cridenbel from his nightly taunting of the Dagda and was angered to find the heavy man slumped on the floor. Immediately upon seeing the body and without knowing facts, the accusation was thrown, "You have killed Cridenbel for no reason and so this is death for you." He grabbed the arm of the Dagda and took him to Bres.

"Your head will be taken and presented for the land to see at the top of the fort," Bres commanded.

"You are not acting as a king!" the Dagda yelled at him, breaking free of the grip of the Fomorian warrior. "Cridenbel stole my food and then choked on a coin that was in it. How is it my fault that he eats like a pig?"

Bres stopped the warrior from placing his hands on the Dagda again. "If that is the case, then there will be gold within him, in his throat and in his stomach. I see the only way to give fair judgement is to cut him open and look at what is in his stomach and throat."

The body of the dead Fomorian was carried to the front of Bres's home and then brought in the house by a crowd of spectators. Cridenbel was cut open, as the king had ordered, and the witnesses in the room stood around as his guts were pulled from his body and a hand shifted into the cavity of his throat. The coin from his throat was produced quickly and, after shifting through his stomach contents, two other coins were soon found.

"The Dagda is not to fault for a man's gluttony," Bres said, and motioned for the body to be removed.

He then spoke to the Dagda. "You have nearly finished your work on Kath Brese, so see me when you have, and I will pay you. Until then, I do not want you to make any more of a show of yourself."

He dismissed everyone in the house and went to his supper on his own. Two women later would join him, and he would have his strength to please them and himself. His taste for all the wonderful things, gold and women and the power of leadership, was never satisfied.

Bres, as beautiful and perfect as he was to look at, had become the absolute opposite within. He did not play music anymore and refused to sing or hear a word of happiness. The only thing he had loved he had driven away, and he felt a horror inside for doing such a thing. When any of the whores came in to pleasure him, it was Brigit he would always think of, and only her that he saw.

ᔅ 7 ᔒ

Dian Cecht had worked for a considerable time on Nuada's arm. He finally had healed it and had fashioned an artificial hand out of silver with the help of Creidhne. It had been nearly seven years since Nuada had lost his hand and had given his throne to Bres. The silver hand was made to be so perfect that the fingers could move, and it was all but a real functioning hand.

The Tuatha praised Nuada as he walked the streets. The longer the praise went on, the more Bres soured against Nuada. Bres watched Nuada, and when Nuada went about his work, with the Tuatha praising even his smallest movement, Bres's eyes glared at his once-king.

What Bres did not know was that the hand, which had been fashioned for Nuada from silver, was making Nuada sick. There was nothing that Dian Cecht seemed to find that could stop the poison's effects. He tried many herbs, plastered in-between the silver and the flesh: This only caused the hand to move awkwardly and continuously in a loose and painful manner. The hooks that Dian Cecht had fashioned up to secure the hand to the arm blistered and oozed pus. The more the healer thought on it, the less sleep he got, and the more crazed his behaviour became.

Nuada's eyes showed the effects of the silver the most. By the time Nuada had worn the hand for a year, his skin was turning a blue-grey shade. He did not act as sick as his body looked ill.

Dian Cecht did not know what he could do to fix Nuada's problem. His children found him several times, talking to himself as if he were speaking to someone else, and he skulked away to the caves more and more.

Bres's kingship did not matter anymore to the people; they had seen Nuada's new hand and declared that, by the silver hand, Nuada was whole again and Bres no longer had a right to sit in place of him.

When Bres heard of this, he argued the hand might be of pure metal; however, it was not of flesh and blood.

But the Tuatha Dé Danann felt they had a right to the king of their choice, and that if they saw Nuada as whole and their law said the purity of silver and gold was as pure as the people, therein, were they not the same? Nuada did not want the decisions of some to lead to a division in his people. One day the debate spilled into the streets until all in the township got involved.

"I cannot take the kingdom if the kingdom falls apart because of my own vanity," Nuada insisted. His modesty did not matter, as the clan had begun to ignore Bres as king and only respected Nuada as their leader. Even without ceremony, he had once again been made king of the people.

One day, a man amongst their gathering stepped forward. He wore the hood of a druid. "I can help with any concerns you have about your hand," he announced to Nuada. "I will free you of any who may say you have a lesser right to be king because of your silver hand. I know a way that a real hand of flesh and blood can be made for you, and there will be no one who can say anything again against your kingship."

Ronan stepped forward to the young druid and asked, "Who are you to say such things? Who taught you?"

"I am Miach, son of Dian Cecht. My sister, Airmed, aids me," the healer said, pointing to a young woman. "What our father taught us we know, yet we have taught ourselves more."

"If you have such ability, before you touch the king, you should prove your skill," Ronan said. "We must be sure."

"I understand," Miach answered. "What would you have me do?"

The Tuatha considered what they could make the young Miach do to prove himself. As they pondered, an old warrior came by and wondered aloud what it was that they were doing, talking aside, as though hidden away altogether. When the old man was told about the healer, he happily related that he could do with an eye, as one of his had been taken in the war with the Firbolg.

"Fine," said Miach. "It is chosen. If you wish, I will take the eye of the cat that you carry and place it in your head."

The warrior looked at his cat. "This cat serves me well, and I have to depend on it to keep rats and other such things away. But if you can give it, I would truly love an eye as keen."

"I will see that your cat has what it needs for the rest of its days. Another cat will be given to you to rid you of any rats. My sister Airmed and I will make it our responsibility," Miach assured him.

The man looked again at his cat and then handed it to the healer. Miach touched the cat and ran his hand across its face. With a scream, the cat leapt from the arms of the healer and directly into those of Airmed, who caught it with her quick hands.

Miach then took the head of the old Tuatha warrior in one hand, and at the same time he drew herbs and powders from his pocket. He pushed the head of the warrior back, and when it came forward again, a new eye had replaced the empty socket in his skull. The eye had the shape of a cat's, and the vertical slit in the middle looked near demon-like to behold, but with each blink the man hollered and yelled with joy.

"Oh, it works so much better than my other eye," the man thanked Miach.

"Why wouldn't it?" said Miach. "After all, cats do have better eyesight than we."

"Now I will just need to shut it well when the wife stands naked before me," the man joked as he hurried off to show his friends.

"Very well," Ronan said. "We have seen your skill. As you can do such miracles, we will send word to all the Tuatha Dé Danann that Nuada is made king again."

"It would be best to use the original hand of the king," Miach said. "Was it kept?"

"According to the Tuatha tradition, we buried it near the battlefield where he lost it," said Ronan.

"We want to go and get the hand of the king. Can you take us there?" Miach asked.

"Surely we can," Ronan said.

"We must take that silver hand before it causes you any more trouble," Miach said to Nuada. "We will take you to a nearby home where we know you will be safe. A place where the Fomorians do not go, a place even the Tuatha do not know of. Come with us."

The people followed the pair of siblings into the forest. The paths were crossed and what little understanding of direction anyone had was soon lost. Nuada looked to Macha, who marched on with such grace while her hand hovered above her sword as though she was not sure what to expect.

"Are you well? " Nuada asked in a hushed manner of his wife.

"'Tis the lack of path and unsettling silence within this great forest," Macha whispered to her husband. "Where are all the animals? It is not natural."

"Ahh!" Miach exclaimed from the front of their line. "But, do you not remember, Macha, we are not natural ourselves?"

Macha eyed her husband in shock. She could not believe that Miach had heard her speak from where he was, and she blushed slightly at being caught in her doubts. Nuada suddenly found himself smiling once Macha had turned away. In his understanding, it took a bold man to embarrass Macha. For the cheek he dared speak, Nuada liked Miach.

"I like him," Ronan said from behind Nuada, to which Macha whipped her head around and observed him briefly with narrow eyes.

"Better you say that than me," Nuada said to Ronan once his wife had turned back around.

The forest went on. Some of the underbrush looked as though it had never been stepped upon. In other areas, the trees appeared to lean down toward them as though to devour them. It seemed a cursed area, dark and frightening. It was in this place that they came to a cave that had been provided with all of the comforts of a round house, and they went in. Miach pointed to a place along the wall where there had been carved out a long bench.

"Sit over there," Miach said. "Airmed will bring you something to eat and some mead. You, Nuada, you will drink until you fall. It is best that way. "

Nuada nodded and happily began to drink. The mead was plenty and sweet and soon, as he drank with his friends, he got drunk. Ronan laughed as Nuada lunged from side to side as he tried to speak.

"It could be a thousand years," Nuada said with his eyes half-open.

"A thousand years?" Ronan smirked as he winked at Macha, who giggled slightly.

"A thousand years since last my bladder felt this full!" Nuada roared.

He was making little sense, but his drunken revelry provided good humour to them during such a serious time.

"Then be about it and relieve yourself, you fool," Macha said as she shoved her husband to hurry him out of the cave.

"Never you mind," Nuada slurred as his chin touched upon his chest and he looked down to his lap. He stood and, shaking, made his way to the front of the cave, where he urinated at the entrance and then fell back in drunken limpness.

As Nuada's intoxication became a stupor, Miach quickly pulled the silver hand off Nuada's wrist stump. As he did this, he joked about his father's workmanship on the artificial hand.

"These sharp hooks like nails that held the silver hand on to the flesh are what one would expect fish to be caught on. Not a warrior, " Miach said.

He then spoke to Macha. "Keep Nuada filled with drink so any agony will be dulled. 'Tis nothing else we can give him. Any more herbs will simply make his blood sicker. His blood needs to start cleaning itself. We will ride and find the severed hand."

"Finding the hand will be easy," Ronan said. "We know exactly where it is. "

The Tuatha took horses and rode as fast as they could to the field where the hand was buried. It took days to get there, and then they had to find the exact place where they had buried the hand. As Ronan had said, finding the hand was easy, as it had been buried with a ceremony, and a small pile of rocks marked the place.

They did find the pile of stones quickly enough. When they dug down, they came only to bones that had turned yellow and had no flesh upon them. The warriors carried the hand back to Teamhair and stopped only to wash the bones in the river nearby. They took the pieces to Nuada and told everyone that none should enter the cave. Even Macha was asked to leave.

The brother and sister druids worked on the hand for three days. No one truly knew what they did, as they kept their methods secret. Rumours and beliefs and superstitions circulated within the Tuatha clan, but none in truth knew what Miach and Airmed did.

On the morning of the fourth day, Nuada rose and walked out of the cave. All eyes went to his hand, which looked as sure and good as it had ever been. The hand that they saw looked old and dirty, as though hide had been stretched on the skeletal remains and reattached to the arm. Still, it was a hand, and Nuada was seen as whole by all who beheld him.

"It will grow more meat on it as the days pass," Miach promised. "It has not been used for some while and the strength must return to it. As the sick must take time to recover to match their old selves, so your hand must take time to recover and match the other one. "

"It is perfect, as sure as any is," Creidhne said with a nod.

"'Tis true," Macha agreed.

"All can see its truth," Ronan nodded. "A miracle, for sure, but it is whole and a real hand."

As more people saw the new hand of Nuada, the Tuatha Dé Danann celebrated and praised Miach. The word got quickly around how the wonderful healers, Miach and Airmed, had made Nuada whole.

It was not long until Dian Cecht himself heard the news and visited his son's house. His eyes twitched, and he looked ragged and worn. His appearance had sunk, his wild stare showing him to be a madman who had lost his mind over a question he could not answer.

Dian Cecht had felt he could answer the riddle of restoring Nuada's hand and health if he thought hard enough. This had been his only thought for seven years. He was horrified to hear his son had solved the riddle he had spent so much time on, without success.

"Why did you do such a thing without first talking to me?" Dian Cecht asked.

"What was there to ask?" Miach replied. "I was simply passing by when I heard the people talking about Nuada's hand and as such, I offered my aid. My sister and I know the herbs all the trees and plants and all of the rocks, and all things as they come together and what they can do. Why was it wrong to help an uncle we have not seen since we were babes?"

"It was my right to take the knowledge to Nuada, not yours!" Dian Cecht roared. He turned to his side and rocked as he scratched his shoulder.

"You truly believe that it is only your right to heal?" Miach asked. "Then because of your vanity, it would be also your right not to heal if others knew how and you did not."

"It is not your right to say!" Dian Cecht screamed, pulling on his lip.

"I can heal, and I will, any and all who need it," Miach said calmly.

Dian Cecht pulled his sword and struck his son in the head. "Well, heal yourself!"

The blow knocked Miach to the floor. His hair flapped forward where the sword had grazed along his skull. With shaking hands he pushed his hair back. He stumbled to a shelf, from which he took several ground herbs that he applied to his head. Dian Cecht, meanwhile, stood and stared with a fresh anger growing in his chest. His eyes twitched faster.

"I will and can heal myself," Miach said defiantly. He stood taller now. The herbs had instantly caused a calming in his body, and he appeared completely healed.

Dian Cecht so reviled his son that he took his sword and hit Miach again and again. He struck his son's head four times, until Miach's brains lay on the floor. Dian Cecht squinted his eyes and spat. "Heal yourself now," he said as he left.

Hidden in the corners of the house, away from her father's eyes, Airmed had seen all that happened. When she knew Dian Cecht was well gone, she cried loudly until some of Tuatha men in the forest heard her.

The men came to her and saw what had happened. They helped Airmed take her brother's body and bury it. By her choice they left her there at Miach's grave, while they ran to tell all of the Tuatha Dé Danann the story of Nuada being made whole and of Dian Cecht's jealous rage.

Airmed did not leave the vicinity of her brother's resting place, and, in honour of him, she never again practiced any major act of healing, except to help her father regain his mind.

Within days of the restoration of Nuada's hand, Teamhair filled with people demanding that Bres leave the throne and return it to Nuada.

"What right does any that come to me have to demand such things?" Bres queried in an aggressive voice to the Dagda who entered the high king's round house on his command.

"It is not my place to demand anything of the Tuatha," the Dagda replied as he moved to stand in front of the king.

The round house was empty except for the pair and the crackling of the fire between them was a distraction to the conversation. The smoke rose above their heads and disappeared into the thatched roof as it drifted out into the clement weather.

"I do not understand," Bres grumbled. "They listen to you. Why do they not listen to me? I am trying to keep them safe!"

The Dagda leaned forward and picked a stick from the fire. The yellow and orange of the flames licked across the stick while it lapped also the air for the oxygen that fed its power.

"The fire is mighty and usual for so many things," the Dagda said. "We cook our food on it. We warm by it. We worship it for our own health. Yet, too much, burns."

"Am I the fire?" Bres queried, not at all getting what the Dagda was trying to say. "I don't understand. You do not need to eat. You are different to us. You don't need the warmth. You will go on forever. Are you saying that I am useless?"

"Not at all," the Dagda smiled. "You are as needed to these people, the Tuatha, more than you could know. That is yet to show. But, it not necessarily by being king that you show them your greatness."

"You talk in gibberish, and I cannot interpret your riddles," Bres said with great irritation as he rubbed his hands across his face.

"You will know eventually," the Dagda said. "Let me show you this. The people of the Tuatha are angry at the way things are. Let us say that they are my hand. This fire is you. You burn with a great desire to make things right. You try to make them love you by burning as hard as you can. You feel you can break them if you burn hard enough."

The Dagda placed two of his fingers in the flames and they caught fire. The flames leapt higher. "If few people come up against you, you can easily burn them, and burn you will, ever higher."

He pulled his fingers out of the flame blew them out. "But, if the entire Tuatha come down on you," he said as he shifted his hand to grip the entire stick and in doing so, put out the flames upon it, "they will stifle you to death."

Bres nodded. He understood.

In the early morning, Bres exited the king's round house and left the king's chair in the streets: a sign to say he had given up the kingship. Nuada was recrowned and taken on his chair around all of Teamhair so that all of the Tuatha could see their true king had returned.

During the celebration, Bres hid himself at his mother's house and watched with envy at a distance. He saw the people strike at the harp, and they began to play the horns and their whistles. They danced and they looked happy. He had forgotten what it had been like when everyone was happy and at ease. The Tuatha would rather listen to music and poetry and dance and celebrate every day of their existence than be forced to work in the fields and on the rock walls and other such things.

Bres felt a sorrow at what he had done, at how he had lost the love of his wife, and at how he had ruled. He believed if he had another chance he could do a better job of ruling the Tuatha. First, though, he needed the chance.

"Mother," Bres said, "I believe that I can be a better king if they give me a chance. Perhaps I could win my wife's love back."

"You must be at peace with all of this," his mother, Eri, said. "Regardless of all, you will be recorded as one of the great kings of the Tuatha Dé Danann."

"But I was not great," Bres said softly. He whispered wistfully, "I used to dance. I used to be the best musician and poet. What happened to me?"

"Too much of the Fomorian showed in you, but now you can return to ways of the Tuatha. Dance, play your harp, and speak poetry. Soften our hearts. Win your wife back."

A thought occurred to Bres and he smiled. "I can be king again. A good king. I will appeal to my Fomorian allies."

Two weeks from the day Nuada became king again, Bres slipped out of the harbour unnoticed and set his boat in the direction of the Fomorian lands. He travelled with his mother, his six cousins, and his favourite dogs and horses for himself and each of his companions.

On arriving in the land of the Fomorians, Bres and his entourage located the great plain, where the Fomorians had gathered for the Midsummer celebration. Bres made his way through the clans, looking for the one he would recognise as his father's family. He was stopped by a hideous-looking man with muscles twice the size of his own, who stood at least a head higher than Bres.

"With your strange look, where are you from?" the giant of a man asked Bres.

"I am from Teamhair across the water to the south. I am of the Tuatha Dé Danann, and my father is Prince Elatha of the Fomorians."

"Really?" the giant said with a raised eyebrow. Then he considered. "Did you bring any dogs with you?"

Bres, surprised at the question, answered, "Yes."

"It is our custom to have a friendly challenge with any stranger we may meet, and you here are a stranger." The huge man waved to gain the attention of the people around him. "I say put our dogs to his dogs."

Bres saw the Fomorians' dogs, which were as muscular as their owners and as scarred besides. He did not want to, yet he had no choice but to agree to the fight if he wanted the Fomorians' respect— even if it cost him his favourite dog. "I agree."

"Bring them down, then," the man growled.

They took the dogs to a woven sapling structure that would serve as a cage for the dogs. The Fomorian brought his dog to the pen and put it in.

"We will place our dog, Cü, against his," Bres said softly to his youngest cousin, Egan.

"I will fetch him," Egan nodded.

"I will present my favourite dog against yours," Bres said openly to the Fomorian as his cousin fetched the animal.

"Don't care if it is least favourite, for they all die the same," the Fomorian snorted.

Bres had his favourite dog brought to the pen to fight against the Fomorian dog. The dogs fought hard and terribly. It took some time, but Bres's dog won, leaving the other dog with a tear that ran from its throat through to its stomach.

The Fomorians cheered, pleased with the competition. Another Fomorian stepped forward. "Did you bring horses?"

Bres nodded toward his boat. "They are over there."

The Fomorian grinned. "Let's race our horses, then, and see which of them are the best."

The Tuatha horses looked a little shaky in the legs as they were led to the land. The Fomorians found this altogether hilarious and laughed loudly that the animals were so unbalanced. Despite the animals' confusion, Bres was not deterred from racing the horses, and he pulled them around to line up with the Fomorians' horses.

The race started. It was obvious from the beginning that the Tuatha horses were superior to the Fomorians' animals when it came to speed. None of the Fomorians said a word after Bres's horses crossed the finish line far ahead of the other beasts. The Fomorian horses came in so far behind that the Fomorians felt a little foolish in being beaten so convincingly.

"Are you any good with a sword?" the giant Fomorian asked. His eye twinkled as a sign that he would be willing to slash the Tuatha men down if given the chance.

"Oh, yes," Bres said and began to reach for his sword, as he knew there was a fight afoot. "I could say that I am one of the best, and would definitely show, by having so few marks upon myself, that I have never been bested, even in play."

The Fomorian man jeered at him. "Sounds a lot like a man who needs to find his place, then, and it might be that your place is under my foot."

"You will stop that!" The command came from behind the giant. "Put away your sword and leave him. I am Prince Elatha, son of Delbaeth, and that is my son king Bres of the Tuatha Dé Danann. Who are you to handle a king as such?"

"I ..." the monster of a man stumbled across his words and lifted his hand as if to stop an attack on himself. He cringed and pushed his sword back into its sheath. He moved out of the way as a man on the back of a blue horse rode up next to him.

Prince Elatha, , son of Delbaeth, sat on his steed and looked as noble a man as any of the greatest warriors in history. His golden hair had plaits within it and was pulled away from his undamaged face. He, indeed, looked very much like his son, and though he may have been much older, many could say that Bres and he looked more like brothers than like father and son.

"What are you doing so far from the shores of your kingdom?"

"I am here to ask you for help," Bres answered flatly.

"And what is this help you would want?" Elatha eyed his son.

Bres did not feel he should be ashamed of his request and that he had every right to what he asked. "I have been displaced from the kingship of the Tuatha Dé Danann, though I have been in rule for seven years. The people placed Nuada back as king and ousted me. Now, in the clan, I am no more than the warrior that I was before."

"It seems strange that they would do such a thing. From what I know of the Tuatha Dé Danann, they are noble, and that is an important quality to them. They prefer music, poetry, and dance and sleep over war and the fight. Why would they do such a thing?"

Prince Elatha asked with an unconvinced look on his face. Bres understood then his father wanted to hear what had happened in Bres's own words.

Bres chewed at his lip and then spoke. "I taxed them heavily, and they had never had a tax before, nor had they paid tribute to any. I was unjust and drove them into hardships. I took all they loved from them. I took their music, their poetry, and their dance. I even gave a third of their children to the Fomorian king Balor to become his, and other Fomorians', slaves. I took a third of their treasures and anything they might love."

He could see his father looked unimpressed. Bres went on, "I know what I did was wrong. I, too, lost the one that I love, and I forgot how to sing and to play the harp." He rubbed his index finger on his brow. "I know I can be a better king and, if I am given the chance ..."

Prince Elatha snickered. "What is it you would do?" He turned his horse to leave, but did not depart immediately. With his back to his son he spoke. "As a king, your rule was meant to be for the people, to make their lives as pleasant and full of joy as you could. It was for you to be blessed by them and for their love of you to remember you after your time, and for history to recall you as a king who was righteous and loved. What is it you will be remembered as?" He did not wait for a reply. "I fear to ask. What is it that you have come here to request?"

Bres stepped forward and tried to get closer to the front of his father's horse so that his back did not face him. The giant stopped him from stepping any closer. "I have come to ask you to raise me an army that I may again be king of the Tuatha Dé Danann."

Prince Elatha looked down at his hands as they held the reins of his horse. He shook his head and spoke sadly. "I will not help you. You have no right to gain something by injustice when you cannot keep it by justice." He kicked the sides of his horse and began to move away.

The desperate Bres called from behind him, "Then what am I to do?!"

His father snorted. "Why do you not go to King Balor and ask him?" He rode away, and Bres watched him disappear.

Bres was not put off his mission, and he thought about what his father had said. Plans came to his mind, and he decided to follow exactly the advice his father had sarcastically given. He would go to king Balor and take his case there. Of all the kings who would raise an army against the Tuatha clan, Bres knew Balor would be the one who would do it.

One of Bres's cousins asked him, "Should I put the horses back on the boat and get ready for us to head home?"

"No." Bres smiled crookedly. "We are going to seek out king Balor."

Balor lived in an area of the Fomorian islands composed mostly of rock. The clan built their homes out of the abundant stone. The edge of this island was ringed with rock that was dull and grey and painful for bare feet to stand on. Bres found the island; however, he discovered it hard to find a place to bring the boats to shore. After traversing the island, he saw an inlet leading to a safe harbor. Nevertheless, the inlet had a narrow entry point, and there, guards on either side of the inlet stopped them, refusing to let them steer the boats farther.

"What is it you want?" one of the guards asked, his voice husky from the cold winds that blew around him.

"I am Bres, son of Prince Elatha, and I have come to seek council with king Balor," Bres responded.

The other guard laughed. "Not much of a noble's following you have there."

"Go and tell king Balor that I am here and wish to see him."

The first guard grunted and nodded his head upward at the other. "Go on, then."

The guard quickly returned to the inlet's mouth to tell them they could enter. He jumped down and landed on the boat. "Best I steer here. Many a jagged rock will rip a hole in this vessel. The water is deathly cold, and you will die of it quick enough if you end up in it."

Bres and his companions followed a crooked path through the inlet, and within a short while found themselves in the harbor, where a large, dirty village lay before them. The people of the village came down to the shore to see who was entering the harbor. Their faces looked as grey as the rocks of the island, and they walked with fur-covered feet on the stones. They all looked tired and worn, with bodies that were pale and sickly. Bres hid his shock; his mother covered her nose because of the stench that came from the Fomorian villagers.

King Balor sniffed at Bres and his followers as if they smelled bad when they entered the room where the Fomorian king waited. The building was big and jutted out over the cliffs below. The large windows at the end of the room gave the feeling of being in the clouds, as mist and fog drifted all around. There was no view for any that stood in the window, and a lookout on a hill would be useless in such conditions.

"What are you here for?" Balor demanded. "Do you bring tribute?"

"I do not bring any tribute, and you will not likely receive any more, as I have lost the throne of the Tuatha Dé Danann. Nuada is once more king in my place."

"Then of what use are you? Why are you even here?" Balor asked as he shook his head and indicated that his guards take the Tuatha out of his presence.

"If I am king again, you have tribute," Bres said, holding up a hand to forestall the guards. "If I am not king, you have none. Without tribute, you will have to try and raid the lands for what you need, and that will lead to your men being killed. If I am king, your men live, your people prosper, and you will remain strong and the most powerful of the Fomorian kings. If I am not king, you will be seen as the king who failed his people, and you will be remembered as such in history when they speak of you in stories."

Balor laughed. "What do I care of such things? The life I live is the life I live and there is nothing more in it."

Bres did not know what else to say to convince the king, yet still he tried. "Without me as the king, what do you have for that life you live? You will lose so much of your pleasure that you will be as the swine in the street. You will be no different. You will have to seek from peasants that which you sought from kings."

This made Balor think. After a time of silence, he heavily exhaled into the frigid room. The steam trail extended from his mouth like the breath of a dragon. "There is something in what you say. I will talk to my council, and I will speak to the kings of the Fomorian clan. It is from them I will seek further arms." He moved to pass by Bres. "We will see where all of this may lead as to the levy placed on the Tuatha."

Balor's council did not think war with the Tuatha a wise thing to do. The thinnest of the advisors looked at Balor and said emphatically,

"We have heard that the Tuatha will fight with such fury that their infants could slay us all when in their battle frenzy!"

Balor laughed mockingly at the narrow man. "Why should I fear death? By prophecy, there is only one who can kill me, and that cannot happen. For the one to end my life must be my grandchild, and for me to have a grandchild, my daughter, Ethlinn, would have to bear a child who would live. No man will ever touch her again where she is now, and it would not matter if one did, for you cannot make leather without a hide."

"It is rumoured that the one son she did bear did not die when it was thrown into the sea on your orders. The stories have come from far away. There are so many of these rumours it is impossible not to believe them to be true," another counsellor said.

Balor scowled. He was not one to be contradicted. "The whore is no more a risk, and her child went under the waves when he was thrown from the high cliffs. So, if the child was not dashed upon the rocks, it would have drowned in the waters. There was no escape. There was no risk of failure for us, and no possibility of salvation for the child."

"Did you see the child go under?" the thin advisor asked.

Balor grew angry. "Do not tell me I am wrong," he growled. "Do any of you have the strength to tell me I am wrong? If I say it is so, then it is so. Do not say the sky is any other colour than I say it is, or I will take your heads and paint them the colours I would like them to be."

The council fell quiet and shifted in discomfort at their king's temper. They all knew and had seen his rage at seemingly inconsequential things. The appalling tantrums when anything did not proceed the way he wanted it to, and the death that would always come as a result.

"It would be wise to go first to the other Fomorian kings," said the thin adviser, "just as you suggested. You know how to convince them, and then they always fight to impress you, vying to be the first at your side in such affairs. High-king Indech will be the hardest to convince."

A heavy-bodied, old adviser made an expansive gesture with his hand as if he were not nervous of the king's disposition. "We are all blessed for the better, having such a king as the mighty Balor. What would the Fomorian clan be without him?"

"This is true," Balor said, his mood improving. "They had but the moss from the rocks to eat and the sap of trees to drink before. Look now. We have food and wine and treasures."

"An abundance of, my king," the thin man said.

"That is right." Balor stood from his chair and pulled his cloak around his shoulders. "This day I will go to the kings, and I will have them send troops, with me at the fore, if the Tuatha tribute is not paid. The Fomorians will not have any fear of losing with me in command."

ᔓ 8 ᔓ

Nuada sat on his chair in his round house, giving hospitality and making conversation with a room full of warriors. Teamhair had become happier once more, and the people went about their work with a lighter step. They had come together to discuss what they should do about the Fomorian soldiers who were due, within days, to arrive and collect the tax they expected.

The Dagda had several ideas regarding what the Fomorians could do with their tribute, but only in a jeer were they said. The Tuatha planned carefully, and only the most trusted of Nuada's Tuatha warriors attended the war-council meetings. They had to be cautious, for they did not want the Fomorians to hear word of their plans until they had the full strength to fight, if war it was to be.

"We have still too few men and women who are trained well enough to fight such a large force as the Fomorian army. We have lost so many over the years, first from the battle with the Firbolgs and then with the punishment and starvation set upon us by the Fomorians. We have to wait until the younger fighters have grown enough and have trained," Nuada said to them.

"Against the tax," Ogma said, "how will we have our strength?"

"This," Nuada replied with a smile, "I have thought about. The Fomorians do not enter the deeper forests to the south. Within these forests we will make our fort, and take half of all animals birthed in the next year, before the Fomorians come to collect their third. They will think it a poor year by their inventory. We will pay much less, and we will grow stronger for it. We will do the same the next year and the year after, until we are ready."

The Tuatha discussed further, and it was decided they had best pay the full tribute for the year and follow the plans of Nuada. They would have a few years to make their schemes complete. So, to the hill near Teamhair the assembly went, taking to the Fomorians the gold they demanded. The enemies then all went away, back to their homes on the islands of the north.

Nuada placed a careful watch all over the country, including in the territory of the Firbolgs who, since their epic war, had been quiet neighbours to the Tuatha for many years. Very few Fomorians actually resided on the Tuatha's shores. Nuada could tell a change in the way the Fomorians acted, and that they all were aware of the Tuatha's hate.

Thirteen years passed by, and the Tuatha continued with the plans Nuada had set into play. The Fomorians never went near the forests, as they had great fear of spirits that might live within. The forests were so big that the village the Tuatha created in secret could not been seen, nor the animals heard. If the Fomorians ever did hear a sound emanating from the forests, they would run in fear of the spirits that might come to attack them. They believed completely that no Tuatha could live in such deep forests and no paths or other evidence of occupation showed, so they left the area alone.

"I think our enemies are slowly getting bolder. They are becoming frightened of what might be in the future, and this they fear more than any spirits that might find them in the forests," Ogma remarked one day.

"I agree. There is something spurring them on," Nuada said with a nod. "I have had the land searched, and still none have seen or heard from Bres. Not even in the great forests or on the lonely islands to the west has he been found. He has been missing from his home, and with him he has taken his mother and several cousins. None of them have been seen in a long while. These years have gone by, and he no longer is heard of."

"It is said they have gone to the Fomorians," the Dagda said. For a moment he thought, then added, "It may be that he has decided to go and live amongst those he feels most likened to." He shook his head and groaned, "More likely, I think he has spoken to them in hope that they will place him back as king of the Tuatha."

"King, indeed," Ogma scoffed. "He could have kingship of the swine pit, where he can sit amongst his kind with his beautiful face and share all the poetry he can spout from that treacherous throat of his."

Dian Cecht sat at the edge of the meeting, his hands to his sides and his mouth half-open. He was drunk and was enjoying the look of one of the serving lady's breasts. He yanked down on her top and snuggled his face in her cleavage. She pulled back, and Nuada stood to gain his brother's attention.

"Brother," Nuada said. "Have you any word on the location of the Fomorian spies?"

Dian Cecht looked at Nuada with glazed eyes and smiled a drunken smile. "Yes, I do. There has been word that a young man with yellow hair has come to our land from the south. I have heard that he is big and a delight for the women to look at. He has been asking about you, though whenever he is told to find you in one location, you leave and go to another."

"I have heard of this, as well," Ogma said. "I do not believe the newcomer is a spy. What spy would ask the whereabouts of that which they wish to spy upon?"

Dian Cecht raised his horn and laughed. "A fox is he."

"I have heard there is something strange about this warrior and none have an understanding of where he comes from and who his father is," Ogma said, ignoring the drunk beside him.

"His name is Lugh, and you will meet him within two days," the Dagda said. "Now, if you don't mind, I need to sleep."

No one asked the Dagda, as he left, how it was that he knew the name of the warrior. Neither did they ask how he knew that Lugh would find them. There were things the Dagda could not tell people like Nuada and others of the Tuatha. They were not of the Sidhe, as he was, and they probably would not understand his methods even if they were told. Such is the way of the people of the hills.

The conversation was all but set aside and forgotten, with the aid of many a horn of mead. Two days passed by. The Tuatha had just arrived back in Teamhair from the secret place in the forest where they held their meetings. The night came, and Nuada was hosting many of the warriors in his round house, when the doorkeeper, Gamal, came in.

"There is a warrior called Lugh. He says he wants to speak to you and give you aid against the Fomorians. When I asked him what art he did, for no one may enter Teamhair without an art, he answered that he was a carpenter."

"We have a carpenter of our own: Luchtar. Tell him to leave," Nuada said.

"I said you would say as such, and he argued further. He said he was also a smith …"

"That is for our Colum Cuaillemech of the three new ways," Nuada overrode the doorman's speech.

"Oh, but I said no to that too, and then he said he is also a poet, a harper, a druid, a healer, a brass worker, and great swordsman."

"We have all of these," Nuada said, curiously knowing the conversation was not at an end.

"I said as such too, and then he said, perhaps you do have all of these great artisans, but do you have all in the one man?"

Nuada was taken aback by the question, and he smiled. "No, we do not." He thought and then said, "Let him play a game on the board so we may see where his skill lies there. Bring him in, and every man who wishes to play can play against him. If he wins, then come back and tell me."

The doorkeeper did as he was told, and Ogma followed him out so he could play a game against the supposed champion. They were gone for some time. When they returned, it was with great excitement.

"The warrior has beaten us all!" Gamal exclaimed.

"He told us poetry and stories of the bards," Ogma told his brother.

Nuada was more than curious by this stage. "Let him come to me, for no one in Teamhair has ever been able to claim and prove themselves to be a master of arts. Lugh will be ours."

"There is still the challenge of strength he must pass for him to sit with us," Ogma said.

"I would agree with that," the Dagda said. "His might has not been proven by a game played on a board."

When Lugh entered the room, the warriors who had not seen him before were surprised by his look. He was tall and muscular, with hair as bright a yellow as Danu herself sported. His clothes were coloured in red and blue, and his shoes were made from the soft brown pelt of a baby deer. He was, in manner and form, a perfectly noble warrior.

Ogma stood, and the other warriors in the room moved aside as he bent to a large stone on the floor. With a show of his strength, he lifted the flagstone and tossed it as far he could. Ogma said nothing, but indicated to Lugh that it was his turn to prove his strength.

Lugh did not say anything, either. He moved to the rock. With less strain than Ogma had displayed, he pulled the stone up to his chest and cast it back to the middle of Nuada's house, where it sat as if it had not been moved. The warriors cheered the feat, and many raised their horns, demanding more of a challenge be made.

Nuada nodded, and from within a chest was brought the Dagda's harp, which was given to Lugh. Nuada pointed to the warrior. "Play and see if you impress us."

Lugh flexed his fingers and then began to play. The room went silent, and they all listened to a lament that he played. Then Lugh livened the music to a dance, and he played happily. When fingers slowed, the mood of the room saddened, and when he quickened his pace, the warriors applauded and danced. The Tuatha convinced him to keep playing, and so he did.

They laughed with some of the songs he sang, and they cried with wretched sorrow at the laments. Lugh relayed songs of the Tuatha's happy times and sad times, and sang of events across the waters in lands that came to them only in dreams. Eventually, he played a soft song until they slept.

In the following days, Lugh became greatly appreciated and loved amongst the people of the Tuatha. Nuada soon considered him as a son, as did Macha, and their two sons treated him like a brother. This was not unusual, as the Tuatha all acted towards Lugh in a similar way.

Soon the time of tribute came. The Tuatha would either have to pay the Fomorians—or go to war with them. The plans of Nuada and his men were still not complete; that is, they did not believe they had enough well-trained warriors to defeat the Fomorians. They trained each day in hidden areas around the land and in the deep forests. The king had to concede that, for another year, the Tuatha Dé Danann would have to pay the levy set upon them.

Lugh left without warning as the tax-collecting time grew close, and the Tuatha felt saddened to find him gone. Nuada was hurt most of all.

On a spring morning, Nuada and his select warriors went to the hill where they were to pay the taxes. While they were waiting, they saw from across the plain that a band of warriors approaching. They could not see who it was from such a distance at first. Then they saw the long yellow hair, and they knew immediately that it was

Lugh of the long arm. The extreme lashings that Lugh's arm could administer, was how he had received his nickname, "Lugh of the long arm," and those who witnessed his feats of strength would attest to it being a well-deserved name.

As Lugh advanced, they could see he was riding the unmistakable horse of king Manannan, a magnificent animal called Aonbharr. Nuada also identified the breastplate of his old friend Manannan. At Lugh's side, Nuada then saw the sword of Manannan, known as the Answerer. With all the riders beside him, the Tuatha could only wonder what Lugh came for in such a way.

"You have been gone for a while, and we thought you might have returned to wherever it is you came from," Nuada said as he embraced Lugh.

Lugh raised his hand to silence the excited crowd. "I returned to my adopted father, Manannan mac Lir. These—," he turned on his horse and indicated to the warriors behind him, "—are the riders of the Sidhe from the land of promise. These—," he pointed to four noble men who shone in the sun as their clothes reflected the light around them, "—are my brothers, the sons of Manannan: Sgoith Gleigeil, the white flower; Sine Sindearg, of the red ring; Goitne Gorm-Shuileach, the blue-eyed spear; and Donall Donn-Ruadh, of the red-brown hair."

"Why do you come here in such a way and on such a day as this? This is the day of our tribute," Nuada said. "The Fomorians will see all of this as a threat rather than anything besides."

Lugh laughed. "A threat it must be, then."

"A threat?" a voice climbing the hill asked.

The warriors turned and observed, coming up the hill, eighty or so Fomorian messengers who had come to ask for the taxes. At the lead were four of the more brutish Fomorians who had been known to punish the Tuatha the hardest of all. Several Tuatha had been beaten to death for entertainment when these men had found the tax paid was not enough. Others who had displeased the tax collectors had had their noses removed, so they now spent their days with the hollow look of skulls.

"You do not threaten us, Tuatha Dé Danann," the lead Fomorian warned. "Your children are our game for the death pits if we so chose, and you are no better."

"You speak of children in such a way. Curse your tongue," Lugh said, much to the shock of the Tuatha clan. "I feel I should cut you down myself."

Nuada was shocked, and tried to control the temper of the young warrior. Their plans for the rising against the Fomorians were not yet complete. "You will have us all killed, and our children, and they will take all, not just the third they take now."

"You listen to this old man," said the most scarred of the Fomorian leaders. "I will cut your heart out and eat it before you even know you have lost it."

These words angered Nuada, yet he remained silent and eyed the balding man.

"These people do not need you anymore," Lugh went on. "I say, you have oppressed them far too long, and they are strong, and they are of gods, and they will not be oppressed any longer."

Lugh pulled his sword and struck out suddenly, tearing the throat out from the Fomorian who had threatened to eat his heart. Within a moment he was cutting and ripping through the flesh of every Fomorian who rose before him. His legs soon turned red, and the blood of his foe dripped to the ground.

His brothers called their war cry, and with great force they descended upon the Fomorian tax collectors. They used both hands and weapons made in strange shapes. With their legs, they clung to their steeds and used their weapon-laden hands to cut down all around them. Their fight shimmered and burned like a blaze, and it became too hard for anyone to concentrate on the individual actions of maiming and killing. Like a fire, the red blood rose from the ground and dropped back to the grass. Nuada watched with his Tuatha clan in shock.

Of all the Fomorians who came for treasure to take back to their land, only nine were left alive when Nuada stepped between them and their hunters. He addressed Lugh. "You must stop."

Lugh stared at the nine Fomorians who snivelled behind the king. He smiled sinisterly at them. "I would kill you all, but there must be someone to take a message to your king. Tell him his bleeding of this land is done." He looked to Nuada. "We will not kill them." He paused. "Unless they return."

The nine men were released, and they scurried off. Their faces showed their terror, and they did not stop to collect any horses. Nor did they seem to care that they had to return to Balor without the tribute. They knew something that none of the Tuatha did. There was something that they were aware of gathering on the high rocks of the Fomorian lands. They had been waiting, the kings of the Fomorians, for the day the tax did not come.

Nuada frowned at the young warrior and, even though he showed himself mighty with the sword, he pulled Lugh up and held his horse to his. "You are young and hot as melted metal. For that reason, you do not understand what it is that you have done. King Balor will now send out his forces, and we have not done all we can to prepare. We have still only trained laypersons who are to play as warriors on the battlefield. We have those whose backs have been broken by the weight of Bres, who are still healing from their loss of their children, and many of the youth we have are still too young to fight. What are we to do when, in time, the Fomorians return and bring their fury down on the Tuatha Dé Danann?"

Nuada deliberately pulled on Lugh so that he might be able to see him, eye to eye. "The worst for you will be that he will send against you and those of the Sidhe, to whom I have sworn loyalty. He will come for you."

Lugh laughed and slapped of Nuada's back as if a joke had been told. His brothers laughed along with him and, most oddly of all, the Dagda joined in. "I might know something of king Balor that you do not that causes me to have no fear of him. He will fear me when he hears who sent from here this day a few of his men and slaughtered the rest."

"It is known that you are the grandson of king Balor, but you were thrown away and taken in by Manannan, son of Lir. You have never seen Balor, nor have you spent time with him. How would you know something about him?" Nuada asked.

"Let us go and see these creatures off. I will tell you soon enough," Lugh said. With that, he spurred his horse on to watch the Fomorians leave.

The Fomorians had nearly reached their boats, and had slowed slightly from the rushed pace they had set as they left the hill. They thought they had got far enough away that they could catch their breath. When Lugh, his brothers, and those that followed got close enough for them to see, they suddenly gained speed again.

They jumped quickly in their boats, which had been pulled up on the shores. Regarding the approaching men with horror, they flung one of their own men out of the boat to help push it off. The terror of Lugh being nearly upon him again gave the tax-collector so much strength that, within half a breath, he not only pushed the boat into the water, he had also leapt onboard and taken up an oar, which he paddled as fast as he could.

Lugh stood on his horse and pointed his sword at the boat. "Back to mother's breast," he mocked the men, "and no more shall you come to where real men live."

All those who had seen what had happened cheered Lugh and jeered at the fleeing men. Nuada again took Lugh aside. "Now you will tell me why you behave in such a way, and what you know about Balor of the evil eye."

"Let us go back to Teamhair," the Dagda said. "He will tell his story there, and we will be able to prepare for war."

Nuada had a sudden realisation that he was preparing the Tuatha Dé Danann for war against the Fomorians. Badb had given a prophecy many years before that had caused him shivers about such a war. Nuada had tried to avoid the confrontation, but prophecies tend to always come true eventually.

They returned to Teamhair and to Nuada's round house. A large assembly filled the house, and Macha sat behind her husband with a neutral expression. Visually, she had not seemed to age. A few wisps of silver hair marked the sides of her head.

Old friends who had come from the ancient islands of the Tuatha clan sat near her and across from her. Now their children and even their children's children joined them. They waited for Lugh, and soon he arrived with his four brothers and sat amongst those in the house. Food and drinks were brought, and soon Nuada asked again for Lugh to tell them all his secret.

"I have been across the lands and have been across the seas," Lugh said. "All that I am and all that I know is from my adopted father's mouth."

"Manannan is a reliable man and always truthful," Nuada said.

"My true father is Cian of the Tuatha Dé Danann. He was kept as a slave for many years by the Firbolg, and then he was saved in a battle long ago." Lugh took a drink from his horn and then continued. "He was saved by the Dagda because the Dagda had word of the future, and knew that Cian could not die."

Nuada remembered that night—Cian, the skinny shape-shifting boy, and the fight where his arm had been torn off, and the way the Dagda had insisted that this boy's wounds be tended and taken care of.

"Cian was taken in and made whole and healed," Lugh said. "When he was healed, he came with you to this land and helped you in the battle against the Firbolg again, always in silence and hidden in the shadows nearby. He thought he had peace, and he settled himself on the ridge of fire with his brothers Goibniu and Samthainn.

Cian was lord of the land, and he was good with his cattle, and they were strong and beautiful. It happened that one cow was treasured most of all, and rumour of the cow came to the ear of Balor. The king stole the cow and Cian made to take it back, for the sake of his family. He saw his favourite beast heading out to sea and was told it had gone to the land of the Fomorians."

"Lost, then," Neit said.

"Not completely," Lugh disagreed, and took another drink. "Cian sought advice from a druid. She told him that as long as king Balor was alive, the cow would never be Cian's again. But he was determined to get it back, nevertheless, and with the druid's guidance he set out to try.

She told him, because no man was allowed to enter near the Fomorian lands without being overseen by Balor, that he should dress, instead, as a woman. He sailed by himself, and came close to the Fomorian lands. He did not want to moor where he would have his boat taken, so he anchored his boat, took to the frozen waters, and swam. When he got to the rocks, he was freezing. He, dressed as a woman, was taken in and given shelter.

When everyone had gone to sleep, my father went to speak to Ethlinn, Balor's daughter, about the cow, in the hope that she would be able to aid him. When he saw her, and she him, they both said that they had seen each other in dreams."

"Not hard to imagine what happened next!" Dian Cecht grabbed at his crotch and raised his drinking horn to the room. The other warriors cheered and raised their drinking horns in response.

The room hushed quickly to hear the rest of the story. Lugh went on, "He was not in the Fomorian lands for very long, but long enough that Ethlinn gave birth to me some months after he left. When Balor heard the news of my birth, he raged into her room and seized me after he had cut her stomach so that she might never have any other children. He then, with his most trusted and gravely evil druids, took me to the tops of the cliffs, where they were to throw me into the currents of the sea."

Cian went silent and drank more of his drink. The occupants of the room waited. Lugh said nothing. Irritated by the suspense, Macha called, "How is then that you are here?"

Lugh looked at the queen over his horn and smiled as he drank. On lowering it, he spoke again. "There had been those who had expected me and knew of my coming. Perhaps by magic, or perhaps through the word of a mother who knew the fate that would befall her child if he was left to it. It does not matter, nor do I have the right to ask or say, yet under those cliffs, in the water, someone was waiting. They caught me as I was thrown and threw a decoy rock into the water so Balor and his henchmen could hear the splash of something falling in.

"I was taken first to my father Cian and then, on word from a seer and a great warrior, they took me to Manannan, who had been waiting for me because of a promise to those who had known my destiny even before Cian was saved on that battlefield, all those many years ago."

Nuada looked away from Lugh and gazed at the Dagda as a flash of a memory came back to him. He was not sure of its full detail, and was not even sure if the thought were real or a dream that he had had. There was something in the way Lugh spoke that signalled to Nuada that, somehow, the Dagda had a hand in the events of Lugh's life more than anyone knew.

There had been so many years and so many wars. There had been battles and death, and those who had come close to the edge of this life only to have that life breathed back into them. There had been warriors who had come from battle with no wounds, but had suddenly fallen down to die as if their lives were meant to have stopped on the field. Sometimes the warriors had bided their time for a little, just long enough to finish the fight.

"Why do you believe you are so important?" Macha asked Lugh, truly intrigued.

"There is a prophecy that by the hand of his grandson, king Balor will die. That is why he locked his daughter away. That is why he tried to kill me as a babe, and that is why he will fear on hearing that it is Lugh of the long hand, his grandson, who comes to the aid of the Tuatha this day. He will fear. He will say he has no fear and there is nothing in the few words of a prophecy that he cannot undo by his own hand. But in his heart, he is already defeated."

In the days that followed, the Tuatha prepared themselves. They sent out word of the war to all of the provinces, and all were told that they must be at the ready for the Fomorians if they came. In Teamhair, they made weapons and strengthened their fort. The Tuatha put more warriors out to watch for anything that might be coming, whether in the day or by night.

Fifteen days after the tax collectors had been sent back to king Balor, a rumour reached Nuada. People had seen the Fomorians attack the west, destroying all in their path. The Dagda's son, Bodb Dearg, was king in that region, so six men on horseback went to see if the stories were true. They returned to say that they were, and that the entire area had been destroyed completely. The Fomorians had taken what they would and set fire to the rest.

"We must take battle with the Fomorians as they stand on these shores," Lugh appealed to Nuada upon hearing the news. It was still night, and birds had not even sung their morning greeting to the false dawn. "Give me the forces I need. You stay and keep Teamhair. Let me and my brothers do our work. We will end this."

Nuada thought, and part of himself smiled at the young man's words. They were words he had said once. "There is nothing that I can do for you at the moment," Nuada said. "I have to prepare myself and Teamhair for the Fomorians. Do you not think that when they are done marching and stomping the ground of Bodb Dearg that they will seek somewhere else to go? Teamhair is their destination, and you know that as well as I do."

Lugh argued with Nuada, but nothing came of it, and he was told again and again that he would not be given any warriors because they were needed to protect Teamhair. In his mind, Nuada knew that Macha and his family were the heart of his cause. He could not admit it to himself.

Lugh rode away from Teamhair and went westward. As he rode, he came across his birth father, Cian, and his two uncles. Along with them were the three sons of their good friend, Biróg. They were surprised to see a rider out so early and asked him what he was doing.

"There has been a raid done by the Fomorians on Bodb Dearg, and they have destroyed everything in their path. I am going to raise the army that will be the answer to the Fomorians' attacks and will end all their raids forever."

"You are committed to such a cause? My nephew, you are still so young," said one of his uncles with a smile.

"He is not that different to us," Cian observed. He thought a moment. "I will fight alongside you, my son."

"As will I," said the youngest of Lugh's uncles, and his wards said the same words of support at the same time.

The last uncle shrugged. "Why not? I grow tired of these raids and tribute and the like. There has been no true peace in these lands since we began here. I say, let us fight."

Lugh smiled and hushed their enthusiasm. "I believe having your aid is a great thing and that I am far better for it. I will ask you though, before we commit to fight, to ride out for me to the far corners of this land and appeal to all of the riders of the Sidhe to come to me. They also will aid us, and their fight is as no others'."

The men agreed and, like children going out to play, they hurried to their horses and went to find those they were sent to find. Lugh continued on to the west and kept going until he came to an area that had been burnt until there was nothing to look at. Trees were sooty and stood against the black of the earth. He rode to the top of a hill, and he finally saw where the Fomorians had set up camp.

He rode down and approached them as if going to meet a friend. Lugh headed straight for where he believed he would find the leader of the gathering. To his surprise, the one he had been told was called Bres stood among them. Lugh eyed him, raised his hand, and saluted him.

"I know who you are. I have heard of you. The Fomorian speak of you bringing an end to tribute. Why are you here, Lugh?" Bres asked. "Why do you think you can approach us as you have?"

"Why should I not?" Lugh asked, as if not understanding. "I am, after all, half Fomorian, just as you are. I have come for the reason of asking you to put back all you have taken and to make coinage for that which you have destroyed."

The Fomorians laughed at Lugh and thought that he must be simple or some other type of fool. The chief warrior standing closest to Bres started to pull his sword. "You will get nothing here, and neither will you get anything from over there." He pointed to another area of the camp. "Nor from over yonder."

Lugh looked at the man who talked as though he thought he was clever and felt anger rising in him. He pointed to another area of the camp and said mockingly, "If I should go over there, then?"

The Fomorians laughed at the chief warrior, and he did not react well to his own men laughing at him. "There is nothing here for you to have," the chief said angrily. "What you can take with you is a curse of all the ill luck and misfortune that there ever may be."

"So be it," said Lugh, controlling himself as best he could so as not to strike out and cut the men where they stood. He turned his horse and headed out of the camp. No one touched him as he left; they all stared and stopped their tasks until he was well out of view. They had all heard the story of how Lugh had driven away the Fomorians who had come to collect the yearly tax.

Lugh watched the activities of the Fomorians for the next three days, and he made sure that he knew as much as possible about what was going on in their camp. When he woke on the fourth day, he saw men riding in from the distance. The riders of the Sidhe had come, and along with them rode the western king, Bodb Dearg, with about three thousand of his men. Lugh went to meet them.

"What caused you to wait and not go straight into battle?" Bodb Dearg asked. "I have heard you are never too shy to fight anyone, or any force, at any time."

"I was waiting for you," Lugh answered.

They did not wait any more; neither did they stand around to plan their attack. The Fomorian camp was surrounded by small hills. Lugh and his followers would have the advantage if they surrounded the camp and then came down upon the Fomorians.

They were a wildly lot, those who went to battle the Fomorians that day, and it was hard to deliver any plan to any of them, as their only goal was to fight. Still, eventually, they took to the hills and came down over their enemies with the sound of thunder at their feet and the projections of death at their arms.

Lugh was first to strike as the Fomorians took to their arms and their horses. The warrior Lugh struck stood still for a moment and then his body fell in two, his head going one way and the rest of him the other. Lugh's reach seemed to extend an unreal length from his body, and he could manoeuvre himself naturally on his horse, as if the animal were almost part of him.

Two men with spears came at him on their horses. The spears were far longer and had more reach than Lugh's sword, the Answerer. He did not catch his breath and, instead, leaned to the side of the horse until he was nearly flat on its underside. He slashed upwards, flicking his sword while continuing to hold the reins between his hands so he could do the same to the rider on the other side. The Fomorians' horses fell, screaming in pain. To the ground rolled their riders.

Lugh held onto his horse with his legs around its neck, and he pulled his dagger to match his sword. With a thrust of each weapon at the Fomorians, both collapsed. One had a gaping wound to his throat, as he had been crouched on the ground, and the other's stomach had been opened. His scream was cut off by the sword of a rider behind Lugh.

The golden-haired fighter pulled himself upright on his horse using the animal's mane. He sat boldly, with weapons still in his hands. His horse had slowed and was all but motionless in the crowd that had come upon him and the battalions within the Fomorian camp. Lugh lashed from side to side, cutting and maiming.

In that moment, from another side, more ally battalions rode in, their battle cries so loud that the Fomorians were stunned. Several turned to fight the new threat, pressed in all sides.

Lugh saw that Bres had joined the fight. The ex-king was surrounded by fifty or so Fomorian soldiers who did not seem too concerned at the press of their enemy upon them. They fought with spears. Lugh could see the spears being cut off, leaving the Fomorians with swords as their only weapons. They pulled their swords from their sheaths and they fought, harder and faster.

Lugh plunged his sword into the open mouth of one of the elite guards surrounding Bres, pushing the dead man back with his foot into his own clan member's sword. With a flick of his wrist, Lugh drew from a pouch darts like the end of an arrow, and he threw these between the eyes of the Fomorian men.

More of the enemy arrived to protect Bres. Their weapons were strange and unusual, but Lugh, his brothers, and the riders of the

Sidhe had been to many lands and they themselves had their own unique weaponry, and so the Fomorians' weapons did not shock them.

Swords with curved edges and rings upon them were carried by some of the larger Fomorian men; others produced spears with weapons on both ends. These unusual spears consisted of a dagger upon one end and a strange knife on the other featuring a curved hook-like blade. Another special weapon was shaped like the fork of a tree, a 'V' shape, sharp on all sides, called a hucha.

Lugh and the riders of the Sidhe answered these weapons with their own, weapons that the Tuatha Dé Danann had never carried before as their own arms. Chains of metal with thorny ends were lashed out, used either to smash at the faces of the enemies or to rip their weapons from them. It would a slow death when hooks with handles, like sickles, carried through the jaws of the Fomorians, pulling the jaws clear away from their faces. Battle-axes and the heads of arrows and darts were thrown.

The female warriors of the Sidhe carried double-edged cutting blades with hooks on the ends. Their hands were sheltered by metal that acted as a sword-catch against the enemy. The Sidhe women slashed the Fomorians down as quickly as the Formorians tried to run.

Soon there stood only Bres and four of his druids cowering beside him. Bres stared at Lugh, who had dismounted from his horse. Bres would not pull away; instead he flexed his chest forward with pride. "What would you do with me?" Bres asked.

Lugh looked at Bres, and then at his warriors, inviting them to speak. The riders of the Sidhe, with their masked faces, stood with the gold of their clothes stained red and yellow. Instead of giving an answer to Lugh's question, they turned to go and clean the enemy's flesh and blood from themselves. The silence of the Sidhe warriors was their way. The Tuatha warriors had vowed to follow Lugh, so they did not answer, either.

"I want this ended," Lugh said. "I do not need to converse to find what is needed in this land."

Bres gave the crooked smile he used when he was nervous. "If you spare me my life this time, I swear to you that I will bring all of the Fomorians to fight and you will have the answer you crave. All the kings will come, and their battalions, and every warrior that they might gain allegiance of. It will be ended, as you wish. My word is truth, even through all my treachery and wrong that I have done. My word is always truth."

Lugh eyed Bres for a while longer and then pulled his blood-covered horse to him. He heaved himself onto the back of the beautiful steed and looked down at Bres. "I will believe your word and I will give you my protection." He then pointed to Bres's druids and flicked his wrist to indicate their lives should be ended.

"Not us," one druid pleaded.

"Spare us as well," another begged.

Lugh addressed them. "I saw you fight, and I saw you cut the men with no mercy, and your faces looked as if the act gave you pleasure. You even cut your own men to get through and have your feast of blood."

"It is the way of battle," the first druid said.

Lugh made a "hmmm" sound as if not sure on what to say to a point that seemed absurd to him. "If I protect you, so highly trained and sought after in an army, then I might as well give protection to all with less training, and you would mount up and destroy us."

"No. That is not what we ask," the tallest druid replied.

Lugh tapped his sword's hilt and then pointed to the druid who had sacrificed his own Fomorian brother in battle. "I would say all may leave this country, even you, but first, by the hand of your brothers you must give your head."

"I will leave and never return," the bloodthirsty druid pleaded.

Lugh eyed him carefully and said, "It is, as you said, the way of battle."

On those words he rode away. The cries of the druid were cut off as the other druids surrounded him and took his life, separating his head from his body to take with them as they fled.

Lugh rode on until he came to Teamhair. He went to the round house of Nuada. Night was near, and he entered the house of the king, he saw Nuada, Macha, and their sons preparing to eat. They were all glad to see him, and invited him in to share their food and drink. He sat down willingly, and pulled faces at the young boy across from him, who laughed.

"Nuada told me you went across to see if there was anything left of Bodb Dearg and to aid him," Macha said.

"I did aid him, and there was battle and death. I joined with the riders of the Sidhe and the warriors Bodb Dearg brought, and we crushed our heels into the very neck of the Fomorian camp. Bres sat as traitor amongst them, and I spared him his life that he would bring to this land the end of the Fomorians. All the clans will be brought together and come to shore. War will see an end to them."

Nuada stopped eating and cast a sideward glance at Macha. He could see she was enthusiastic for the fight, and he saw in this the return of the woman he had bedded down with as wife to the king. In his heart he knew that he could not stop her from entering battle, not even at his command. He thought on this fact. He stood and went out the door of the round house.

"Where are you going?" Macha asked.

"War is upon us, and Balor will be along with the other kings, and there will be many a warrior to battle against. We cannot prepare ourselves by sitting in the shadows with our supper. I go to call an assembly of kings and the highest warriors in the land. It will be done, and then I will have my supper."

King Nuada knew what he must do.

Three days from the time Nuada sent out messages to all corners of the land, men began to gather. Teamhair soon filled with the strongest and mightiest. Nuada had his chair taken out into the thoroughfare of Teamhair, that he could speak to all his people that were there. He did not sit in it, however, but stood beside it on the top of a large rock. Macha stood next to the rock with her sword and spear in hands and her arms strapped for battle.

"Tuatha Dé Danann! My people! Children of Danu!" Nuada called. "We are here to speak on the matter of war and the Fomorians who come to attack! It is well that they come, for they have taken our sustenance and our treasure! They have taken our children and made slaves of them! They have sucked the land and taken all they could, and when they could not take, they lied or killed for it! Do we claim any more years of this torture?"

The crowd shouted, "Nay!"

"There is no more hope for peace against such, for they wish it not. For the murder or skin of our families! There is no justice in that, and any claim they make is as the last! A lie!"

The crowd sounded their agreement. "A falsehood!" Again, more loudly they called. "They claim what is ours is theirs and yet, why do

we call it ours in the first place if it is not ours!"   N u a d a
thumped his chest, and the multitude began to roar their anger.
"We stand to fight for ourselves and our children and our children's
children! They've stomped these lands for long enough with their flat
feet and their misshapen selves!"

Nuada called to the crowd to calm, and then he went on. "I
am not the man to lead you this time! I have seen the wonders of
another who can wield a sword and slay fifty men while playing
board, pleasuring a woman, and eating his breakfast!"

A soft chortle across the crowd was heard.

"He will be your king! I have chosen ill in the past, but not this
time! You all see his face and feel stronger for the vision! You all have
known his skills and have felt prouder for his birth being that of a
Tuatha Dé Danann! Lugh will be king!"

The crowd exploded into a roar of approval, something that
had not happened when Bres took the kingship. Nuada recognized
instantly the difference and felt an inner calm flow through him for
the first time since leaving Finias.

Lugh stepped forward, seated himself in the chair, and was taken
on his tour around Teamhair, which would lead, finally, to Lia Fáil.
Macha and Nuada followed at the rear of the procession.

"Why?" Macha asked. Nuada reached to touch her hand, which
still held her sword. She sheathed the weapon immediately and took
his hand in hers. Again, she asked him as they stopped walking,
"Why?"

"We have lost enough. Now it comes to the loss of one or the
other. Prophecies seem to always make their way to the surface,
no matter how we try to fight against them." He kissed her hands.
"I have seen you take the life of a man and even drink the blood
from his skull, and I have seen your gentle touch as you care for our
children. Your warmth at night was warmer than the sun on my face,
and your kiss like the sweetest of drinks to my lips. If I can have just
one more day with you by no longer being king, than it is a day well
worth the sacrifice."

Macha stared at her husband and smiled. She kissed his hands
as he had hers and they both began to walk again, following the new
king to the stone of virtue.

↜ 9 ↝

Two full moons passed by, and two days after the second moon, a cry went up that the Fomorians' ships were approaching. The alarm was sounded, and the warriors all prepared themselves for the battle. It was a beautiful summer's day for the Tuatha Dé Danann, yet to the Fomorians it would be ghastly and hot, for they came from lands where it was colder, and some areas had ice all the year.

Lugh sent out spies to watch the armies as they came ashore. By no means could they allow the Fomorian clans to escape their view. The orders were given to them, that if they had any opportunity at all to create havoc or delay the attack, then they should take it.

Lugh and Nuada had worked together to train even those peasants from the fields that they might add numbers to their cause and fight for their freedom against the Fomorians who outnumbered them so greatly. Numerous warriors had arrived at Teamhair. Several warriors were still on the march and had yet to arrive, so the Tuatha needed the delay of battle for many reasons.

Nuada took the Dagda aside and spoke to him. "You are the most knowledgeable in the art of spying. It might be this day that you should go to the Fomorians and see if they hold true to the noble way of battle. I know that if they give you trouble, then you will be able to deal with them and return to us."

The old king watched as his friend rode out, then went to arrange for his youngest son, who was too young for the fight, to be taken away where he would be watched over by a warrior whom he trusted and whose fight this was not. He trusted his son to the care of the noble Sreng of the Firbolg, or a man of Sreng's choice.

Nuada sighed and went to his work.

The Dagda proceeded forward. While other spies made their way around where the Fomorians took camp, the Dagda went to the entrance of the encampment. When the Fomorians readied to attack, the Dagda stood his ground. He did not try to use his art to kill the Fomorian guards. Instead, he asked to speak to their high king. They took him to where the kings were assembled in conference and planning. King Balor sat amongst them, and his chief warrior stood behind him.

"What are you here for?" king Balor growled.

"I have come to ask for a delay in battle," the Dagda stated flatly.

Balor laughed and pointed him to the hill where Teamhair was situated. "If you need a delay now, you should have waited until the right time to attack the Fomorians who came before us."

"A delay will be given," another king said, and the other seven kings said the same soon after. Balor stared at the king who dared countermand his decree. The king returned Balor's stare, unafraid. "I am Indech, son of De Domnann, and I do not need your look, Balor. I have choice and voice in the way of the noble fight. It is right and it is done."

Balor grunted. "It is done." He waved for the Dagda to go away, then reconsidered and stopped him. "I give my support, too, but only if the Dagda eats some broth. Is it not our way to have broth and drink with such decisions? Our hospitality should be upheld, and then he will not return to the Tuatha Dé Danann and tell them that he was not received well."

"That is right," Indech agreed. "To you, we show we are hospitable and noble. It is the tradition that you have broth with us and if you do not, this is seen as a sign of a man who is too proud and has no nobility. In tradition, you will be put instantly to death if you do not eat the broth, and all of it, and then we will march upon your people immediately."

The Fomorians all avered it was their custom, and Balor went and spoke to some Fomorian men about the meal. They took the Dagda to a cauldron on the fire, in which they had been preparing some food for the battalions. The cauldron was massive and looked as though it held more than enough for the village. The mains of the broth were made with milk, goat, pig, and mutton.

Balor looked into the pot and then eyed the Dagda mockingly. "You are such a well-stuffed man, this small pot will not be enough. Bring another," he told the dirty slave who cooked their food. He then summoned another slave who was cutting bits of pig. "You too, go and fetch a third. We do not want to be told that we have not the manners to be hospitable."

The Dagda watched as the Fomorians dug a pit in the ground, which they carefully lined with gravel. This done, they poured the three cauldrons of broth into it. The Dagda was presented with the stirring ladle, and he sighed as he moved to start the supper, with men gathering around him. There would be no magic to aid the Dagda in this challenge; it would be a true test of his power, without spells or illusions.

He ate as quickly as he could at first and maintained his eagerness for some time; however, as he filled, he slowed more and more. His stomach bulged and his face became damp with sweat. Soon, he removed his shirt because it had grown tight against his stomach and inhibited his eating. Each time he thought he could take no more, he thought of the Tuatha Dé Danann, and again he ate. The men teased and jeered him at each break he took, and each time the Dagda said something in return to show he was not being defeated.

"It is a good food, this, and it tastes as good as it looks," the Dagda said. Once, his hand quivered as he brought the ladle to his mouth. "I am just shaking the broth and enjoying the smell that it lingers for longer. After it is all gone, I fear I will miss the scent."

And even as the ground beneath the broth appeared and the Fomorians might have thought there was nothing else to eat, the Dagda defied them and scraped the ground as if still hungry, even against the pains in his stomach.

The Dagda stood alongside the pit for a moment after he had finished, and he swayed. Eventually he sat down, and then lay on the ground. The Fomorians laughed and pointed at his stomach, the skin shiny from being stretched as far as it could go. Comments about him being with child or with calf were thrown at him. He simply smiled and waved his hand as if hailing a friend.

The Dagda felt so heavy that he knew he should not ride for a while, and that even if he moved he would surely be sick, so he lay where he was and slowly began to doze. He could not fall asleep completely, being in the enemy's camp, and after a while he got to his feet, gave thanks for the Fomorians' hospitality, and took to his horse.

The Dagda's horse snorted in protest as the big man got upon the animal's back. "Now, what is this show for?" he asked of the horse. The warrior's impressive stomach extended well beyond its normal perimeter and he had to lean forward slightly, as sitting directly upright made the weight feel greater.

He pulled his clothes back on in a disorganised fashion. His leather-hide shoes were inside out, and his cloak he carried on his arm. His shirt had not been able to cover his stomach, so he had decided to put his brown coat on back to front, and he looked like a simpleton as he rode along. He was careful on any descent, as the lurching of the horse and the way he was forced to lean backward to keep his balance, pushed the food inside his stomach closer to the surface of his mouth.

Nuada waited at the top of the fort for the Dagda. He had been gone for some while, and the night was moving in. He was concerned that something had happened, and what had been made of the Dagda, he did not know. He reassured himself that the Dagda was different to men like Nuada, and he was sure to go on for a long time after the king of the silver hand, Lugh of the long arm, and the other kings had gone. Ronan came to him and they began to discuss possibly rescuing the Dagda when they saw the warrior riding along with his giant stomach and his strange dress. They went down to him.

"What have you been doing?" Nuada asked. "Get down." He gestured to Ronan for help. "Come on and we will help you."

"You look as though you are with child," Ronan laughed, slapping the Dagda's stomach.

The Dagda groaned, "Yes. I have heard enough of what I look like, but I can say that the delay has been given."

"What happened?" Nuada asked.

"Let's just say I sacrificed my gut and my good looks for a time. Now if you do not mind, I feel I need to be sick and then sleep." He slapped Nuada's back and stumbled his way up the street towards his home.

For seven days the enemies delayed the battle, and both sides had their spies trying to seek the others' battle plans. This came up with no success on either side. A battle plan was easy to cast, but was not always easy to keep in place with the enemy close at hand. All the warriors, especially the lower-ranking peasants, found that the heat of battle often dismissed any intention of following a plan. Fighting for one's own survival became more important than even the survival of the clan when on the field.

The day of the battle came, and the Fomorian men and the Tuatha Dé Danann walked towards one another until they came to the plain. So closely packed together were they that they could hear the threats they shouted to each other from the far side of the field.

Nuada paid no heed to the other end of the field for the time; instead he walked his horse alongside his men. He viewed them with pride and knew each of them, even the peasants who had joined them. The Dagda pulled against the reins that held Nuada's horse and he pulled him in close. Ogma, Macha, and Badb moved in to hear what was being said against the noise and the metal as the Tuatha began to beat on their shields.

"We should keep Lugh out of this," the Dagda said to Nuada. "It will not give the Tuatha much courage if something happens to their new king."

"A king should fight alongside his men," Ogma said.

"And," the Dagda said sharply to Ogma as he saw Neit join their company, "what would it be to the peasants, or the Tuatha who are too young or too old to stand on these fields? What of the women who are this time in birthing, to hear that their newborns have no high king and that there fails the Tuatha Dé Danann?" He glared from warrior to warrior. "That their shining light, whom they have heard will, by prophecy, defeat the Fomorian, is lying in the midst of death and crows to pick his bones. Would they hear of it well ... their leader ... gone?"

"The Dagda is right," Nuada said. "Without Lugh on the field, the Fomorian will discern no better than to believe that I am still the king and their target. Macha, take Lugh and eight others to guard him against coming out to battle."

"Me?" Macha raised her voice in protest. "I am the leader of nearly six hundred warriors, and you want me to leave the field. I am one of the most experienced of all the fighters, and never has any laid a scar upon me."

"It is even better for that reason then, is it not, for someone so experienced to be watching over our king?" Nuada shrugged off his wife's objections. "We will see hands of it if you wish. The people will speak by the raising of their hands, and we will do as they bid. What say you?"

"I say," Badb voiced her opinion, "you cannot change that which has already been determined." She looked with an empty stare at Nuada.

"It is not determined yet!" Nuada spat. A hand rested on his shoulder, and the jostle of the horse beside him changed his attentions to focus on Neit.

"I will take her and eight of my men, and then I will return," Neit said calmly, as he always did, unless in the battle frenzy. "I feel this is a fight for the ages, and my bones tell me what I do not want to hear. Still, the Tuatha will have victory." He thought about it for a moment. "They will, will they not?" He looked at Badb and then the Morrigu, who had arrived beside her.

Badb caressed his arm and did not say anything. The Morrigu spoke assuredly, "The Tuatha Dé Danann will be victorious."

Nuada pushed his wife away and pointed for her to leave. Neit took her horse's reins, and they both went their way to take Lugh from the field. Nuada laughed softly, amused by Macha's persistence.

He spoke to those warriors remaining with him. "We have assembled thousands for the fight, and there is no room for us to all enter the fray. The riders of the Sidhe have not come to aid us this day to end the battle as fast as we can. We know that they do not always wish to enter into mortals' affairs, and it is our fate now we must fight for.

"It would be best for us to start with the peasants and hurlers. They have been trained and have as much skill in them as any warrior. Let the Fomorians see the might of the common people, and then they will realize if these are the least trained for the fight, then they will truly be in desperate trouble in days to come."

The assembly agreed, and they rode out to the leaders each battalion and each king to tell them all Nuada had said. Each section agreed also, and the people who had most to lose that would fight first.

Armed with their arrows, darts, spears, and daggers, the peasants had a look as menacing as any swordsman or war band. It was the battle they had joined to see the end of the tribute to a race who cared not whether they lived or died, so now they brought the fight within them to he fore. All were as determined as any not to die, but to kill.

The battle horns trumpeted, and there was rage in war cries that the Tuatha Dé Danann screamed as they ran out onto the field. The

Fomorians responded by charging out in the same way. They sent forth a strange assortment of men and women. Some were dressed as swordsmen, and some were obviously of lesser rank. None looked to be of the peasant class, and yet all looked poorly. The heat was affecting the Fomorians, and it showed in their fight. By the end of the day, there were many losses on each side, and no greater strength showed by either.

The night came with a disturbingly peaceful atmosphere. No music was played aside from the sound of a solitary harp strummed by the Dagda. The Tuatha Dé Danann saw to their dead and injured.

Dian Cecht, his mind suddenly cleared by the events of war, dressed the wounded and made the injured as well as possible. Many of those warriors the healer tended stood ready to fight in the next day. Nuada inspected all, and gave his approval to most for the next day's fighting.

The second day of war was more solid than the last. The wall of opposition the Tuatha met still equaled their forces. The Tuatha fought hard, and Nuada rallied close to the fight, yet he stayed back far enough to keep the Fomorians aware that even the Tuatha's weakest warriors were still strong enough to beat them into the ground.

The end of the day still saw neither force to be any stronger than the other. Again, Dian Cecht saw to the injured and his mind seemed even clearer; the madman was dissolved away by the necessity for the healer.

Nuada made sure that Lugh remained unable to come to the battlefield for the third day of battle, as he had for the days prior. Macha, much against her desire, guarded the king's round house with Badb, the Morrigu, Dian Cecht, and two of the Dagda's sons, Midhir and Bodb Dearg. This left Nuada and the Dagda in charge of all of their battalions. Thousands stood on the strand, and they waited their turn to gut the enemy. It was the point of showing that their minds about the tribute were set, and they acted as a whole.

The third day did not any more decisively than the days before. Those who walked at the end of the day knew they had no advantage on their side. There was none given to the other side, either.

It was a fight of balance, but Nuada knew the Tuatha had more advantages than the Fomorians, as the Tuatha had not yet committed their best men and women to the fight. He knew the Fomorians were worn from their travels and suffering in the heat, as the days warmed continuously. The Morrigu reported that evening and told Nuada that the next day would be the hottest day of the year. Nuada knew in that moment that the war would be sorted on that day.

When morning came, Nuada dressed himself in his finest battle armour. Macha recognized the change in her husband and asked what it was she saw in him. He said nothing at first. As his clothes were pulled over his naked body he seemed to carry himself with pride. Finally, when he reached for his bronze chest plate, he spoke.

"The Morrigu and I talked, and the weather will help us defeat the Fomorians. It is the hottest day of the year today. If the peasants and those with less training than we have can keep the Fomorians from advancing, then I say with such high warriors as we have, the Fomorians will fall dead, and they will be cut down like the harvest grass."

"If you are to fight," Macha said, "then I am, too."

Nuada looked at his wife as he strapped his breastplate to him. "Who then, will make sure the king stays in safety? Is not the position you hold as important as the battle is for the rest of us?"

He could see that Macha would not answer the question.

"Goibniu daily makes more swords, spears, darts, daggers, and all of our arms. He and his brother work very hard and long hours. He does sit in a sulk because he cannot fight. Instead, he works with the Tuatha to make sure all have strong, fresh arms every day of this battle. He has hardly slept, and still he attends the forge. He is as powerful a warrior as you, and I am sure the head of a Fomorian he would love to hunt. He does as he knows is best for the clan."

Macha rolled over on the soft skins that lay on the ground, her naked body fully exposed in the early morning light. Nuada paused in his preparations and moved to her. He touched her skin and stroked her hair. He felt the twines of plaits within her dark hair. Each plait represented someone close to Macha who had died. Four of the braids were permanent: two for her lost children, one for her mother, and one for her real father. The Dagda had raised Macha as his own child, but she always knew she was just a little bit different to her sisters. Her softness and sweetness mixed with the passion for the people, but, most of all, for her family. Nuada felt that his wife, unlike her sisters, was breakable. He placed a kiss on her head and they moved closer to each other, and for that moment there was no Tuatha and no Fomorian, just them.

The morning sun rose to a higher point and it was nearly time for the battle to start again when Nuada heard a horrible scream against the quiet of the new day. He and several others rushed to see what had caused some woman to cry out in such a way. Nuada feared the Fomorians had entered the camp and had made away with the lives of many a warrior. It was to the forge he noticed that the Tuatha ran, and he pushed his way through to see what was within.

Brigit was knelt on the ground, her heart breaking as she cried to the sky. She held her son, Ruadan. She looked at Nuada with eyes that pleaded for help as he came to her through the crowd that had gathered. The young man had a spear shaft protruding from his chest, and he was panting in shallow breaths as he came to the bridge of the dead.

"What happened?" Nuada roared for an answer to be given.

"It was Goibniu," Cron, the old mother, said. "The boy wanted to see a spear, and when he held it—," she looked dazed as she spoke, "—he threw it at Giobniu. We could all see that Ruadan wanted death upon Giobniu, and Giobniu saw it, too. Giobniu pulled the spear from himself and threw it back at Ruadan."

"Why, boy?" Nuada asked, not angry; confused. "Why would you do such a thing?"

The young man's eyes were starting to glaze. He heard enough that he tried to answer. "My," he breathed for a moment, "father," he heaved a little more, "to please." The words were said on his last breath, and reached to stroke a tear of his mother's eye as he shifted across the bridge of the dead and to the other side.

Brigit wailed and rocked while she held tightly to her child. Nuada looked around the gathering and did not see Goibniu. A fear grew within him and he bolted to his feet and called, "Goibniu! Where is he?"

The people moved. None could say that they knew where Goibniu had gone. Nuada pushed his way through the crowd and outside. He saw Luchta, the carpenter who aided in the making of the spears, and he asked him if he had seen Goibniu.

"I followed him out of the forge, but was met with so many that I could not continue forward. He is on his way to the well of Sláine."

Nuada ran as fast as he could. The thoughts whirled in his mind—how Bres had used his own son to try and take down the reason the Tuatha Dé Danann enjoyed a constant supply of fresh weapons: Goibniu. The shock of seeing Brigit, the Fiery Arrow, most loved of all the Tuatha women leaders. Like a sister to some, a mother to others, and even like a daughter when the time was right; that was how the Tuatha viewed Brigit. Her pain was everyone's pain.

Goibniu was stumbling back from the well when Nuada came upon him. He could see that the smith had an injury on his side. The wound was more towards his back than his front. The spear's point had bounced on a rib and pushed the weapon towards his spine rather than towards his heart or lungs, and that had saved his life.

Nuada checked the wound. "I want you to go and see Dian Cecht to make sure there is no filth in it. What are we to do for weapons?"

"I am strong enough, and I will not fall down when my clan needs me to stand up," Goibniu said. "It is more that I have been near-skinned than mortally wounded. The water was soothing and has made the wound clean and clear. It will heal me."

"I will still see it bound," Nuada said. "It is good that you are well. This will give the Tuatha encouragement."

Goibniu went first to Dian Cecht, and then back to his work in the forge. By the time he took up his hammer again he felt no pain from the attempted murder, and all the people had left to go to battle. Ruadan had been carried away, and Brigit prepared with vengeance in sight for what would be the final battle. She strapped each piece of the leather and metal armour to herself with purpose and care.

The line of the Tuatha Dé Danann that day was constructed of the strongest men and women of their clan. Some warriors wore breastplates that glinted in the sun, and others wore boiled leather that had been polished with oils to increase the chance that a sword or spear might be deflected. Several breastplates had decorative studs serving further to aid in deflecting weapons. Not many fighters wore helmets, but enough did that a flash of sun reflected across the fore of the Tuatha formation as all of the chosen swordsmen lined up.

Nuada sat on his horse and tapped the end of this sword on his foot. He lifted his shield and looked at the Tuatha battalions with pride. The horns sounded over the hills, and the battle commenced.

Nuada rode with his target in sight. King Balor, who had taken his horse to the front, believing he was invincible, led the Fomorians. Even with his horse and his determination to crush the Tuatha, Balor remained surrounded by the men who protected him. Nuada threw darts that he kept in a pouch by his side with fatal accuracy. Arrows whistled overhead, and the Tuatha ducked down on their horses so that none of the missiles might touch them, but would strike the enemy instead.

Brigit's arrows of fire exploded upon the Fomorians, and she drew and lit them at a pace that it seemed like an endless stream. Her anger and her heartbreak carried through the air and settled mercilessly upon the Fomorian warriors. When she ran dry of arrows, she took darts, and found the eye of every man she targeted.

Nuada saw Ceithlenn of the crooked teeth, her face wrinkled with age and bitterness, she on her horse, as she fought on her own, away from the Fomorian clan. She struck her own brother, then took the sword covered with his blood and wiped it on her brow. She turned her gaze to Nuada, and her resentment offered him a grimace.

Nuada threw a spear at the woman. It missed, as she moved well on her horse. Instead it hit the Fomorian king, Indech, in his upper chest. While this was not his goal, Nuada smiled at the strike. Indech was thrown to the ground, and his horse trampled upon him. To the Fomorian leader, the wound might not have been completely fatal, yet as the hooves of the other warhorses came upon him, his bones broke and his skull splintered into the ground.

Some warriors who had seen their king fall jumped from their steeds and dragged Indech out of the fray. Blood spat from the Fomorian king's mouth, and the only words the warriors could make sense of were his call for his poet.

His poet arrived at a run. Indech could say nothing more. Probably he wanted to tell the poet about how he wanted to be recorded, or something of the like, for vanity's sake. Nothing came of it. The poet could not talk either because of the repulsion and faintness he felt when he looked at his king's crushed body.

Out of nowhere, the Morrigu rode. She cut the throat of one of the men who had tried to shelter Indech as he died, and she threw a dart into the face of the second and third warriors. Both fell to the ground howling in agony.

The Morrigu dismounted from her horse with sword in hand and strode towards the poet. He ran away as fast as he could, stumbling as he fled. She was left beside the king, ignored by those fighters still in battle. She pulled Indech's head up by the hair and, from within her shirt, she drew forth a small wooden bowl.

As Indech coughed, his eyes wide with horror, the Morrigu collected the blood in the bowl, and dropped Indech's head back down with a force that smashed his skull further on the rocks below it. She then used her sword to end his life. She did not take his head, but, with her hand cupped across the top of the little bowl so as not to spill the contents, she rode at speed back the way she came.

The Tuatha had seen the Morrigu and were inspired, as they knew she had been guarding Lugh. The cries of battle had brought down the great fighters. Nuada shifted on his horse even as he struck another Fomorian, as he knew that Macha had joined the fight, and his fear of losing her grew.

Dead and dying warriors lay around his horse's feet, and the animal slipped on the bodies it trod on. Nuada had no choice. He had to dismount and fight on foot. Other warriors did the same, and the fight continued over bodies and blood. The wounded who groaned underfoot were soon hushed as they were crushed under heel. Blood and flesh streaked down the fighters' faces and bodies. Armour that had glowed that morning had clotted with scabs. Bones lay broken on the ground, gradually crushed into a mash of reds and browns.

Lugh suddenly appeared on the battlefield to fight, and the Tuatha surged with force. The shape of Macha caught Nuada's eye as he saw her approach king Balor. She cut between him and an attempted death-blow to Badb. To the back of her sister she fought. Badb tried to change places with her sister, but Macha continually disallowed it.

Nuada's love for his wife projected him forward until he was level with her. King Balor kicked at Macha, knocking her to the ground. Nuada came between them and raised his shield to protect her; this, however, opened his side up to exposure. Macha saw the sword-blow coming from Balor and threw her sword at the Fomorian king. It hit him on the side. It caused only a small gash and did not disable him.

Anger at being damaged compelled Balor forward, and he landed the point of his sword in Macha's throat. Nuada cried in anger and horror and thrust his sword back at Balor. Balor saw the sword and parried it just as was about to impact. The men struggled with one another and began to fight hard and heavily.

"Macha!" the Dagda called from behind Balor.

The Dagda's call was enough of distraction for Nuada to finally impact the Formorian king. Nuada brought his sword down across the Balor's side and struck half his nose off. Balor reeled backward in shock. Nuada raised his sword to cut the king's throat, but he stopped. The sword of Balor had found him first, and he fell. As Nuada's legs buckled, he saw the Dagda struck by a spear sent from the hand of Ceithlenn.

Nuada lay on the ground, his pain overwhelming. He saw Macha just to the side of him and reached for her as the sword of Balor cut his throat and took his head.

King Balor roared in satisfaction, pulling the head he had cut above him. He called to his horse, which would not come across the field of bodies. So many warriors were still fighting that the sounds of battle caused the horse the terrors. Balor did not care, and he raised the head again and called to the Tuatha clan. "I have your king's head! This is done! No one can stand against me!" He shook Nuada's head. "No one!"

It was the fate of the battle that Lugh, who had been fighting fiercely, stood at that moment in front of his grandfather. "I stand against you, grandfather! I am high king. I am Tuatha Dé Danann!"

He drew back his arm, and with all his strength he threw his spear. The stunned Balor had not expected anyone to break through the line of Fomorians around him, much less stand before him. His face was not protected, and he did not have the time to raise his shield, nor could he dip to avoid the spear. It thumped into his head and pushed his blind eye that he had been so proud and bitter of, back into his head. Balor's face folded in with the impact and he was lifted from the ground. He flew back and landed on his own men and their weapons. As he did so, he released Nuada's head. It rolled out of the dead tyrant king's hand and lay near Macha.

ᔐ 10 ᔐ

Lugh roared at the Fomorians in rage at all the death before him; in horror at Nuada's death and in his sorrow for the loss of those he had come to love as family. Tears started to run down his face. His anger pulled him to the dead Fomorian king and he cut down every enemy in his path without even thinking there might be a wound in it for him.

Brigit came to fight alongside him, and their combined passion stopped the Fomorians' assault. Lugh slipped his hand down to the corpse of Balor and, with his dagger, he sawed at the neck. All the time he cut at the dead king, he fought with his other hand any enemy who dared to come near him. As the Fomorians caught sight of the dead Balor, fewer and fewer approached until, with crack of the neck bone being displaced, Lugh lifted the dead king's head and boomed an explosive, enraged sound across the field. He shook the head and continued to cry out, over and over again, for his emotions caught all his words and his tongue failed him.

The Fomorians all stopped their attack as they came to an understanding that all of their kings were dead, and their most furious warrior and leader was being displayed as a trophy. They began stampeding to their boats. They did not care to stop for the horses or anything else they might have salvaged from their defeat. They ran purely to salvage their own lives. Some slipped on the dead and fell down. This was their folly, as the Tuatha Dé Danann soon showed them to their halls of the dead with quick, violent actions.

As Lugh watched his enemy flee, he saw Brigit with her hands on Bres. She did not kill him, although her face showed that part of her wanted to. He could see that there was still something in her that had mercy for the one who had caused her so much pain: Lugh knew that there was a time when Brigit had found in Bres all that she could ever love in a man. He felt for her.

"Come, and we will take Bres up to have judgement passed on him," Lugh said to Badb, who was kneeling by her sister Macha, wailing and crying out in pain.

"I will do as you ask, not because you are king, but because there has been enough death. The land stinks like a bitch's heat and it is only the scavengers that gain anything this day," Badb said quietly. She let go of Macha, whose eyes stared in death. Carefully, Badb kissed her head and closed the dead woman's eyes.

She and Lugh then walked down across the bodies, picking their way as they went so they did not fall. They watched as Bres reached his hand out and touched Brigit's face, then brought her hands to his mouth. They could see the tears as they flowed down both their faces. Neither Lugh nor Badb felt anything for Bres.

Bres stepped away from Brigit when he saw that Lugh and Badb had come for him. "If you wish to end me, end me now. I am still the son of Prince Elatha, who did not fight this day, but has taken care of the Dagda's harp and has played it during the battle. He has proven that Fomorian and the Tuatha can be in peace. It is your rule. I argue for my life that I may leave with my father or live in peace here with my wife."

"You argue for your life and would compare yourself to your father, who has proven himself honourable and good?" Lugh laughed, tears of anger and heartfelt pain rolling across his flexed jaw. "What part of you came to the understanding that there is anything the like between you and him?"

"I may not be my father." Bres shook his head. "I do not know what to say. I have given myself now, to you, and have not fled with the other Fomorians. They, at the shore, row away and back to their lands. They will not return here. I had the chance to go, but I remained and waited for what was next."

Lugh tried to control his anger. He clenched his jaw, and the muscles at the side of his face flexed yet again. His blue eyes were bloodshot and his face was flushed red. He breathed and then took a moment before speaking. "We will go and take it to the judgement of the Tuatha Dé Danann, and they will decide. Maeltine Mor-Brethach is the oldest of the wise ones, and we will have council with him. He will decide your fate."

The Dagda, whose wound was covered, and the Morrigu had arrived at Lugh's side by this time, and they walked with Bres as they made their way back to Teamhair. Brigit walked behind them, her head hung low, and she seemed to be suspended in a silence that had enveloped her.

Badb returned to her fallen sister's side and carried her from the field, and then she returned for Nuada. Her grief caused her to rock back and forth as she walked, and when she stopped, she cried to the skies. The sound was so sorrowful and filled with pain that others came to aid her.

They took the bodies of Nuada and Macha to a dell filled with summer flowers. They placed the couple next to each other in a grave, making sure that they lay in each other's arms. Dian Cecht had carefully sewed Nuada's head into place. Many stayed by the fallen couple's grave until evening, when the other Tuatha Dé Danann arrived for the burial. Those who did not linger went back to Teamhair for the trial of Bres.

Bres was placed before the people, and he saw how they loathed him. He did not care. Instead, watching Brigit was what made him weep. He stood tall and behaved as if the tears on his face were not there. He waited for the judgement.

Maeltine the wise one was brought forward with the aid of Lugh and the Dagda, who appeared to no longer suffer from an injury at all. Maeltine was an old man, grey and mostly bald. He was hunched and stood on wiry legs. Spots of age dotted his face and he wore a thin moustache, plaited in narrow strips, that ran down the sides of his mouth. His hands shook, and when he smiled at any who aided him, as he did often, he displayed a mouth empty of teeth except for the occasional black stump. He sat in the chair that had been brought for the judgement and groaned when his knees made popping sounds as he bent them.

"Bres," the old man said, more clearly than his look would suggest he could speak, "Step forward. I have heard enough of this over the years. It has been near twenty summers since the time the Tuatha trusted in you to be their king."

The Dagda whispered something in the ear of Maeltine, to which the man's long eyebrows lifted in surprise. "Really? It does not matter the time, as there will be those who will record the time as being twenty years and others that will speak of the time as one-hundred years. It does not matter. Time is time, and it something that only we, as people, recognise. The plants do not plan a day or for time, nor do the animals. The heavens and all have their own understanding. It is only we who say, in our vanity, that it is *time*." He shook his head, dismissing the thought. "What rule do I, and the Tuatha, rule? It is ruled that Bres will die by drinking the death mushroom unless he can state a case for living." He eyed Bres.

Bres exhaled heavily. "I cannot say I have a defence that will give the right for life." He paused and still did not move his gaze from Brigit. "There is but one I have ever truly loved, and I failed her. I failed my son. I failed my mother and I failed my father. The Tuatha Dé Danann, who I thought of as my people even in my days of craze …" he trailed the thought off as if he did not know honestly how to finish the thought.

He took a deep breath. "If I am to live, I will teach you the best that I have learnt. I can teach you about when it is best to dig your fields and to plant your crops and when to harvest. I will be able to teach you how to make sure your fields do not run dry of crops for the harvest, and I will teach you how to always have the best of yield. This is the knowledge I have, and it is in the fields and in the forest that I find my peace. I know more about plants and that which grows from the soil than I do of the emotions of the people and my wife."

Maeltine thought on what Bres had said as he rubbed his hand across his moustache. Then his eyes twinkled—he had thought of something. "What you say will aid the Tuatha Dé Danann and make then stronger and grow. I now cast the judgement to the one who has been damaged the most—your wife, Brigit."

All eyes turned to Brigit as she stood with a flat expression upon her face. It was as if she had not heard what had been said, and she looked at Maeltine, confused. She gathered her wits quickly enough, closed her eyes, and sighed. When she opened her eyes again, she gazed at Bres, who no longer looked at her, but at his feet.

"I cannot say that I want for any more death. I do not know exactly how I feel. I do know that the death of another does no more than create hate, for his mother will cry out and his father will curse. In my mind, I had lost myself, but I am still here. I am Brigit. In him, in his mind, he lost himself, but he is still here. He is Bres. Let it always be that way."

The Tuatha murmured together and they gathered closer to Brigit, for if she found compassion, then they would, too. Lugh waved his hand, and Bres was allowed to be set free where he would remain with the Tuatha Dé Danann and teach them his knowledge.

Immediately after the trial, all of the Tuatha returned to the battlefield. The stench of death blew across from the ground, and the Tuatha had to take away the dead and finish off those who lingered. They dug pits and long trenches; both Fomorian and Tuatha shared the same graves, as the damage done to the victims made it too hard to tell which was which. The death birds had come and had started their scavenging as the Tuatha filled the pits.

The evening brought all the Tuatha down to the graves of Nuada and Macha, where the druids and priestesses chanted and made rings of flowers that they shared with one another. The biggest of all the warriors, including the Dagda, brought the largest boulders they could find and created four stone walls around the couple. One of the walls was shorter and made space for a doorway. They created a tunnel leading to this doorway by using other large rocks.

During the days and nights that followed, the fires burned, and the Tuatha brought huge amounts of soil, placing it against the stone walls of the grave to give them strength to stay standing.

When the mound stood high enough, they placed the largest slabs of stone on top as a roof for the couple's room. The Tuatha then brought more dirt and soil and covered all but for the entrance tunnel. It looked like a small hill with a doorway by the time they had finished. They ended by fitting a wooden door to the front of the tunnel. It took them thirty-three days and nights of heavy and continuous work. Bres helped with the building as all Tuatha did, even from as far afield as they came.

On the evening of the thirty-third night, the druids and priestesses entered the room containing the once-king and his queen, taking with them the couple's most prized possessions in life—this included the remains of their two lost children and a keepsake of their daughter who had been taken from them and sent across the seas. Nuada's eldest son stood by the door as it was sealed, and he planted his sword at the entrance. Lugh held the spear of the people and placed it alongside the buried sword.

In the night sky, a cry that went up from birds of the night, and the Tuatha Dé Danann wailed in reply. They tipped mead on the burial mound and marked the door with the blood of their strongest cow before a lament was played by the Dagda and other musicians.

As music was played, thoughts soon turned to the remembrance of happier times; the life that was not the death that is. The Tuatha began to dance and sing. Poetry was spoken, and laughter of the Tuatha was heard once more across the land. They stayed the night and burned great fires to their once-king and the queen he loved so very much. They celebrated Nuada, the great king, who had brought them to their beautiful new country, to a land where the Tuatha Dé Danann could finally find peace.

ᔄ EPILOGUE ᔄ

Ireland has gone on, as has the people. Stronger and ever good, they are. New cultures, people, and even religions would come. Some would try to the make the ancient bloodlines bend and break in mind and spirit, yet this never did happen. Though the stories began to fade until they were told by very few, still they continue.

Nuada was a legend who now is often no more than a hint on the breeze or a mention in a movie. This legend believed in his people and the future of the place, the great land in which he found himself. His belief that there is a better way than war is now echoed in the voices of many around the world. Where there is a choice between crushing the life out of an enemy or forming peace by releasing ego … the choice is simple.

THE OLD LANDS

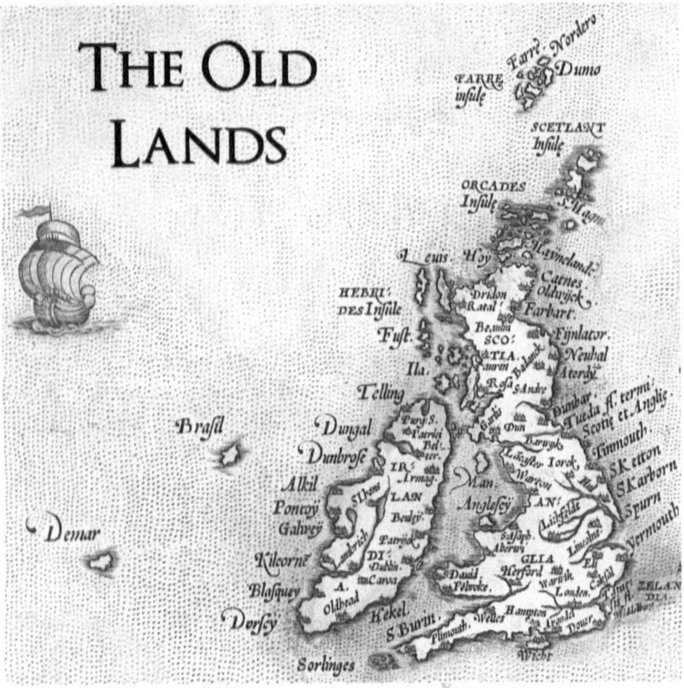

ERRIS

Irish Names Pronunciation Guide

Aengaba:	Oon-gubĕ
Aengus mac Og:	Eng-gus mac ō
Aibhne:	Ab-nah
Airmed:	Eh-r-mid
Aonbharr:	Ane-varr
Aoife:	Ec-fa
Aos-Si:	Ace-she
Arias:	Are-e-us
Badb:	Bābe
Balor:	Bel-or (with throaty 'r')
Banda:	Ban-dah
Belgatta:	Bell-yatt-ah
Bres:	Br-ĕ-s
Brigit:	Bri-git
Boann:	Boh-an
Bodb Dearg:	Bov-jar-ug
Cesarn:	Ses-sa
Ceithlenn:	Keh-lin

Cian:	Key-en
Claiomh Solais:	Clīve-sol-ish
Colum Cuaillemech:	Col-lum Kay-el-mek
Conand:	Konn-un
Corpre:	K-or-prĕ
Craisech:	Cray-shek
Creidhne:	Kred-neh
Cridenbel:	Kree-den-bel
Cron:	Krõne
Dagda:	Dae-da
Dalbaech:	Dal-bek
Danu:	Dan-oo
Dea:	Dõ
De Domnann:	De-Dom-nan
Delbaith:	Del-bee
Dian Cecht:	Dee-an Kairt
Donall Donn-Ruadh:	Don-al Don-Rū-h
Eadon:	Ā-don
Eire:	Air-eh
Elatha:	El-a-tha
Elcmar:	Elk-mah
Emrys:	Em-er-is
Eochaid mac Eirc:	Y-ð-ich mac Erk

Eri:	Eh-r-ah
Ermas:	Ern-mass
Ethlinn:	Ă-linn
Falias:	Fel-ee-as
Finias:	Fin-ēē-is
Firbolg:	Feer-bolg
Fodla:	Fod-la
Fomorian:	Fom-or-ian
Gaillimh:	Gyle-lee-ah
Gann:	G-arn
Goibniu:	Gov-noo
Goitne Gorm-Shuileach:	Gō-nee Gor-em Soo-leech
Gorias:	Gor-ee-ass
Indech:	In-dek
Lia Fáil:	Lee-ah Foy-l
Luchta:	Loo-tah
Luchtaine:	Loh-ten-nāy
Luchtar:	Loh-tah
Lugh:	Looh
Macha:	Mah-ha
Máel Sechlainn:	Mall-Sheck-len
Maeltine Mor-Brethach:	Mall-tin-eh Moor-Brr-ĕ-tek
Magh Nia:	May Nee-ah

Magh Tuireadh:	May Too-rah
Manannan, son of Lir:	Man-an-an, son of Leer
Miach:	Merh (accent on the 'h')
Midhir:	Mith-ir
Morfessa/ Morias:	Mor-fes-sah / Mor-ris
Morrigu:	Mor-ig-oo
Murias:	Mor-ris
Nechtan:	Nek-ten
Neit:	Net
Nemed:	Nev-ed
Nuada:	Noo-uder
Ogma:	Og-mah
Ráith na Ríogh:	Ror na Rerh (accent on the 'h')
Ronan:	Rōe-narn
Ruadan:	Rōe-da
Samthainn:	Sam-hīenn
Senias:	Seen-ēē-is
Sgoith Gleigeil:	Scot Glīe-gīel
Sidhe:	Shee
Sine Sindearg:	Shen-nee Sin-djah-ig
Sláine mac Dela:	Slon-nuh mac Dee-lah
Sreng:	Shreng
Teamhair:	Tev-ir

Troighid (measurement):   Troy-id

Tuatha Dé Danann: Too-ath-a Djay Danann

Torc: Tark

Urias: Oor-ēē-is

Author Biography

Gillian Bridé Madell (Duce) was born in Taree, New South Wales, Australia to newspaper owners Mr. David Thomas Mills Madell and Jeanette MacDonald on the 27th of November 1973. When she was four her family moved to the town of Mareeba, Queensland; a rural area of the north, where she grew up.

As the third child of seven, she learned to amuse with words from a very young age. Raised with the newspaper industry around her, she found herself drawn to the word and writing her own brief stories and thoughts down and sharing them with her young friends.

She ran a successful business with her partner, Barry Johns, for several years, but eventually she decided to go back to her true passion of writing. She has had several articles published and her first book, *Magic and Mayhem: Tree of Knowledge* was published by Saga Books in 2006.